TALES of PIRATES
SMUGGLERS and .BUCCANEERS.

Nos. 1 & 2.]   **THE SCOURGE OF THE SPANISH MAIN.**   [One Penny.

With a shout of triumph Harry Seaborne sprang forward and thrust straight at the throat of the buccaneer chief.

MORGAN the BUCCANEER; or, the Terror of the Seas.

CHAPTER I.
THE CAVE OF THE BUCCANEERS.

THE opening scene of our tale is laid in a lovely island where reigns perpetual summer. 'Tis the small isle of Tortugo, one of the West Indian group, now little known and rarely visited, but, at the time we write of, celebrated as the realm of the buccaneers.

Like a brilliant emerald set in a sapphire sea,

Tortugo lay bathed in eternal sunshine; and on the bright June evening on which our narrative opens, well might it have been taken for one of those isles of the blest of which Mahomet dreamed, and, in his Koran, so poetically described.

The aroma of its spice groves might have been scented many miles out at sea, and beneath the waving, fan-like leaves of its cocoa-nut and bread-fruit trees the warrapeet sang her evening song, and the fireflies quivered and glittered and flashed in the gathering shades.

Oh! how beautiful, how exquisitely beautiful it was.

And is this earthly heaven devoid of inhabitants? For not a house, not a hut, not a tent meets the view.

Surely, if human beings tenanted this earthly paradise, they would be enjoying the calm and tranquil evening hour on the golden sands, or 'neath the shade of the giant trees, or down in the valley beside the rippling streamlets?

And yet, whence come those loud, discordant voices, those occasional bursts of revelry, or snatches of song, interspersed with oaths, and frequently with the clashing of arms?

Ah! amidst the citron and the orange-trees afar down in the valley yawns the mouth of a cavern, the one black flaw on the surface of the emerald.

It is from thence that the uncouth sounds issue.

Let us enter this seeming portal to the abode of the damned, brushing through the citron and orange bushes, and stooping to avoid the drooping branches of the lime trees, that strive to hide this blot on Nature's escutcheon.

Then down the dark, tunnel-like passage, beyond where the horned bat flaps his leathery wings o'erhead, and the toad and newt croak a hoarse response underfoot.

A noble subterranean hall presently reveals itself to the astonished gaze, and within it a numerous and a richly-garbed, if not a noble, company are assembled.

Who are these men, who, like the bats, the toads, and the newts we have just mentioned, prefer the darkness to the light, who linger here like moles within the bowels of the earth, when the gorgeous sunset, the rippling sea, the shady grove, the song of birds, and the musical murmur of the insect world, call them forth to enjoy the beauties of creation?

Who are they?

Why, King Morgan and his mighty buccaneers; the scourges of the world, the demons of the sea, and, above all, the heroes of this our true and terrible tale.

And yet, right winsome and courtly gallant do they look beneath the fiery radiance of the three-dozen glaring and sputtering firewood torches that are affixed high up around the walls of the cave.

Gayer dresses, richer laces, or a greater profusion of velvets and cloth of gold, could not well have been beheld at a royal court.

And how white were the hands of the caballeros, and how their fingers blazed with rings!

Perhaps their hands were so white from their being so frequently bathed up to the very wrist in the blood of their foes; and the rings, all glittering with diamonds, and rubies, and pearls beyond price, that decked their fingers, had once belonged to the dark-eyed senoras and senoritas of New Spain.

Yet no love gifts were these gemmed circlets; they had been torn from the quivering, stiffening fingers of violated and assassinated innocence; for the buccaneers spared no man in their anger, no woman in their lust, no living thing in whose veins coursed one drop of Spanish blood.

Though many of them were so effeminate in appearance they were all warriors staunch and true.

No one was admitted a member of their confraternity until he could indisputably prove that he had at different times overcome nine foes in personal combat, and had remorselessly slain each one.

But let us individualise some of the band.

Amongst that array of a hundred and fifty plumed and brocaded cavaliers, three or four personal introductions will be alone at present necessary.

The leader of the host might have been discovered at a glance, as leaders of hosts generally may be, by the extreme plainness of their dress as compared with that of their companions.

'Twas thus with Alexander and with Cæsar; 'twas thus in modern times with Napoleon and with Wellington; and 'twas equally so with Sir Henry Morgan, King of the Buccaneers, and Scourge of the Spanish Main.

He was seated before a rough deal table, clad as soberly as a Puritan in a suit of dark brown cloth, but his plain steel cuirass was polished to the brightness of a mirror, as was the heavy helmet, which was scarcely lifted from off his broad, massive brow.

By his side sat a gigantic black woman, who overtopped him by a head, for Harry Morgan was not very tall.

She was young, and, for a negro, lovely, and yet her sex would not for a moment have been guessed at, for she was dressed à la cavalier, and wore a sword at her side and pistols in her belt, while a snow-white broad-brimmed hat was slouched over her eyes, from which waved a splendid ostrich plume.

This woman was supposed to be the only human being whom Morgan the Buccaneer had ever loved.

She had been a slave in New Grenada, and had poisoned her former master in order that she might the more readily elope with Morgan.

The buccaneer had since taught her navigation, seamanship, gunnery, and the use of rapier, cutlass, and boarding-pike. With these weapons her match could hardly be found. She was also a dead pistol shot.

She fought by Morgan's side in battle, whether on ship-board or ashore, and had twice saved his life.

The third most important person of the group was Walter Evandale, first lieutenant of Morgan's great war-ship, the Death Cloud, which lay in a little bay on the south of the island, with her crew on board, her guns shotted, and her snowy canvas ready to be expanded to the first favourable breeze that blew, for the buccaneers hoped that this would be their last night on the island before putting to sea.

Walter Evandale was about twenty-five years of age, and particularly handsome.

His features bore a noble expression, but there was something in his keen black eye singularly repellant and forbidding.

He seemed to be as much attached to Morgan as the black Amazon who sat at the great freebooter's side, and had on many occasions done him signal service by delivering him out of sore straits, where consummate skill and desperate courage could alone have effected that object.

He was attired in a rich costume of blue and silver, his buff funnel boots were adorned with spurs of solid gold, studded with jewels, and the diamond aigrette that fastened his heavy black plume to his wide-brimmed cavalier hat was worth a king's ransom.

By his side sat a stripling, even more handsome than himself.

He was a mere youth, certainly not more than fifteen years of age, even if so old.

His frank, open, sunny countenance proclaimed him to be English born, and his dress also showed that he had served on board an English man-of-war. Such was indeed the case.

Harry Seaborne had been two years in the navy, serving in the flag-ship of the brave Duke of York, High Admiral of England (still later England's last ill-fated Stuart king); but then he had been transferred to a gunbrig, and this gunbrig had six weeks ago been captured by the great buccaneer ship, the Death Cloud, under the command of Morgan.

All on board her, with the exception of our hero, were slain in cold blood after they had surrendered.

Lieutenant Evandale had disarmed our hero at the close of the action, and struck by his heroism and almost girlish beauty, had carried him below, thrust him into a state-room, locked him in, and borne away the key.

After the English captain and all his crew had been slaughtered, their bodies committed to the deep, and the blood-longing of the buccaneers had been appeased, he had first exacted a promise from Morgan that the boy's life should be spared, if within six weeks he would consent to become a buccaneer, and had then let him out of the state-room, conducted him on deck, and introduced him to the great chief.

To-night the term of six weeks had expired—to-night Harry Seaborne was to become a buccaneer or be shot.

Such was the decree of Morgan, and Morgan's decrees were immutable as those of doom.

Though the life or death of a boy was but a trifle in comparison with the affairs of moment that needed the consideration of that august assembly.

The gunbrig captured from the English had been turned into a buccaneer vessel, and the great question now was who should command her.

Morgan was puzzled to decide. Amongst so many brave and bloodthirsty gallants it was hard to say which had deserved promotion to a captaincy the most.

The matter was presently under strong discussion.

The gallants were not backward in putting forward their claims.

Modesty and diffidence are rare virtues amongst buccaneers.

"By the gods! 'twas I who took Maracaibo, burnt the town about the cursed Spaniards' ears, and after roasting five hundred women and children in the great cathedral of San Josef, hung the priests in all their vestments around the battlements of the great tower, with the bishop two hundred feet above them, on the gilt weathercock, out of due respect for his exalted rank. From that town I brought you a hundred and fifty prisoners, and two thousand Spanish dollars. Does not such a feat as this entitle me to the captaincy?"

So cried L'Olonois, one of the most bloodthirsty of the freebooters; but scarcely had the words escaped his lips when Monsvell, a grey-bearded Dane, sprang to his feet, exclaiming, fiercely—

"Listen to the vaunting Frenchman! A rare feat of arms to brag about, truly! Look at my head, comrades. How is it so bald? Not from age, but because I have plucked out a hair for every foe that I have slain, and, by the god of battles! in a few more years I shall have parted with every one. Why, L'Olonois, in my last raid on Nata, I, with my own hand, plucked out the tongues of five hundred women, because they would not reveal where their husbands and brothers had buried the treasures of the town, and then I began to flay the backs of the men with red-hot sword blades, and at last one confessed, and so I enriched our treasury with ten thousand pieces of eight."

"Fury! do you dare to urge your pretensions against mine, grey beard?" cried L'Olonois. "Ah! thou dost. Then, by every fiend in the devil's army, I will give thee a clean shave with my sword blade."

The gleaming steel was bare in an instant, and the Frenchman, quick as lightning, made a slash at the old Dane's chin, but the descending stroke was caught on a blade as firm and ready as his own.

Cut and thrust were then quickly given and returned; but ere worse could come of it, with a roar like that of an angry bull, Morgan leaped over the table, and struck up the opposing blades with his broadsword.

"What!" he exclaimed, furiously, "are there not enough Spanish throats to slash that we need be cutting our own? Put up your swords, or I will cut ye both down where ye stand, and so end the dispute."

The Frenchman and the Dane sullenly complied, and then Morgan resumed—

"By my right hand, you shall neither have the ship, for I shall promote my trusty first lieutenant, Walter Evandale, to the command I have purposed it from the first. Come hither, Walter, my friend."

The courtly gallant arose from his seat beside the English boy prisoner, and, with his gold lace and superb diamonds glittering in the twilight, approached his redoubtable chief.

"How is this, Walter Evandale? Thou lookest

but ill-pleased at the honour I am about to confer upon thee?" said Morgan, as the young lieutenant bent his knee before him. "Dost thou not want the ship?"

"Captain, I have but one wish, that is, to be ever at thy side whilst thou livest, and when thou diest never to be away from thee. Grant me this, then I shall be happy, and give the captaincy to whom thou wilt," was the soft reply.

Walter Evandale had spoken in a voice of deep feeling and pathos, and the expression of his countenance acted in unison therewith—all but one feature—his eyes.

Those keen, dark, lustrous orbs, that were as impenetrable as night and almost as awe-inspiring, were fixed—it might have been appealingly, it might have been threateningly—on his great leader's countenance.

Morgan himself had never been able to fathom those eyes.

"Thy self-devotion pleases me, thy attachment to my person wins my warmest gratitude," said Morgan. "Thou shalt be still my lieutenant, but with the pay and a share in all plunder equal to that of a captain. I have said it—you may return to your seat. And, hark ye, employ the next quarter of an hour in bringing that stubborn English lad to his senses, for if he does not elect to become one of us he dies this very night."

Lieutenant Evandale kissed Morgan's hand, sprang to his feet, and, returning to his seat, did as his chief had bidden him.

But Harry Seaborne was not open to conviction. He was as stubborn as ever.

A moody silence followed Walter Evandale's rejection of the proffered captaincy.

L'Olonois, the Frenchman, and Monsvell, the Dane, had resumed their seats, and sat scowling at each other like two tiger cats, impatient to be at each other's throats ; but between them still stood Morgan, leaning on his naked sword, and well they knew that he had the strength of a lion, and was not particular whom he smote with it.

He now beckoned up a tall, stately warrior, by name Rupert Russel, who was clad entirely in a suit of black velvet, and who was renowned as much for his retiring habits as for his bravery.

"Rupert Russel," said Morgan, "I appoint you commander of the new buccaneer ship Pestilence, lately a gunbrig in the navy of his most Christian Majesty, King Charles of England and then yclept the Bulldog ; and I nominate you her captain for two reasons—firstly, because I have often seen you perform gallant actions ; and secondly, because I have never heard you afterwards brag of them. Does the appointment please you?"

"Captain Henry Morgan, I am clumsy at giving thanks," replied the cavalier in black velvet. "I will express my gratitude by deeds. Believe me, that in less than a week the Pestilence shall have stricken sore."

"'Tis well," answered Morgan, with a grim smile. "I like your reply. We both set sail at sunrise."

Rupert Russel, with a faint smile, retired to his seat, and the momentous business of the evening

having been thus disposed of, the buccaneers betook themselves to various employments to kill time.

Some took up the dice box, others devoted themselves to cards and tric-trac, which they played upon inverted casks and barrels, and the yellow gold suddenly shone forth in great heaps ; and out of gold and silver goblets, set with gems, pillaged from many a sacred shrine, they drank the purple wine as though it had been limpid water.

In the midst of this scene of revelry and confusion, Morgan, who never drank and never played, summoned before him the English boy-prisoner, Harry Seaborne.

On hearing the voice of the terrible buccaneer king address him by name, Harry sprang to his feet, and would have walked up to him alone, but that Lieutenant Evandale also arose, and grasping his arm, said—

"I will go with you, boy, for I am your friend. Nay, I will be, whether thou will or not. Now, do not throw thy young life away ; and the only way to preserve it is by joining our band. It may not be for long, for chances of escape will, doubtless, offer themselves ; but once beard a lion in his den and he will rend thee in pieces."

Harry Seaborne made no reply, but he grasped the lieutenant's hand convulsively.

The next instant they were standing before the terrible Morgan.

"Boy," said the buccaneer king, addressing our hero, and as he did so making his great black brows meet over his hooked nose, "you have had six weeks to elect between two things—namely, the life of a jovial buccaneer or death. Which way hast thou decided?"

"The lad will become a buccaneer, most assuredly," said Walter Evandale, nudging our hero.

"But I must have the answer from his own lips," said Morgan, petulantly. "Speak out, my lad."

"I would rather die a hundred deaths than lead the life of a rascally pirate," was the brave reply.

"Fiends of hell! dare he beard us to our very faces?" cried Morgan, turning black in the face with rage.

"Dare I? Yes, of course I dare. I am an English boy, and I have fought under the brave Duke of York, who will one day be England's king, Heaven bless him!—aye, fought with chivalrous Frenchman and with brave Hollanders, and if I have not quailed before such foes, is it likely that I shall do so before the bloodthirsty buccaneers of the Spanish Main?" answered the brave Harry Seaborne, whilst his cheeks flushed with anger and indignation.

"Have a care, lad, or your tongue will wag away your life," roared Morgan, furiously. "Death and fury! why will you not join us? Dare you say that there is any disgrace in leading the wild, free life of a buccaneer?"

"There have been buccaneers who have won the world's admiration and respect," answered Harry Seaborne ; "but they were not the men who burnt women and children wholesale in churches, who hung God's ministers from the towers and the spires of God's temples, or who tore out tongues, or branded with red-hot sword-blades helpless prisoners, in order to make them turn traitors to their kinsmen. And yet all these things I have heard thy villainous followers confess to have done—aye! and they have boasted of it with pride."

"True, boy; but their victims were only Spaniards," hissed Morgan savagely between his clenched teeth.

"Spaniards or no, what matters it? Are not Spaniards fellow-beings? By Heaven! would that I were on the deck of our admiral's ship, the Great Harry, and had the hanging of all you cut-throat villains from the fore-yardarm; then, when the last man of you had expired, I could die happy,' said the prisoner.

"My poor boy, you have signed your death-warrant," whispered Walter Evandale in our hero's ear.

"Abusive puppy, thy life shall atone for this! Perchance if I had your admiral here I would serve him as you seem anxious to serve us. May the devil take him and his brother, King Charles, also!" cried Morgan.

But, before the words were well out of his mouth, Harry Seaborne had whipped Walter Evandale's sword out of its scabbard, as it hung at his side, and had assailed Morgan with the fury of a tiger, crying—

"Ah! wilt thou dare mutter high treason in the presence of an English officer and gentleman? By the light of Heaven! I would force the words backward down thy throat with a sword point wert thou thrice a buccaneer king."

Morgan was seized with the most intense surprise at this conduct on the part of our hero; but in his long career of crime he had been too often suddenly set upon to be taken off his guard.

His great sword was raised in an instant to ward off Harry Seaborne's slashing cut, and, as Walter Evandale was about to pinion our hero from behind, he cried—

"Hold! lieutenant, he has invited me to give him a lesson in sword play, and, by Heaven! I will —a rough one, maybe; but, anyhow, one that will last him his life."

"Follow the counsel you just now gave to one of your men, Captain Morgan, and perform deeds instead of uttering vaunts," exclaimed our hero, while he continued to slash, and thrust, and guard, with consummate ability.

Presently Morgan's sword was dashed from his grasp, and flew upward to the very roof of the cavern.

With a shout of triumph Harry Seaborne sprang forward and thrust straight at the throat of the buccaneer chief.

The lunge would have been fatal had not Walter Evandale hastily interposed, and received the weapon through the fleshy part of his left arm.

Seeing that he had severely wounded the man who had saved his life—the only being amongst the whole piratical horde who had shown him any kindness—Harry Seaborne relinquished the hilt, the emotions of youth asserted themselves, and he burst into a flood of tears.

Soon he was roughly seized upon by a dozen hands, and felt himself helpless in the power of his foes.

Walter Evandale plucked forth the sword from his arm and calmly returned it to its scabbard, the black Amazon came forward and commenced to bind up his wound, and Morgan, recovering his breath, said—

"Lieutenant, I owe my life to you. That young limb of Satan has the strength of his father, the devil, in his single arm! I was never disarmed before, and by him I will take care that I am never disarmed again. Cast him quickly into the Cave of Despair, ye who have charge of him; and, ere we sail in the morning, see that he be buried in the sands of the seashore above high-water mark up to his head, batter them hard down around him, and there, hatless, let him remain until the hot tropical sun pierces to his brain and drives him mad, or, failing that, till the vultures pluck out his eyes, or the swamp alligator scents him out and takes off his head at a gulp. Away with him, I say! and see that all is done which I have commanded."

"Captain Morgan, let me beseech you not to consign the poor boy to so terrible a doom," said Lieutenant Evandale. I have received most hurt in the encounter, and surely if I can forgive—"

"I cannot!" cried Morgan, interrupting him. "Lieutenant Evandale, 'tis easier to shake a tower of granite than Henry Morgan. The malapert boy shall die as I have commanded, though you begged me to the contrary until the day of doom. Have I not pronounced justly?" he added, glaring round on the assembly.

"Aye—aye! most justly," shouted all.

"Death!"

Walter Evandale bit his lip until the blood flowed, but his face was passionless as ever.

"Forgive me, my only friend, for having unwittingly hurt you," said Harry.

"I do, my poor boy. I will see you before you are led forth to suffer, and, if you have any dying wishes, perhaps I may be able to fulfil them," was the reply, and he held our hero's hand for a moment in his.

The English middy was then led away to the dark and cheerless Cave of Despair.

After he had departed a kind of listlessness and apathy seemed to fall over the assembly.

They drank their wine in silence.

Cards, dice, and tric-trac were now thrown aside.

"Death and the devil! let us arm and out!" suddenly cried Morgan, half drawing his great sword, and then clashing it back into its scabbard. "Methinks that day will soon dawn in the east, and there is much to do aboard both the Death Cloud and Pestilence before we can put to sea. This will be no common voyage, my brethren. Our first prey shall be the gold-laden Spanish galleons; and thereafter I have sworn to lay waste, to burn and destroy, every Spanish seaport from Cordova to Costa Rica. Ah! ah! we will have rare sport and rare spoil, too."

With wild cries the buccaneers seized their arms, and, thirsting once more for scenes of blood, followed their great captain out of the cave.

CHAPTER II.

THE CAVE OF DESPAIR—LIEUTENANT EVANDALE MAKES A CONFESSION.

THE rock-bound dungeon into which Harry Seaborne was thrust by the fierce buccaneers was a kind of inner cave, the entrance to which consisted of a huge rock, nearly a ton in weight, which had to be rolled back by the joint efforts of about a score of men ere the terrible prison chamber could be reached.

When he was fairly within it, and the stone was rolled back to its place, so closely did it fill the aperture that not a ray of light was admitted from the outer cavern, and every sound was also excluded.

The darkness was so intense as to be almost palpable.

'Twas difficult to breathe in such a place, for the air felt as heavy as lead.

Well did it deserve its name of the Cave of Despair, for bondage therein, though it lasted but for a few hours, was enough to crush the stoutest heart, and exclude hope from the most sanguine breast.

But this was not the reason that it had won its terrible name.

It was because the buccaneers confined no prisoners therein but such as were destined to suffer, within twenty-four hours, a death of torture.

It answered to the condemned cell in New-gate, only there was no reprieves at the Isle of Tortugo.

King Morgan was not a monarch who indulged in prerogatives of mercy.

Hour after hour passed by, and to Harry Sea-borne each one seemed an age.

If he sat down it was upon an oozy bed of wet slime ; if he stood up the roof of the cave was so low that he often, in his apathy or thoughtlessness, knocked his head against it and nearly stunned himself with the blow.

It seemed, however, to be of great length.

He guessed that by the echoes of his voice as he spoke aloud ; but he had no desire to investigate its intricacies.

He knew full well that had there been any exit therefrom the pirates would not have immured him therein.

That was a very safe conclusion.

At length he discovered that the great stone which had been rolled back to allow of his being thrust into this loathsome den was again in motion.

Presently the aperture was once more clear, and a tall, elegant cavalier entered, holding in his hand a lamp.

Directly he had done so the rocky door was once more shut, and Harry Seaborne, who had been momentarily blinded by the strong glare of the lamp, after having been so long immured in the pitchy darkness, recognised the form and features of Lieutenant Evandale.

"Oh ! sir, this is kind of you," faltered Harry. "What news do you bring me, my only friend ?"

"None, my boy," replied the buccaneer lieu-tenant. "The doom that Morgan has threatened, will, without doubt, be inflicted upon you ; and did I attempt to save you I should be involved in the same fate, without effecting any good by the sacrifice of my life. Morgan would turn upon his best friend if he endeavoured to thwart his designs."

"Oh ! what a monster he is. Why did you interpose to save him when I had my sword-point at his throat ?"

"Were I to tell you, boy, you would scarcely believe me," replied Evandale, with a strange smile.

"But I would believe you, my friend, no matter how strange the reason," replied our hero.

"Well, then, my lad, I will tell you. Secrets are safe in the keeping of the dead, and you will be dead in a few hours more. Even if 'twere not so I believe I could trust you, under all circumstances, Harry."

"Of course you could. Did you not save my life, Mr. Evandale ?"

"A doubtful service, since I but preserved you for a more terrible death," sighed the lieutenant.

"Never mind that now, but tell me why you saved Morgan's life at the risk of your own."

"Because I hate him."

"Because you hate him ? That is a very strange reason," stammered Harry Seaborne.

"Yet, nevertheless, a true one. I owe him a terrible debt of vengeance, and I will suffer no one to cancel that debt for me. Listen," and the young lieutenant's utterance was choked by gasping sobs as he spoke ; "that man slew my father on his own doorstep ; he crucified my mother on the roof of our hacienda ; he thrust three baby brothers and sisters into a heated oven, and baked them to death with slow torture ; and, lastly, a great hole was dug, and therein every house-servant and slave was buried alive. And all these horrors were perpetrated because this man-fiend found less money and less treasure in the hacienda than he had anticipated."

"Horrible—horrible ! But how did you escape the wholesale massacre ?" inquired Harry.

"By being absent from the hacienda at the time, on a visit to an uncle, who dwelt far away in the in-terior. As I grew older, the terrible tale was told unto me, and the name of the perpetrator of all these barbarities, and I swore that when I had grown to man's estate I would avenge my slaughtered kin-dred. That is why I am a buccaneer."

"But why have you delayed your vengeance so long ?" asked our hero. "Surely you must have had many opportunities of slaying the bloodthirsty free-booter since you have joined the band ?"

"Aye, many ; but I am waiting until his life is more valued by himself.

"Until lately he has been as reckless of it as though it was worth nothing ; but now he begins to appreciate it at a higher value.

"He has fallen in love with a young and beautiful girl, and one of the objects of this expedition, on which we are about to start, is to capture her and carry her off.

"Then, with the immense wealth that he expects to amass from the plunder of the gold-laden Spanish galleons, and of the towns along the coast, Henry Morgan means to buy a fair estate in some foreign land, and there, in company with his young and beautiful wife, to lead a life which he deems will exceed in happiness that of the seventh heaven."

"And can such a wretch as this buccaneer chief really love?" exclaimed Harry Seaborne.

"All men who can hate deeply can love strongly, and that he loves this beautiful Spanish girl there can be no doubt.

"I have even heard him rave of her in his sleep. Well, I will help him to fill his cup of happiness to the brim, I will aid him to raise it to his lips, and then, 'ere he can taste one drop of its honied contents, I will dash it from his grasp, and at the portals of the earthly heaven he has so long sinned and sighed for I will avenge father, mother, brother, and sisters, by despatching him straight to that nethermost pit which is yawning wide to receive him.

"But first he shall have a foretaste of its tortures at my hands, such as I have been maturing for years."

"Oh! it is all very horrible," muttered our hero, with an involuntary shudder.

"It is all very just," was the cold, stern reply.

"That man's life is as much my property as the rings on my fingers or the diamond buckle that secures my plume.

"Woe be to him who cheats me of my long-hoarded vengeance.

"Better for him had he never been born.

"And that black Amazon, Zoabinda! Over her I must keep an especial watch, for if she hears Morgan rave in his sleep, as I have done, of Donna Catalina de Guzman, her hatred towards him will grow as bitter as my own; and, instilled by a paltry jealousy, she will endeavour to take a life which is forfeited for very different reasons.

"Yes, Mistress Zoabinda, I will take especial care that you do not thwart me."

At this juncture a great noise was heard in the large cavern without.

CHAPTER III.

THE SAILING OF THE BUCCANEERS—ALONE ON A DESERT ISLE—THE ALLIGATOR.

THE great stone that blocked up the entrance to the Cave of Despair was again rolled backwards, and revealed a number of the buccaneer sailors, all armed to the teeth, standing in the aperture.

"Lieutenant Evandale," said one, touching his forelock, "Captain Morgan requires your immediate presence aboard the Death Cloud. We are about to weigh anchor, sir. Prisoner, you are to come along with us."

"My poor boy, in talking of other matters, I have forgotten to ask if you have any last wishes or dying requests to make," said the handsome lieu-

tenant, laying his hand upon Harry Seaborne's shoulder; "because, if so—"

"I have not, sir," replied our hero, sorrowfully. "I am an orphan, and leave no one in the wide world to mourn my fate. I am glad that I do not, for it is a very terrible one; yet, nevertheless, I have enough courage to endure it."

"That is well," answered the lieutenant. "Let us on then, for 'tis useless to trifle with fate."

The buccaneers closed round our hero with their swords drawn, the lieutenant placed himself at their head, and in this manner they quitted the cavern, and bent their steps towards the seashore.

How beautiful appeared the face of nature after Harry's long immersion in the gloom of the cave!

The sun was just rising from behind the mountain peaks, and threw his first rays of chequered light upon the towering branches of the bread-fruit and cocoa-nut-trees, leaving the valleys still in partial shadow.

The birds were singing in the tree-tops, bees and other insects were merrily buzzing among the myriad tinted tropical flowers, and the murmur of the sea fell soothingly on the ear.

Here, in a little bay that was almost land-locked at its mouth, and formed a secure haven in all weathers, lay the great war ship, Death Cloud, and close by her consort, the brig Pestilence.

At the mainpeak of the former vessel fluttered in the breeze an immense black banner, on which were emblazoned a skull above two crossbones.

'Twas the dreaded flag of the buccaneers.

It had waved over a hundred victories, but never over a defeat; and that white skull had grinned from its lofty perch upon such scenes of cruelty and ruthless slaughter as never before had disgraced a conqueror's arms.

Cheerily came the song of the sailors as they manned the capstan bars and wound up the great anchor from its bed. On the towering quarter-deck paced the watchful sentries, and slanting sunbeams flashed and sparkled upon their steel morions, corslets, and the points of their shouldered spears.

Her ports were all open, and the bright-polished brass carronades flashed in three lines from her sides.

Those grim bulldogs were silent now, but in a few hours, at most, they would be belching forth destruction and death.

Morgan was plainly distinguishable, standing on one of the high battlemented round towers, that rose one on each side of the richly-carved and galleried stern.

He was surrounded by many of his chief officers, whose showy raiment and profusion of gold lace, feathers, and jewellery, were very pretty adjuncts to the gay and spirit-stirring scene.

"Farewell, Harry Seaborne; I must aboard at once, for no doubt Morgan is chafing at my delay. May Heaven give you grace and strength to bear the tortures that are in store for you," said Walter Evandale, seizing our hero's hand.

The brave English boy returned the pressure, and the next instant Walter Evandale was gone.

Harry felt a strange and bitter pang as the only

being who had shown him any kindness during his captivity quitted his side.

He could have cried like a child, but he checked the bitter tears and strode manfully on.

In a few minutes more they had reached the beach, and there, far above high-water mark, they halted beside a small round hole of about five feet in depth.

The hole was Harry Seaborne's living grave.

He was grasped by two strong sailors and his arms pinioned tightly to his side with a cord.

They then raised him in their arms and dropped him, feet first, into the hole.

He exactly filled it.

His head alone appeared above the level of the ground.

Situated as he was, he could by no earthly possibility have clambered out of the hole unaided ; but, to render his living grave more secure, the fierce buccaneer sailors proceeded to trample the clay-mingled sand tightly down around him, until it was as firm as adamant, and the pressure upon his body nearly stifled him.

Then one of them, with a malignant grin that might have become a mocking fiend, placed a jug, full to the brim with cool, limpid water, on one side of his head, and a dish of luscious fruit on the other.

Harry shuddered, for he felt that these tempting things were placed so near to him that, when a few hours hence he was raving with thirst and hunger, they might increase his torment, for, like unhappy Tantalus, though they would be almost within reach of his lips, yet he would be unable to put out a hand to convey them to his mouth.

The sailors now left him and hurried aboard their ships.

Five minutes later Harry Seaborne was the sole human inhabitant of the beautiful Isle of Tortugo.

Slowly and majestically the shapely bows of the Death Cloud and the Pestilence swung round seaward.

Then clouds of white canvas bellied out from the square black yards, and the ships began to glide up the bay like two stately swans, the Death Cloud leading the way, with the mouths of all her brass carronades flashing in the sunlight, and the Pestilence following in her wake, with a blood-red flag waving at her peak.

It was a fair and gallant sight, and Harry Seaborne forgot his own hapless condition in contemplating it.

But when Morgan, quitting his plumed and jewelled warriors, stalked to the stern of the vessel, and, raising his hat, waved him an ironical adieu, he remembered all, and his heart throbbed for an instant, as though it would break.

Then, clenching his teeth and knitting his brows in fierce anger, he muttered to himself—

"Walter Evandale's narrative affords me some consolation now. In avenging his slaughtered parents, and brothers, and sisters, he will also avenge me. Aye ! cruel murderer, thy days, like my own, are numbered, and thy end will be equally terrible."

He watched the two vessels gliding down the bay until they passed the headlands and were hidden from his view.

Then he turned his thoughts inward, and tried to realise the full horrors of his position.

It was no difficult matter to do so, since a moment's consideration assured him that escape was absolutely impossible, and that if the heat of the midday sun did not by sunstroke put a speedy termination to his miserable existence, he must still perish by the slower process of starvation.

Slowly the glorious luminary crept up the cloudless heavens towards its meridian, until at length it looked like a great golden boss in the centre of a vast shield of glittering steel.

Then Harry Seaborne's tortures commenced. His brain felt like a mass of burning lava, for the perpendicular rays of that tropical sun were streaming down upon his uncovered head.

Already an intolerable thirst consumed him, and his tongue seemed to cleave to the roof of his mouth.

He heard the melody of the song birds, the buzz of the summer insects, the musical murmur of the sea, as one in a dream ; but sometimes his eyes would wander to the cool cocoa-nut groves, scarcely five hundred yards away, with an intense longing, and then would turn with greater desire still to the limpid water that sparkled in the stone jug by his side, or to the plate of rich and luscious fruit, that only required an outstretched hand to reach them.

But alas ! both his hands were pinioned down tightly to his sides, and if his arms not been bound with cords, the weight of the clayey sand would have prevented him raising them, even had he possessed the strength of a giant.

So hour after hour passed away, each one increasing and intensifying the sufferings of the poor sailor boy, until the overpowering odour of musk suddenly assailed his nostrils.

He opened his eyes and glared wildly around him.

Well he guessed what caused that ill-omened smell.

He knew that it came not from a plant, or its aroma would have reached him long before.

The only living things naturally giving forth that strong and overpowering perfume are the musk-rat and the alligator.

One of these creatures he knew it must be who was approaching him now.

He looked around, and his terrors were no idle ones, for an alligator, at least twelve feet in length, was approaching him at a sluggish trot.

His scales glittering in the sunshine, his great mouth open wide, displaying its formidable rows of double fangs, regular as the teeth of a saw.

Escape was, of course, impossible ; his body was protected and out of harm's way, but at one snap the alligator would tear his head from off his shoulders.

Well, he could but die once.

These thoughts passed through his brain with lightning rapidity.

Yet, when he looked round, the unwieldy brute was close upon him, so near that he could feel its hot, nauseous breath upon his face.

At the very moment, however, when Harry Seaborne thought that the next would be his last, the report of firearms reached his ears, followed by the most unearthly howl and shriek that he had ever heard.

He opened his eyes, and the first sight he beheld

them still grasped fusils that were smoking at the muzzle.

But who were they, and what brought them here?

The boat was a large one, and propelled by eight long-bladed sweeps or oars.

At the moment when Harry thought the next would be his last, the report of firearms reached his ears.

was the alligator lying on its back and struggling in the agonies of death.

The second, a large boat lying broadside by the shore, and full of armed men.

It was evidently some of these who had fired upon and killed the alligator, for one or two of

Its occupants could not have numbered less than a score of men, some of whom were evidently common sailors, others assuredly common soldiers, and the rest officers in both services, of some rank and distinction.

These latter sprang ashore directly the boat

grounded on the beach, and advanced straight towards the prostrate but still struggling alligator.

"A splendid shot of thine, Don Pedro. It has evidently pierced the brute in a vital part. As for my bullet, it glanced off its scales and flew upwards like a hailstone from sloping glass," said one.

"Yes; I flatter myself on the general correctness of my aim and the steadiness of my hand," replied another voice, which must have been that of Don Pedro. "But now to give the mighty saurian his *coup de grace*. That pleasing duty pertains to my rapier's point. Now, gentlemen, behold !"

The speaker unsheathed his long, slim rapier as he spoke, and glanced keenly at the animal's upturned yellow belly, to detect the exact spot where throbbed its heart.

At last he found it.

But just as he was about to thrust home, the brute in his dying agonies, and without any malice prepense, with a sudden flap of its scaly tail tossed Don Pedro high in the air.

At the same instant another cavalier thrust his sword into the alligator's body up to the very hilt, thus giving the monster its quietus, for it stiffened out and lay quite still in death.

The discomfited Don Pedro picked himself up from off the wet sand, his brilliant dress all soiled and crumpled, returned his rapier to its sheath, shook himself to see if any bones were broken, and then ejaculated—

"The alligator had his revenge there ; delicate attention in return for delicate attention ; but I see, Don Guzman, you have effected my self-constituted task for me. You have slain the monster."

"Yes, that I have," retorted he who answered to the name of Don Guzman, with a laugh. "But ah !" he ejaculated, in an altered tone, "we have arrived too late to rescue a poor fellow-creature from his voracious maw. See, the brute has devoured him entirely, save his head. Let us cut the animal up, and see if he hath swallowed the body entire."

"You may cut him up, but you won't find the body there," said our hero, gravely.

"Ah ! the head speaks," exclaimed Don Pedro. "There is some deviltry here."

And he crossed himself devoutly.

"There has been some deviltry here," replied Harry Seaborne, "but not of the kind you dread. My body is attached to my head, never fear ; but I have been buried alive, and left here to starve by the accursed buccaneers."

"Ah ! say you so ?" exclaimed Don Guzman. "That little plot of theirs we will, at all events, frustrate. Ho ! there, you in the boat. Send two men hither at once with a spade and picks."

They speedily came, and in a very few minutes our hero was unearthed and pulled out of the hole.

"Now tell us quickly who you are," said Don Guzman, in an authoritative manner.

"I am an English midshipman. My vessel, the Bulldog, was captured some weeks ago by the buccaneers. All were slain but me. I was reserved for the still more terrible fate from which you have just rescued me. Whom have I to thank for that timely rescue?"

"I am Don Juan Perez de Guzman, captain-general of the sea and land forces in New Spain of his most Catholic Majesty Alonzo III.

"For months my most ardent longing has been to discover the island which harbours the blood-thirsty buccaneers who pillage and destroy our seaport towns.

"I have done so, and I know it is at present deserted by them, because we saw their two war vessels leave the bay and steer seaward, while we were creeping up close under the shadow of the shore.

"Now, our object is to sack their cave of as much pillage as we can carry away with us, and then quarter in it some eight or nine hundred Spanish soldiers, so that when, after their present cruise, they return home, they may find themselves made prisoners in their own stronghold. Can you guide us to this cave of theirs, my boy ?"

"Most assuredly I can. Follow me, signors," said Harry Seaborne, in an ecstacy of delight.

He led the way confidently from the beach up the grassy slopes ; the path to and from the cave was so firmly impressed upon his mind that he couldn't miss it. Already he thought he saw the top of the great lime tree whose lower branches drooped over its yawning mouth. He never hesitated in his onward course therefore; yet when he reached the spot where the mouth of the cave should have been naught could be seen of it.

Harry stammered out his surprise and consternation ; his manner was too natural for the Spaniards to fancy that he was deceiving them for a moment. Search was made in every direction for the cavern, and in that search he himself zealously assisted, yet no cavern was anywhere discovered.

"The rascals must have a trick of so covering or hiding its mouth with brushwood or some other contrivance that perhaps it would take days or even weeks to discover the cave," said the captain-general. "That time we have not at our disposal. We must return to Costa Rica, in order at once to despatch hither a force of tried soldiers to take possession of the island, and capture this robber horde when they return. Young man, will you cast in your lot with us ? Wealth and fame are to be earned in the army and navy of King Alonzo as quickly as in those of any other monarch. Come, your decision, and quickly ?"

"I will enter any service wherein I may have a speedy opportunity of crossing swords with this wretch, Morgan," replied our hero, bitterly. "By Heaven ! I thirst as much for his blood now as I did for the water which stood beside me, and which I could not reach, when buried in the sand half an hour ago."

"Then I will appoint you to a man-of-war that we are going to send out from Costa Rica on purpose to engage and capture this villain. Then you may have an opportunity not only of crossing blades with him, but of afterwards seeing him hang in chains from the fore yard-arm," said the captain-general.

"Agreed ; I will join that ship," answered Harry Seaborne, quietly.

"Let us to the coast, then, and away," said the captain-general ; "come on, my friends."

At that moment the boom of heavy guns was clearly distinguishable in the distance.

CHAPTER IV.

THE DEATH CLOUD AND THE SPANISH GALLEON.

OUR readers will remember that the last view our hero obtained of the two buccaneer vessels was when they rounded the headland that formed the narrow entrance to the bay and glided out to sea.

Then Harry Seaborne and the Spaniards, after they had relinquished their search for the cave, and whilst they were proceeding to the beach, heard the sound of very heavy firing in the distance.

Let us now follow the fortunes of the two piratical craft, and see how that firing was caused.

Like two graceful, white-winged swans the vessels dropped down the bay, the stately three-master leading the way, and the pretty little gun-brig following close in her wake.

They sailed in company about two miles out to sea, and then the Death Cloud signalled to the Pestilence for her captain to come aboard to receive his final directions.

The Pestilence backed her fore-yard, a boat was promptly lowered, and six flashing oar-blades presently made the scattered waters foam and sparkle as they rose and fell in monotonous but regular cadence.

Morgan and Walter Evandale stood alone on the towering poop of the Death Cloud when Captain Rupert Russel came up the side and ascended the three flights of steps that led to the quarter-deck.

He was still clad in the sombre suit of black velvet he had worn in the cavern on the preceding evening ; his long silver spurs clinked on the oaken planks (it was the fashion even for officers in the royal navy to wear spurs in those days), as did the gilded end of his sword scabbard.

He doffed his black, broad-brimmed, sable-plumed cavalier hat as he approached Morgan, and then, after a low bow, folded his arms on his breast, and silently awaited his commands.

"Captain Rupert Russel," said Morgan, "I have made a slight change in our plans since our anchors have been at the bows, and our ships have been breasting the waves. Our cruising ground is the Spanish Main, as we determined last night; but I mean to attack Chargres, and not to leave of that city one stone upon another, for I owe Chargres a very heavy debt of vengeance, and I am too honest to leave it unpaid."

Rupert Russel (it might have been out of respect of Morgan's honesty, it might have been out of mere politeness) bowed low at this, and his jewelled fingers played unconsciously for a moment with the hilt of his rapier.

"Well, gallant Captain Russel," continued Morgan, "thou knowest the Carribbean Sea near unto the coast line is full of coral reefs, and not adapted for tacking or manœuvring. I therefore send your Pestilence to keep considerably to windward of me, so that if a fleet of Spanish men-of-war should appear on the horizon you may bear down upon the Death Cloud and give us a timely warning to evade them. Do you understand ?"

"Perfectly, Captain Morgan," was the reply. "But am I to be precluded from engaging any vessel in fair fight ?"

"Any vessel of your own size you may, for I know that you will come off victor. Any larger vessel, no, for your destruction might lead to ours. Do you plainly understand me, Captain Rupert Russel ?"

"Plainly, Captain Morgan," was the reply ; "and I will act up to your injunctions in all things."

"'Tis well. Then get thee back on board thy ship. Thy course is sou'-sou'-west, half west ; but keep sufficiently close to the land, the third day from the present, that the noise of a large city being blown up by gunpowder may reach thine ears. Then, should this incident happen, tack ship and bear down upon Chargres."

Rupert Russel again bowed low.

"Thy commands shall be obeyed to the very letter," he said ; "yet, in spite of the injunctions thou hast laid upon me, the Pestilence may have stricken sore ere thou seest me again."

Turning on his heel, he then quitted the quarter-deck of the flag-ship, and was rowed back to his own vessel.

Then the two buccaneers bore away from each other by running down the sides of an isosceles triangle.

.   .   .   .   .   .

Morgan and Lieutenant Evandale, who was the first officer of the watch, stood upon the quarter-deck of the Death Gloud until their consort was pretty well half down on the horizon.

Brightly the sun shone on the calm bosom of the ocean, but the gentle breeze that blew from the westward soon caused the beautiful Isle of Tortugo to lessen far astern, and at last to disappear.

As the heavily-pooped ship careered over, her great white sails bellied before the wind, and the bright blue water flashed from her sharp prow, to bubble in many showers under the expanded wings of the white steed that, with blood-red nostrils and arching neck, upreared beneath the bowsprit.

The sailors, with the lesser officers and the arquebusiers, were grouped in the forecastle and in the deep waist, over which peered the brass arquebuses of the poop, while the sailing-master, with a great gaudy chart spread on the capstan, was intently measuring the distance from headland to headland along the Guatemala coast, and from thence to Chargres and Panama.

And still Morgan and Walter Evandale strode up and down the quarter-deck conversing.

The stern buccaneer chief was telling his younger companion of all his brilliant hopes and aspirations.

"I know that thou lovest me," he said, "or I would not tell thee of these, my day-dreams."

"You may trust me, Morgan," replied Walter Evandale. "Have I not thrice stood between thee and death ?"

"Aye, and on two occasions, when all my other officers stood aloof, because not one of them could have saved my life except at the imminent hazard of his own. And yet you, my friend, shrank not from the danger."

" I shrank not because thy life is very dear to me, Morgan," was the reply.

" And yet why should it be so? I have done no more for thee than for others," said the buccaneer.

" Pardon me, Morgan, but your great heart forgets the many favours it has conferred, the many kindnesses it has granted. I owe you a deep debt, and one day I will pay it."

Had Morgan noticed the expression of the young lieutenant's face as he uttered these words he would have been startled, for assuredly no love illumined that pale, handsome, but saturnine countenance. The momentary clenched teeth and flashing eyes spoke rather of a terrible hatred.

Morgan's attention was, however, taken up elsewhere, for suddenly he exclaimed—

" Ha ! yonder is a sail that beareth towards us somewhat suspiciously. By Heaven! she is Spanish, too."

Lieutenant Evandale sprang upon one of the culverins, and, shading his eyes with his hand, for there were then no telescopes, he peered for an instant intently at the stranger.

" Well, what do you make her out to be?" asked Morgan, abruptly.

" A great Spanish frigate, galleon-rigged, with twenty-four culverins a-side, cross-bows on her forecastle, and hackbuts on her poop, full of men, too. See how many helmets are glittering in the sunshine."

'Twas even as the young lieutenant said, for the noonday sun shone joyously on the bright blue sea, and fell upon the snow-white canvas of the approaching vessel, which was swelling to the breeze above the tier of brass-mouthed culverins that peered from the red port-holes of the bow waist and her towering poop and forecastle, which were covered with a profusion of heraldic and symbolical carving and gilding.

Her masts were each composed of two tall spars, having four large square sails.

She had ponderous basketed top and poop lanterns, a great square spritsail, under which the water that boiled against her bow was flashing as it wreathed and foamed in the light of the meridian sun, and bubbled under the counters of her stern.

Several men in armour were visible above the gunnel, and their pikes glistened as she approached, rolling over the great waves. There was one whose cuirass and helmet of polished steel shone like silver as he stood on the lofty poop.

When she was still about half a-mile distant a red flash broke from the tall forecastle of the stranger, a wreath of white smoke curled aloft through her rattlins and white canvas, and a stone bullet whistled over the water across the foreyard of the Death Cloud.

Morgan signalled that no notice should be taken of this hostile demonstration.

Then the stately galleon, spreading her broad canvas more fully to the wind, sheered ahead, and, backing her foreyard with an air of considerable seamanship, lay-to across the bows of the buccaneer.

A great yellow banner then slowly rose to her main peak.

As it unfolded itself there gleamed thereon the three golden castles of Spain.

And now on each side of her stately bows could be clearly read her name. It was " La Sancta Trinidad " (The Holy Trinity).

One glance at the lofty sides, the grim cannon, tier above tier, and the gigantic poop of the Spanish galleon, with her gunnels lined by pikemen and arquebusiers in their steel caps and coats of mail, sufficed to convince both Morgan and his lieutenant that they were opposed to a ship which it would be next to madness to engage, and yet from whom there was in all probability no escape.

" I think that by putting our head about and steering sou'-sou'-west we might outsail her," said Evandale.

" Outsail her !" echoed Morgan, with an oath. " But I won't outsail her ! The Death Cloud has fully half as many men, and more than half as many guns, as this vaunting stranger, and we buccaneers are unused to run either by sea or land. By Jove ! 'tis just as well that we never learn the way. Let my black banner with the skull and cross-bones flutter in defiance of yonder jaundiced flag ; and hark ye, Evandale, nail it to the mast."

Up went the sable flag in an instant, the great skull grinning as if in horrid mockery at the coming carnival of death. Lieutenant Evandale, with a hammer slung to his right side, and a bag of nails clutched between his teeth, ran up the shrouds and quickly performed his mission.

He had scarcely regained the deck when the red flash of a cannon gleamed from the Death Cloud, and the whizz of the ball could be distinctly heard as it passed through the Don's rigging.

At this prompt reply to her own gruff challenge a dozen bright banners at least fluttered in the wind from the gaff, peak, and mast-heads of the Spanish galleon.

These were the private pennons of the commander and of the distinguished officers who served under him, many of whom were blue-blooded grandees of old Spain.

Both vessels had been going under easy sail, but they now began to shorten way and bear up for each other, making all secure on board as the distance lessened between them.

The trumpets rang shrilly out, the drums beat, and the cymbals clashed in harsh response.

" Open the gun ports ! Shoot home the culverins !" cried Evandale, through a speaking-trumpet.

" Yare, yare ! my yeomen of the sheets and braces. Cheerily, cheerily, ho !" roared Morgan.

" Arquebusiers to the poop and forecastle !" hallooed the artillery master. " Prime pans, light matches."

" Crossbowmen to the tops and yards !" echoed the captain of archers, in a shrill treble.

Thus was the Death Cloud cleared for battle.

Every order was obeyed with alacrity.

The buccaneers, like a pack of bloodhounds, were anxious to fasten their grip on Spanish throats.

The Holy Trinity was coming on under topsails.

Her canvas being hauled up, displayed her steel-bristling decks, and the polished mouths of her great carthouns, that gleamed upon the dark blue water as they were run through the carved and pointed sides of her gunnel.

These primitive cannon were loaded with bullets of stone and iron, and pebbles lapped in lead.

On board the Death Cloud the crossbowmen, with their weapons bent and bows laid, and the arquebusiers, with muzzles pointed and matches lit, were crouching behind the wooden parapets of the poop and forecastle, which, like those around the tops, were all fashioned in the shape of battlements.

The cannoniers stood by their culverins with linstock and rammer, and the waist of the ship bristled with steel caps, short pikes, bared sword-blades, and ponderous axes.

On the poop were now gathered Morgan, Evandale, and a couple of score other cavaliers, glittering with lace, and velvets, and cloth-of-gold, their white bejewelled fingers toying with the gem-set stocks of the pistols that were thrust within their broad silken sashes, or with the diamond-sparkling, gold-hilted rapiers, that hung so gracefully at their left sides.

These are the gay gallants to whom the reader was introduced in the cavern on the preceding evening.

We shall see how long their hands will remain white presently.

It is quite a mistake to assume that a fop is generally a coward.

Experience shows us that it is undoubtedly the reverse.

Prince Murat (*la beau sabreur*) was ever in the van of battle.

So was our own Prince Rupert.

The Cavaliers of Charles I. had more of mad valour than the sombrely-clad Puritans ; and it has been noted in many a modern battle-field that the very richly-uniformed regiments of cavalry have, in most cases, eclipsed in daring, in dash, and in *élan* those less splendidly garbed.

At length both vessels were within three lance lengths of each other.

No sound broke from either but the ripple of the parting waters under their counters.

Their bows were very nearly in the same direction, thus they were approaching each other crabwise—broadside opposed to broadside.

There was very little manœuvring in those days.

Close quarters was the prevailing fashion of engaging, and the sooner yardarm was linked to yardarm the better the combatants liked it.

So the adverse crews continued gazing on each other, both longing for a closer relationship.

All at once a line of lights glittered along the deck of the Spanish galleon.

" Down on your faces, my hearts of steel !" cried Walter Evandale, waving his sword.

Arquebusiers, cannoniers, swordsmen, crossbowmen, and pistoliers had thrown themselves flat on the deck almost ere the flames had shot from out the gaping muzzles of the Spaniard's great carthouns and demi-culverins.

The stone and iron hail that the galleon belched forth tore across the Death Cloud's decks, splintering her bulwarks and rending her rigging and canvas, but, owing to Walter Evandale's wise precaution, did no destruction to human life beyond slaying six arquebusiers, who occupied a little wooden turret at an angle of the poop.

CHAPTER V.

DESTRUCTION OF THE SPANISH GALLEON.

" Now, my merry devils, it is our turn !" roared Morgan, foaming at the mouth, as he always did when he was strongly excited. " Cannoniers, to your lintstocks ; crossbowmen, to your duty. Aim low and aim sure. Remember we all fight with halters around our necks, for the captured will be hung on the yardarm."

A fierce cheer burst from the buccaneer crew, and the next instant a volley from their cannon, crossbows, and arquebuses was poured upon the great quarter and lumbering stern of La Sancta Trinidad, while her people slowly and laboriously re-charged their unwieldy pieces of artillery.

The bolts whistled from the crossbows, bullets whizzed from the arquebuses, and the cannon-shots boomed as they flew over the decks or sank with a heavy crash into the huge hull of the Spanish frigate, causing her to reel for an instant like a drunken man.

But the Dons replied with vigour, and the reports of their answering guns reverberated like thunder across the bosom of that tropical sun-illuminated sea.

From the poop and forecastle the arquebuses maintained an incessant roar, and their bullets, each containing three ounces of lead, being fired point-blank, did deadly execution, beating great pieces of buff and mail into the bodies of those whom they slew or severely wounded.

" Now, now, yeomen of the sheets and braces ! wear, wear ! Look alive, my boys, or we shall all be dead enough in five minutes—wear, wear, I say ! Cheerily, ho ! cheerily," roared Morgan, once more.

He required no speaking-trumpet to make his stentorian voice heard, and he was obeyed promptly.

By rapidity of manœuvre and superior seamanship, the Death Cloud, almost hidden by the dense smoke of the carronades, bore back for an instant. and then sheered down upon the larboard side of the Holy Trinity.

Immediately she had done so she poured in a tremendous broadside upon the Spaniards, who did not expect it from that point, and the sudden crash and slaughter filled them with alarm.

" By Jove ! that is well done, my trusty cannoniers. Fire into them, and fail not, or never again will ye handle sponge or rammer. To it, Mansveldt, with thy bowmen ! At it, D'Olonois, with thy arquebusiers ! Bring down those rascally archers from the galleon-tops, or, by Heaven ! we shall all be riddled with holes like kitchen cullenders," bellowed Morgan.

A loud cheer was the response to his words, and crossbowmen and arquebusiers, knowing that his eye was upon them, strove to outvie each other in skill with their respective weapons.

The deck of the Death Cloud had, by this time, become encumbered with the dead and wounded, and as there was neither accommodation nor due attendance for the latter, they were permitted to lie just where they fell, with their blood streaming away to leeward, and dripping from the scuppers into the ocean, while the shot ploughed and tore up the oak planking of the deck, beat down the bulwarks, rending masts and booms and spars to shreds and splinters. Each time the ponderous stone bullets of the great Spanish carthouns thundered and rushed through the sides of the Death Cloud she staggered and trembled in every rib and plank.

"Sweep down the Spanish gunners with your arquebuses—shoot them dead through their open ports!" shrieked Morgan, hastily traversing the corpse-strewn main deck, and then leaping upon the forecastle, where Mansveldt the Dutchman, like a burly blacksmith, was handling one of those ponderous firearms as easily as if it had been a modern rifle.

"For God's sake do as I bid you, for one more volley from those accursed carthouns will send the Death Cloud to her ocean bed with the rapidity of a flash of lightning," continued the buccaneer chief, whilst in the madness of his anxiety and excitement he bit his nether lip until the blood flowed.

"We are doing our best, and our men can do no more," muttered Mansveldt, who had not been in a good temper since Rupert Russel had been promoted over his head to the command of the Pestilence. "We have been purging the Dons with leaden pills ever since the game commenced, and, I doubt not, we've made some hundred or more of them sick with the dose. But in this sudden darkness which has come on we aim at random."

As he spoke he levelled one of the long arquebuses in its iron sling with his own hand, and applied the match to the open pan.

A shriek from within one of the Spaniard's ports, and the heavy fall of a steel-clad gunner, echoed simultaneously with the report, proving that he was no indifferent marksman.

But, as Mansveldt had remarked, the darkness had almost become that of night.

The clouds had gathered in thick masses, totally obscuring the blue sky, and the red sheet lightning began to gleam from behind the jagged rifts, and from out the oft-recurring rents in the heavens.

Dark as ink grew the calmly-heaving sea, but a low murmuring wind was rising in the distance, that threatened shortly to fleck its surface with foam, even if it did not stir it into mountainous ridges.

But these sudden changes were either unseen or unheeded by most of the combatants. The vessels who were now lying-to, with their foresails backed, and both crews pouring their missiles upon each other with a deadly animosity, that increased as the slaughter and the darkness deepened around them together.

Notwithstanding the superior size of the Holy Trinity, and the heavier metal of her cannon, the Death Cloud stood to her bravely, for those bold and desperate men by whom she was manned fought with ropes around their necks, and this urged them to the highest pitch of rashness and valour.

Meanwhile, Morgan, who had returned to the poop, stood with his arms folded on his chest, calmly surveying the scene, though bullets and crossbow-bolts whistled around him like hailstones in Labrador.

Whenever a barbed crossbow-bolt from the Holy Trinity struck down a brave buccaneer, to writhe in agony and welter in blood within his sight, or when a shot tore up plank and beam almost beneath his feet, he would growl a heavy malediction, but the next instant he was calm and tranquil as ever.

Suddenly Walter Evandale grasped him by the hand, and pointed to the Spanish galleon, saying—

"She has hauled her wind—she is bracing up her foreyard-arm—she is about to give us the slip."

"That she shall never do," roared Morgan. "By that manœuvre she has signed her death-warrant. Ho! my lads, up with her helm; bend sheets and braces. Now, then, helm hard down—hard, I say. Let her luff, and may the devil not be put out at having to find unexpected accommodation for so many visitors."

He concluded with a strange sepulchral laugh, which was drowned in the shout of triumph that burst from his crew as they perceived the object of the manœuvre.

It was answered by a wild shriek as the prow of the Death Cloud struck the hull of the Spanish galleon right amidships.

That shriek was the despairing cry of the strong and brave, who had never flinched when the arrow flew and the culverin boomed around them.

At the moment of the crash the foremast of the Holy Trinity bent like a willow wand, and then went by the board, bringing down with it the main-top-mast and a wilderness of spars and sails.

The heavy culverins and carthouns went surging all to leeward, and, crashing away the lee bulwarks, plunged into the sea.

Then the ship herself parted in two, the towering forecastle floating one way, the castled poop another, with the poor fellows that were left, who clung to them with the blind tenacity of despair and dread.

Again and again, at the sport of the waves, were they dashed aloft towards the cloud-draped sky, and then hidden, as a mountain of foam swept over all, hurrying them down fathoms deep, never to rise more, together with the last fragments of their ill-fated ship.

The Death Cloud, with her white sails expanded, floated triumphant over their ocean tomb.

CHAPTER VI.

IN WHICH THE PESTILENCE STRIKES.

WHILE Morgan is getting his ship into something like order, inspecting the amount of damage done, and ascertaining the number of his dead and wounded, let us see what Rupert Russel is about.

It will be remembered that the Pestilence bore away from the Death Cloud in a sou'-sou'-westerly direction, some two or three hours before the latter ship encountered the ill-fated Spanish galleon.

But, strange as the coincidence may appear, almost at the very moment that Morgan and Walter Evandale from the deck of the Death Cloud sighted the Holy Trinity, Rupert Russel and his first lieutenant, who in like manner were parading the quarter-deck of the Pestilence, beheld a strange sail approaching them.

That this stranger was also Spanish there could be no manner of doubt; she betrayed it in her build, her manner of sailing, and in many other ways that the experienced eyes of a seaman would detect.

It soon became apparent also that she was a much larger vessel than the Pestilence, but then the pleasurable discovery was at the same time made that she was a merchantman, not a war-ship.

"Outward bound to Old Spain, I'll warrant, and laden with gold and diamonds and all the other priceless gems of the New World. By Heaven! we must take that ship, Joseph Bradley. Come, my friend, we must entrap her by a ruse. Let us make ready, so that the Pestilence may strike sore."

Joseph Bradley, the second in command, gave a grim smile at his superior officer's lowly uttered but ghastly joke, and half drew his sword, an intimation that he was ready to obey his commands.

"Hoist the British flag half-mast high, and run up above it the plain blue pennon of distress. Close all our ports, so that we may ourselves resemble a harmless merchant craft, but so lightly that they may open at a moment's notice, and see that all the culverins within are double shotted. Then get all our men out of sight, save some two dozen, whom order to divest themselves of their armour and don their plain clothes. When this has been done, keep firing the smallest of our culverins as a signal of distress, so as to entice this Spaniard to our assistance, when we will board and carry her."

"Good—good! a capital device, Captain Russel," exclaimed Joseph Bradley, rubbing his hands with evident delight. "All shall be done as you bid. But how quickly she approaches us."

"All the more reason for haste on our part. Come, get the men promptly to work," rejoined the captain.

The men did get promptly to work, and in five minutes the smart, bloodthirsty looking little gun-brig was changed, to all outer appearance, into a harmless merchant craft.

No culverin muzzles now frowned along her sides, for the ports had all been closed, while the guns on her deck were covered by bundles of loose sail-cloth or heaps of seeming merchandise.

Her yards, too, seemed to be swinging about anyhow, as some of the less important ropes had been cut, and now waved in the breeze, while such of the sailors as had been suffered to remain on deck lay about in strange and listless attitudes, as though ill or dying.

Yet, in spite of this, a close observer might have seen crouched under the lofty bulwarks of her main deck scores of fierce and bloodthirsty buccaneers, all armed to the teeth and ready for action.

And now a puff of white smoke rises from her bows, followed by the roar of a culverin.

'Tis the the distress gun.

The buccaneers fire it every minute to attract the attention of the Spaniard.

Ah! at last she hears them; she alters her course, and bears up towards them.

A suppressed cheer breaks from the buccaneer's decks, but is quickly quelled.

On comes the stately Don.

She is a three-master—a very large ship—named the Santa Catharina.

The great white sails belly out before the breeze, and the yellow banner of Spain floats proudly from the peak.

Nearer and nearer still; but when about a furlong from the buccaneers she backs her foreyard, and floats motionless on the water, like a graceful swan.

What can be the cause of this?

Does she suspect the ruse?

No; the look-out in the maintop has sighted the buccaneers who lie about the deck of the Pestilence, he has reported what he beholds to his officers, who are assembled on the poop, and the captain, fearing that he may be bearing down upon a fever-stricken, or even a plague ship, thus hauls off.

But the vessels are now within hailing distance.

Rupert Russel guesses what causes the Spanish vessel to hold aloof, and, seizing a speaking-trumpet, he bellows through it—

"Aid us, or we perish!"

"What ship is yours, and what are you afflicted with?" was the response of the captain of the Spaniard.

"This is the English ship Bull Dog, trading from Boston to the Cape," cried Rupert Russell, again. "We are perishing for the want of water; our casks were all washed overboard a week ago in a heavy gale."

"Then you have no infectious complaint on board—no fever, no plague?"

"No; we have none of those things. We are only dying with thirst," replied Rupert Russel.

"We will soon terminate your torments, my friends," replied the Spanish captain, still through his speaking-trumpet. "We will range up alongside and give you a dozen casks; we can well spare them."

A gleam of fierce triumph crossed Rupert Russel's pallid brow. The low chuckling of the buccaneers was audible as they heard the reply of the Spanish captain, and swords and daggers were loosened in their sheaths, to cut the throats of those who were intent on rendering them a kindness.

On came the Spanish ship, careering over the sunny, dark-blue waves—nearer and nearer yet, until, on the tranquil bosom of the great deep, she lay right alongside of the treacherous buccaneer.

Then Rupert Russel drew his sword and cried, in a voice of thunder—

"Fix grappling-irons! Boarders to your feet!

Battle-axe men in front—swordsmen in the centre—pikes in the rear—arquebusiers and crossbowmen to the tops and castles with you, to cover our advance, and see that ye aim quickly and aim sure. Now, my men, I will lead you. Let the Pestilence strike!"

He was in his element now, that tall, pale, black-velvet-clad cavalier, with his small, white hand grasping his sword-hilt, his fingers all sparkling with diamonds and amethysts and rubies.

The Spaniards saw the deadly snare into which they had fallen, and essayed to escape therefrom, but in vain. Before they could glide away from the buccaneer's side the grappling irons had been fixed and bolted, holding both vessels together in their terrible embrace.

The next instant, Rupert Russel, with his sword between his teeth, and a long-barrelled pistol in his right hand, clambered over the enemy's bulwarks and gained her deck.

A pike point was at his throat, but he shot the bearer down. Two more were thrust at him, but he severed their heads with one slashing cut of his terrible sword, and the next instant he had stretched the bearers thereof also dead at his feet.

By this time dozens of his boarders had sprung over the Spaniard's bulwarks after him, and still they continued to arrive, until at least a hundred bloodthirsty demons stood on the vessel's decks.

But the Spaniards, though only merchantmen, were not going to yield without striking a blow. Had they not in them the blood of Columbus, of Pizarro, of Cortez, of Ruy Diaz the Cid? And would they dishonour such illustrious ancestors in an hour like this? Never!

Merchant sailors in those days knew well how to wield pike, brandish sword, and level guns, for often, when pirates infested every sea, they were called upon to protect their cargoes with their lives.

Around each of the Santa Catharina's three great masts were ranged stands of pikes and swords, these her seamen eagerly seized, and turned like a pack of fierce hounds upon the intruding wolf.

Their captain, a man of giant stature and noble bearing, placed himself at their head, exhorting them by every saint in the calendar to defend their lives and their ship to the last gasp, for no mercy was to be expected from their bloodthirsty foes if they once overcame them.

"You say truly, vaunting Spaniard," shouted Rupert Russel, who had overheard the concluding remark; "we buccaneers entertain not such pitiful sentiments, and yet in one sense we do, and loving-kindness to boot, for do we not endeavour to send ye as speedily as possible to that heaven which your cunning priests tell you exists beyond the tomb? If 'tis so then are we not kind?"

"Blasphemer! I will send thee straightway to that nethermost pit which our priests also tell us awaits such as you beyond the tomb. Reviler, mocker, infidel—have at thee!"

As he spoke the Spanish captain sprang at Russel with the fury of a tiger.

"Spanish dog, have at thee in turn!" cried the buccaneer captain, crossing blades with the giant, and with such energy that sparks of fire flew from the clanging weapons.

"Now, my lads, stand back!" he exclaimed to two or three buccaneers who seemed anxious to help him to overcome the Spanish captain with their pikes. "There is plenty of food for your vengeance elsewhere; this little job I have cut out for myself, and no one else must have a finger in the pie. Away!"

Thus adjured, his men left him to fight his own battle, and presently both buccaneers and Spaniards, as if by common consent, leant upon their arms and gazed with strange interest at the personal combat.

The Spanish captain was a master of fence, and he held his own for a long time; but Rupert Russel's cool, nonchalant manner of attack and defence, accompanied all the time by a running fire of biting sarcasm, taunt, and reviling, at length caused him to lose his temper.

From that instant his fate was sealed—the buccaneer captain guarded or avoided all his cuts, thrusts, and slashes with consummate ability and coolness, and when the Spaniard began to feel tired and exhausted he in turn adopted the offensive.

Like quivering streaks of forked lightning were his thrusts, and in a few minutes the life-blood of the Spanish captain streamed from half-a-dozen deep wounds; but he still fought on, protecting head and heart, if he could do nothing more.

But Rupert Russel pressed him home; presently his sight grew dim—he reeled—the sword dropped from his relaxed grasp—he fell to the deck, faint from loss of blood.

"Do you beseech me for life?" asked Rupert Russel, placing his foot on his chest.

"I scorn to beseech anything from my fellow-man, and yet the errand of mercy on which we approached your ship ought to insure it, as well as the lives of my unfortunate crew, without the asking," was the reply of the Spanish captain.

"It was a meritorious and kind-hearted action," murmured the buccaneer.

"Then, in consideration thereof, how do you mean to treat us?" asked the Spaniard.

"In the most considerate, kind, and thoughtful manner," was the reply.

"How so?" demanded the Spanish captain, his face, for an instant, lighting up with a grateful smile.

"By slaying you one and all," was the laughing retort. "When is a man so fit to die as just after he has performed a kind and meritorious action, especially if 'tis towards his enemies? That is the instant for a true friend to strike home, in order to send him straight to the Paradise of the blessed, without the intervention of the tropical and sulphurous purgatory. I am that true friend."

As he spoke he thrust his sword with savage glee into the Spanish captain's heart, and with such force that its point stuck deep into the deck beneath.

The Spaniard expired without a groan.

But this act of Russel's aroused the fury of the Spanish sailors to the utmost pitch

They had furthermore heard him declare that no mercy would be shown them if they yielded, and so the best way was to fight till the last man fell dead upon the vessel's deck he guarded.

TALES of PIRATES
SMUGGLERS and BUCCANEERS.

No. 3]   THE SCOURGE OF THE SPANISH MAIN.   [ONE PENNY.

" Do you beseech me for life?" asked Rupert Russell, placing his foot on the Spanish captain.

MORGAN the BUCCANEER; or, the Terror of the Seas.

They did fight well and bravely; but though in numbers they were nearly equal to the buccaneer crew, they had never made of fighting a profession and so they were at a great disadvantage.

Every buccaneer was a consummate swordsman, and understood the handling of bill, axe, pike, and arquebuse as well as a reaper knows how to handle a sickle. The consequence was the Spaniards were slaughtered like sheep, and at last, with the exception of some half-dozen officers, they were all overcome and remorselessly slain.

"Why are we spared, since our captain and all the rest of the crew have been so barbarously murdered?" asked the principal of these, as he turned indignantly upon Rupert Russel.

"To help us to discover your hidden treasure, if there be any," was the reply.

"Think you we would do so, even if such were the case?" asked the young Spaniard.

"May be so, may be not," laughed the buccaneer captain. "I am not a wizard to foretell problematical events. But we have tortures that have wrung many a confession from at first unwilling lips."

The ship was then searched, and ten thousand pieces of eight, together with five thousand golden doubloons, were found on board of her, in addition to a general cargo of cocoa, coffee, sugar, rice, &c.

No jewels or precious stones were to be discovered anywhere, and Captain Russel, fully convinced that they were somewhere safely hidden away, and that some of the officers above would assuredly know where they were concealed, again ascended to the deck.

"We have not found that which we chiefly sought for," he said, addressing those unhappy men. "Where are concealed the diamonds and other precious stones that form part of your cargo?"

Every one of the six officers declared his utter ignorance of any gems being on board.

"You cannot so persuade me," said Captain Russel, with a bitter smile. "I have put the 'question ordinary,' so now I must put the 'question extraordinary.' Ho, there! are the galley fires lighted?"

An answer was returned in the affirmative.

"Thrust in more fuel!" shouted Russel, "and some of you lead these fellows forward; the air grows chilly, perchance they feel cold."

To resist was useless, so the Spaniards, with calm dignity, rose to their feet and marched, guarded on each side by the buccaneers, down off the lofty poop and on to the main deck.

The galley was soon reached—its top was of gleaming copper—an immense fire burnt within.

Captain Russel placed his open palm within a few inches of the gleaming surface and hastily withdrew it, for the heat was intense.

The top of this galley-stove was large enough to admit of six men lying across it side by side, but then their legs would drop over in the front, from the knee downwards.

Captain Russel saw this at a glance, but it was all the better suited for his purpose.

"Strip!" he roared to the prisoners. "Your bed is ready for you. Behold!"

The prisoners bowed, but they made no commencement at undressing themselves.

"Ah! I see, ye have been delicately nurtured, and are accustomed to valets. Well, here are dozens at hand—clumsy, perhaps, but willing. Lend a hand, my boys," said the buccaneer.

Several buccaneers pounced on the Spaniards and quickly disrobed them, pulling every particle of clothing from off their bodies, cutting with their daggers when any resisting button interfered.

"Now put them to bed. They won't require tucking up, for they will not find it cold," continued Russel.

Scarcely were the words out of his mouth ere the six naked Spaniards were hurled down upon their backs across the bright copper top of the galley-stove. They writhed, they struggled, they growled hoarse anathemas, and then shrieked shrill ones; but all to no purpose, for two brawny ruffians held each of them down on his burning bed by his shoulders, and two more by his knees.

"Now, then, will ye confess where the diamonds and other precious stones are secreted?" asked Russel.

"We know not—we know not," was the response of one and all the prisoners.

"Ah! still contumacious," hissed the buccaneer captain. "Perhaps their feet are too cold, my men. Make them bend those stubborn knees, and strap down the soles of their feet against the red-hot bars. It will draw down the blood from their heads, and perhaps restore their reasoning powers."

With bursts of laughter and applause the buccaneers obeyed this behest. The shrieks of the tortured men now became terrible. Still, however, they professed to know nought of any precious stones being on board.

"Bah! we are deceived after all," exclaimed Rupert Russel, when the smell of the burning flesh had become almost intolerable. "There can be no jewels in the ship, or this ordeal would have wrung the confession from these fellows' lips before now. Take them away and pitch them to the fishes, who, perhaps, like their food cooked as well as Christians or—or buccaneers."

The six poor wretches, still alive, were then tugged off the stove, carried to the ship's side, and hurled over it into the sea, which immediately wrapped them in its watery shroud.

"Now, my hearties, make sail on the two ships, and let us bear away, for I perceive a storm coming on. Ha! ha! the rain will wash our decks, and the wind will blow away the smell of blood. By Jove! the Pestilence has stricken sore."

And with these words Captain Rupert Russel, having intimated to his first lieutenant that he should remain on board the Santa Catharina until morning, and given him instructions not to part company, retired to the principal cabin to wash his hands and polish up the brilliant rings that adorned them.

CHAPTER VII.

IN WHICH OUR HERO ENTERS THE SPANISH SERVICE AND REPAIRS TO CHARGRES.

LET us return to the fortunes of our hero, Harry Seaborne.

Baffled in not being able to discover the entrance to the buccaneers' cave, he had felt, notwithstanding his recent rescue from a terrible death, disappointed and vexed, until Don Guzman had offered him an appointment in the Spanish navy, thereby, in all probability, affording him an opportunity, and at no distant period either, of crossing swords with the redoubtable and terrible Morgan.

He felt no scruples at thus thwarting the deeper hatred and revenge of Walter Evandale, who, it will be remembered, had made Harry his confidant during their interview in the Cave of Despair; for though the buccaneer lieutenant, it is true, had preserved his life on board the Bull Dog, yet had he—or so at least our hero thought—left him to his terrible doom without sufficiently endeavouring to save him therefrom.

"He seemed to take my fate as a matter of course, and scarcely made any effort to avert it," muttered Harry to himself. "I would have shed the last drop of my heart's blood in his defence, for I loved him as a brother; but that is no reason why I should forget my just vengeance upon Morgan. I have as much right to strike the caitiff dead as he has."

He had, therefore, accepted Don Guzman's proffered appointment with joy: and high were his spirits and bold his thoughts when, proceeding once more to their boat, the Spaniards betook themselves to their oars, and rowed down the beautiful bay towards the headlands.

He could not but admire the tall and stately warriors among whom he sat, with their dark, olive faces, clearly-cut features, brilliant eyes, and glossy black moustaches.

Their garb was rich in the extreme.

Their helmets and cuirasses bright as mirrors of steel.

And they were well armed with sword, dagger, and pistol.

He thought of Columbus, Pizarro, Cortez, Vasco di Gama, and Ruy Diaz di Bivar, heroes who had made Spain famous above all the nations of the earth; but then his mind wandered to one, Admiral Drake, who, with a few small vessels, but manned by Englishmen, had scattered and defeated the largest and best-appointed fleet Spain had ever fitted out, even their Invincible Armada, and his pulse beat quickly at the thought that he belonged to the nation that had won this great glory.

Slowly, for the tide was against them, they neared the towering headlands that from the sea concealed the entrance to the beautiful bay they were about to quit.

At last, however, they were passed, and now the boat skirted the shore of the fair island until, after half-an-hour's further row, they entered a little creek, where lay a small war vessel, or guarda costa, at anchor.

A minute later they were alongside, steps were lowered, and they ascended them on to her decks.

Though, as we have said before, a small vessel, this guarda costa our hero discovered to be crowded with armed men.

Don Guzman had brought them over from Guba, determined to disperse by force the buccaneers of the island, whose existence and locality he had only discovered a few days previously.

Harry Seaborne came to the conclusion that perhaps it was quite as well that Don Guzman did not find Morgan and his friends at home, for though the little vessel was so strongly manned, Morgan's forces would yet have outnumbered them considerably, and would no doubt have won a thorough victory over their foes.

Of course our hero did not express these opinions to the Spaniards, for he knew that they were as vain as they were brave, and might possibly therefore have resented them.

A few minutes later the little vessel weighed anchor, set her white sails to the breeze, and stood out to sea, her captain assuring Don Guzman that they would make Havana by sundown.

He was wrong in his calculations, however, for the same storm—that had almost invested with the darkness of night the conclusion of the dreadful combat between the Death Cloud and the Holy Trinity, and which had shrouded in similar gloom the Pestilence and La Santa Catharina just as by Rupert Russel's command the six half-roasted bodies of the tortured Spanish officers were being hurled over the bulwarks of the latter vessel into the sea—also beset the course of the guarda costa, La Tupilso, compelling the gallant captain to reef all her white canvas and to scud under bare poles.

The clouds, none of which had been visible the short space of half an hour ago, had risen from different points of the horizon with wondrous rapidity, and swelling, as they converged towards each other, into the most gigantic proportions, had, in a very short space of time, covered the whole heavens.

The low sound of distant thunder was distinctly heard, and sudden gleams of lightning traversed the black clouds, that every moment hung in lower and gloomier folds over the waste of waters.

The gentle and hitherto imperceptible heaving of the ocean gave way to long and regular swells, denoting afar off the war of angry elements, and the guarda costa began to pitch violently.

The topmasts were struck, the topsails and staysail close reefed, and everything made as snug as possible, as the clouds came careering on, driven before the invisible and as yet unfelt tempest.

The sailors stood at the several parts where the coming danger might most require their presence, conversing in low tones with each other, now watching anxiously the gathering storm, which momentarily threatened to burst upon their little vessel, and then, with an enquiring gaze, marking the face of their captain.

Large, heavy drops of rain soon began to fall, and presently a vivid streak of lightning flashed like a glittering serpent through the murky atmosphere, while the air was rent with a report so loud that every startled seaman placed his hands suddenly before his eyes or ears.

The soldiers and men-at-arms were now sent below and the hatches battened down upon them.

In a time like this they were useless—nay, worse than useless, for they might interfere with the proper working of the ship.

Then a line stretching along the horizon was plainly visible.

It was of white foam.

"Stand firm, and ready all. Here it comes," shouted the Spanish captain through his trumpet.

The heavy ground-swell pitched the guarda costa broadside on to the path of the coming tempest, but the helm was jambed hard-a-weather, and she was brought up readily.

The grey-bearded, steel-capped, corsletted helmsman grasped the spokes of the wheel firmly with his great horny hands, and with calm, unblenching eye watched the approaching hurricane.

Onward it came, ploughing up the sea, which boiled, roared, and foamed before it.

On it swept, with lightning velocity—a moving wall of surge.

The lightning flashed fast and fierce out from the black clouds—which seemed suspended close above their heads—and ran like veins of gold along the heavens.

The thunder came, peal after peal, like reports of artillery, rattling along the skies and reverberating around the horizon, till it died away in the distance in low, indistinct mutterings.

The glassy waves between the vessel and the rapidly-careering tempest began to heave, and while every man held his breath with expectation the guarda costa rolled heavily, and a minute later, with a loud roar, the storm of wind and wave burst full upon her.

The wild waters swept across her bow-waist, filling her main deck with water, and even leapt upon her tall fore and after-castles with the noise and body of a cataract.

The terrible storm-wave swept by as speedily as it advanced, but it left a scene of wild sublimity behind.

The sea was illumined by phosphorescent light, raging with a loud roar, while vast masses of water, rising from its bosom on every side, would swell into gigantic billows, and then burst into cataracts of glittering foam.

The guarda costa plunged heavily into the yawning ocean-furrows that opened on every side, threatening to entomb her.

The whole scene that met the eye was one of sublime desolation.

This state of things continued for hours, the gale neither increasing or decreasing in intensity.

The guarda costa could scarcely hold her own, but struggled like a stout-hearted swimmer to keep afloat, and succeeded, though nobody could say how long she would continue to do so.

She was laying-to under bare poles, while the waves had long ago washed everything from off her decks.

And now the rattle of her pumps, as the crew essayed to prevent the depth of water in her hold from rising higher, could be clearly heard in the occasional lulls of the tempest.

Harry Seaborne had for the past hour been standing on the after-castle beside Don Guzman, both holding on by the same life-line, both anxiously, but in silence, regarding the tempest.

Suddenly they heard a terrible roar, like a violent rush of wind and waves into some vast hollow cavity.

So loud was it that the reverberating thunder crashes seemed to sink into insignificance.

Then, by a lightning flash even more vivid than anything that had preceded it, they saw the hull of a monstrous ship reel and stagger for a moment

within a cable's length of them. Down it plunged, bow foremost, into the angry waters, and disappeared from sight.

The guarda costa spun round like a teetotum, the revolving spokes of the wheel knocking down the helmsman.

Then she sprang forward like a dog when he leaps from a steep bank into a river, and for a minute seemed as though she would also plunge headlong into the great hollow, funnel-like vacuum in the ocean, caused by the sudden foundering of the big ship.

But this vacuum filled up again almost as rapidly as it had been hollowed out, so that instead of diving into it the guarda costa spun round again, this time the reverse way, and finally scudded away with her bow pointing as it had done before.

The helmsman picked himself up, and resumed his grasp of the spokes with a sadly-puzzled expression, for he had seen nothing of the foundering of the strange ship, and was at a loss to account for the eccentric conduct of the little craft he had sailed in for so many years.

But Don Guzman and our hero looked sadly and inquiringly into each other's faces for a minute or two, and then the former remarked—

"That unhappy ship was a Spanish galleon of the largest size. I would that I could have distinguished her name, but she foundered too quickly to permit of my doing so. I noticed, however, the figure of a saint carved in silver between her two stern galleries, together with her three great battle-lanterns, that rose above her after-castle. Now, may Heaven receive her ill-fated crew!"

"Amen," echoed our hero, reverentially doffing his plumed cap. "They number many a score. That dreadful roaring noise we heard must have been occasioned by the waters rushing into her, and causing the pent up air in her cabins to explode, like the roar of a hundred cannon. I noticed that she was dismasted, and a perfect wreck; but yet I wonder that we see no bodies floating about."

"They have all, undoubtedly, gone down with her," responded Don Guzman, mournfully.

"That were to suppose that they were all below at the time she foundered; but surely some of the crew were on deck, and, if so, they would scarcely all be sucked down with her, especially as she was mastless; and, even if they were so sucked down, one or two would assuredly rise to the surface again," replied our hero.

"'Tis hard to say," returned Don Guzman. "Be it as it may, I see no one, and a dark body could easily be distinguished amongst all that white foam. And yet I do see something—there, there, yonder, just in that luminous patch of phosphorescent water! 'Tis a man, and he is alive, battling for his life with the waves, and his face is whiter than their foam. Ah! how awful it must be to die thus, within sight of the succour that can never reach him."

"But I think he might be saved, Don Guzman—he is not a hundred yards distant," exclaimed our hero.

"Saved? Impossible! We have not a boat

that would live for an instant in such a sea, and there is not a man aboard, I dare swear, that is so tired of his own life that he would risk it on the very problematical chance of saving yon stranger," retorted Don Guzman, with a shrug of his shoulders.

"I will risk mine on the chance of saving any drowning man!" exclaimed Harry Seaborne.

"Do not think of it, my boy; you will sacrifice it needlessly," said the Don.

"'Tis at all events as noble to die in attempting to save life as in endeavouring to take it in battle," replied Harry, all the time hurriedly throwing off his outer garments.

Then he cut one of the life-lines, and fastened a coil of it around his waist.

He was now ready for his desperate venture.

"Don Guzman," he exclaimed, "if we never meet again, farewell. I mean to swim out to the rescue of yon hapless stranger; whether I am destined to succeed or no is as Providence wills. When I reach him and grasp his sinking form I will send forth a shout that you will hear, I warrant me; then bid your men haul in the life-line and pull us on board. There's not an instant to lose. I am off."

Without pausing to listen to Don Guzman's further objections, and half-fearful that he might put forth his hand and detain him by force, our hero sprang over the battlements of the after-castle, right into the raging waves, that dashed against the vessel's sides, twenty feet below, and struck out for the drowning man.

Though so young, he was a bold, strong swimmer, and cleft the waves like a swift-sailing boat.

"Keep afloat a minute longer—relief is at hand," he cried, in a voice that was clearly audible above the roar of the wind and waves, and that voice was heard by the drowning man.

A minute later our hero reached him.

He was on the point of sinking, and could not gasp forth a single word; his eyes were open, but fixed and glassy—his face and even his lips were deathly white.

Harry seized him by his long black hair, and, turning round, gave the shout that he had bidden Don Guzman listen for.

Then he struck out for the vessel, dragging the drowning man after him.

Harry's strength was failing fast, for the force of the waves was very terrible; but presently assistance was rendered by the hauling in of the life-line, which made it merely incumbent upon him to keep himself and his now almost unconscious companion afloat.

This he effected by passing his left arm under the right arm of the stranger and treading water. Soon they were under the guarda costa's stern.

They were then hauled up out of the water, and presently were safely on board.

"Ah!" said Don Guzman, slapping our hero on the shoulder, "I never dreamed that you would have succeeded so well. You are a gallant youth, and this action has endeared you to my heart. Spain, I predict, will one day have reason to be proud of her adopted son. But whom have we here? Is he unconscious?"

"Yes," answered Harry Seaborne, "and had I arrived a minute later he would have been unconscious for ever. Who he is I know not, for I was too busy in the effort to preserve both our lives to look at him whilst we were in the water, and here it is so dark that I can only dimly see him as he lies at my feet."

"Drag him within the rays of the binnacle light," said the Don. "I feel a curiosity concerning him."

Harry Seaborne and the Don effected this between them.

The former gazed on the deathly pallid face of the half-drowned man for an instant, and then exclaimed—

"Ah!" I know him, but where we have met I cannot recollect. His face seems to me as familiar as my own when seen in a glass."

"He is no Spaniard," said Don Guzman. "Ho! there. Bring lights and a flask of spirits; we must not let the man perish now he is among us. Lights and spirits, I say!"

The lights could not be brought, for the wind persistently blew them out directly they were raised above the hatchway, but the spirits were, and the neck of the flask being got between the stranger's teeth, a goodly draught was poured down his throat.

Its effect was instantaneous.

Intelligence returned to his glassy orbs, and he moved, he gasped, he breathed. At length he exclaimed—

"Where am I?"

Before anyone could reply to him one of the sailors cried—

"There is another body alongside, beating against the hull of the vessel. It can be easily rescued without anyone going into the water."

"Some of you take a boat-hook and try to pull the poor fellow aboard by his clothing," said Don Guzman.

"He don't seem to have any clothing on, senor," replied two or three men in a breath.

"Well, get him on board, anyhow. If he is beating against the ship one of you can easily lower himself over the side and get a good grip of him," said Don Guzman. "Don't let the poor fellow perish unaided."

"Let me go," said our hero, preparing again to leap over the side.

"That you shall not," replied Don Guzman, detaining him with a strong hand. "You have put us Spaniards to shame sufficiently for a single night."

Then, raising his voice, and addressing the sailors, he continued—

"Get him aboard, you dogs! By Heaven! if he is not laid beside this other rescued man within three minutes I will bastinado the whole larboard watch."

This threat had the desired effect.

A strong, burly Spanish sailor permitted a rope to be fastened around his waist, and was then lowered over the side by his companions.

A minute later he was hauled up again, bearing in his arms a naked, lifeless body.

"I think he is dead," exclaimed the Spaniard, as he gained the deck. "At any rate he is precious heavy. Come, friends, help me to carry him up on the castle and present him in due form."

Three men immediately offered their services, and raising the body on their shoulders they carried their heavy load up the double flight of steps on to the towering poop deck.

"Well, is he alive?" was Don Guzman's first question when they gained the deck.

"I fear not, sir," replied the spokesman of the party.

And they laid him down beside the other rescued man, who had relapsed again into unconsciousness.

"Why, he is completely naked," exclaimed Harry Seaborne; "and, oh! what a terrible expression of agony is writ upon every feature of his countenance. The man is dead, but he has never been drowned."

"How then, in Heaven's name, has he died?" exclaimed Don Guzman, in horror and surprise.

"Indeed, I cannot guess; but what is this? Why, his back is a mass of burnt and blackened flesh, and his feet—good God! the bones are protruding through the withered up, decorticated skin," said our hero. "This man has died by torture, and that torture shows the handicraft of Morgan and his buccaneers."

The gale had by this time somewhat subsided, and the moon shining out betweeen black and jagged rifts in the clouds had aided the faint light of the binnacle lamp in enabling our hero to make these terrible discoveries.

But the same silvery radiance might enable him to pierce the incognita of the man whose life he had himself saved, and whose face had seemed so strangely familiar to him.

He now gazed upon him for the second time, and perceived that he was a tall and finely-formed cavalier, very richly garbed in a suit of the richest black silk velvet.

He was singularly handsome, and of about thirty-five years of age.

His hands were small and white, and covered with rings, some unmistakably of very great value.

His sword hilt was of pure gold.

His dress seemed as familiar to Harry Seaborne as did his face, but even that failed to fix his identity, or to recall to the mind of our hero where they had before met.

Suddenly, however, the stranger for the second time recovered his intellect and consciousness, and for the second time asked, faintly—

"Where am I?"

Then his gaze wandered around and around, being first cast, as a matter of sailor instinct, upon the masts and yards of the vessel, then upon the helmsmen, and then upon our hero and Don Guzman.

He stared hard at Harry Seaborne, with a look of surprise, not to say horror, then he involuntarily stretched out his left arm, and his hand came in contact with the naked body of the dead man.

He turned round and gazed at the agonised, up-turned face, and then shrieked in terror—

"Ah! the very dead have risen to torment and torture me."

"Heavens! I have saved Rupert Russel the buccaneer," exclaimed Harry at the same moment.

CHAPTER VIII.

WHICH TELLS OF A VIRTUOUS SENTENCE ONLY HALF CARRIED OUT.

DILATED with horror were the eyes of Captain Rupert Russel when, first returning to consciousness, they gazed upon the burnt and blackened body of the dead sailor.

Fiercely gleamed the eyes of Don Guzman as he listened to the buccaneer's involuntary confession that he had been the torturer.

As to our hero, his feelings were mingled ones of anger and disgust—anger that he had risked his life to save so worthless a wretch; and disgust that the villain was one of his own country, claiming nationality with a Raleigh, a Drake, and a Howard.

"Don Guzman," he exclaimed, "let the man of blood recover his strength, and then suffer me to avenge the honour of England, that he has sullied, upon his vile body. I shall thus avenge his tortured victims also."

"Boy, it must not be," answered Don Guzman. "I cannot permit you to imperil your life by crossing swords with a man whose blood would pollute even the axe-blade of the common executioner. For him a very different fate than death from the weapon of an honourable and upright gentleman is near at hand."

"And what fate may that be?" demanded Captain Rupert Russel, with a reckless laugh, for he had listened to the colloquy of our hero and Don Guzman with considerable interest, though he had hidden any inner emotions he possessed under a supercilious sneer, that was half real, half assumed.

"Bloodthirsty pirate, you have involuntarily acknowledged yourself to be the torturer and murderer of this Spanish sailor who is beside you," said Don Guzman. "How we came to rescue his dead and your living body is plainly evident, for it was assuredly Heaven's will that the very dead should rise up in judgment against you, to appeal with his mute lips for retributive justice. That justice I will mete out."

"But suppose I had nothing to do with this man's death? Suppose that all I have just said was a mere incoherent raving, caused by weakness or scarcely-recovered reason?" urged Russel.

"I reject such a supposition—the confession was too clear; your horror at the sudden appearance of your victim was too real and unassumed; you are the murderer of this man, and I am your judge. I sentence you to be swung one dozen times beneath the vessel's keel, and then to be hung in chains from the foreyard-arm. A death of greater torture I cannot find it in my heart to inflict even on you."

"Thanks for your remarkable clemency," replied Rupert Russel, with a shrug of the shoulders, then, suddenly changing his sarcastic tone, he exclaimed—

"Now picture to yourself that we change places, and instead of you being my judge I become your executioner. I will show you—thus !"

Swift as a lightning flash the sword of the privateer captain sprang from its sheath, and with a fierce lunge he thrust full at the exposed throat of Don Guzman.

But ere it could take effect a sword just as keen and quite as deftly wielded turned the ruthless point aside, and the buccaneer found himself engaged, up to the very hilt, with no puny antagonist.

It was Harry Seaborne, who had turned the sword aside, and who now cried—

"Ah! would'st thou again do murder, villain? I have foiled thy detestable intention. Beware my lightning blade, or thou diest ; better had I left thee to drown like the dog that thou art."

Rupert Russel was a skilled fencer, indeed, he had been esteemed the best swordsman in the pirate fleet, but he was now weak and faint with having battled so long with the fierce waves.

The consequence was that Harry Seaborne disarmed him almost immediately, sending his gold-hilted sword flashing and quivering over the high bulwarks into the sea.

Rupert Russel then folded his arms on his chest, and said in English, so that Don Guzman should not understand—

"For Heaven's sake thrust your sword through my body, and save me from the terrible fate to which I am decreed by yonder Spaniard."

Harry Seaborne was about to comply with this request, for, in spite of Rupert Russel's rascality, his mind revolted at the awful doom to which he was sentenced, but just as he was about to sheath his steel in the pirate's heart, as the only act of mercy he could bestow, Don Guzman grasped his arm, and thus prevented him from granting it.

At the same instant half-a-dozen Spanish sailors laid hold of Rupert Russel, rendering him powerless.

They dragged him off the lofty poop down into the waist of the ship.

Then others coming around him, they tore the rings from his fingers and the gold chain from off his neck.

A rope was then slung right under the ship, running in slip gaffs, and to one end—that coming over the starboard gunwale—the hapless Rupert Russel was bound by the ankles and by the wrists.

His body was thus curled up like a ring, and, as the reader will remember, the first part of his sentence was that in this position he should be swung from the starboard bulwark, down under the ship's keel up to the larboard or port bulwark, and back again, one dozen times.

This was in itself a very terrible punishment, and to one who had already, within the hour, experienced the torture of being half-drowned, calculated to be even more so ; but it was very commonly in use in those days, so we must not give Don Guzman the credit of having invented it.

Captain Rupert Russel suffered himself to be bound in silence.

He uttered not one petition for mercy.

Perhaps he knew full well that it would be useless.

The next instant the boatswain's horn rang out, and over he went, as the rope was paid out, with a heavy splash into the water.

A minute later, all pale, ghastly, and panting for breath, he was hauled up on the larboard side, suffered to remain for a few seconds above the water, and then down he went again. Then the starboard hands began to haul in instead of paying out, and so he was drawn backwards under the ship's keel.

But all of a sudden the six men who were hauling in fell backwards in a confused heap on the deck, with only a portion of the rope in their hands.

It had been severed—clean cut through.

At the same moment the larboard men also drew in the rope on their side.

That end also had been cut through.

Rupert Russel was gone !

A score—aye, for that matter a hundred—dark and angry faces were at once peering over the vessel's side, but no Rupert Russel appeared.

A boat was lowered, for the sea was now much calmer, but though it was pulled around and about the ship for very nearly half an hour, the body of the buccaneer captain, neither alive nor dead, floated into sight, and so at length it was hoisted aboard again.

The guarda costa then once more spread all her white sails to the breeze, and shaped her course towards Chargres, which her commander seemed in some hurry to reach.

Many and various were the suppositions to account for the fracture of the rope to which the buccaneer captain had been bound.

Some supposed that it had jarred against and been cut through by the vessel's keel ; others, that a passing swordfish had fractured it, whilst some—but these formed a very small minority—expressed an opinion that Rupert Russel might in some manner have contrived to draw a knife from his pocket and cut the rope himself, thereby effecting his escape.

The almost sheer impossibility of doing such a thing caused the supporters of this theory to be intensely laughed at.

But then what had become of the body ?

Tied up as it was, most probably it had sunk at once like a stone to the bottom of the sea.

This was a very reasonable conclusion, and it was readily accepted as the probable solution of the mystery.

CHAPTER IX.

WHEREIN OUR HERO OBTAINS THE COMMAND OF A SHIP.

TWENTY-FOUR hours later the guarda costa arrived at Chargres, and the officers at once landed and repaired to the fortalice of the captain-general. Chargres was a splendid city in those days and very strongly fortified.

Harry Seaborne knew that against it Morgan was about to wage warfare to the knife, as he wished to make it a point of 'vantage in his meditated attack upon Panama, which he had sworn to capture and pillage.

Harry Seaborne hoped very much that he would be permitted to join the land forces here, so that on the landing of the great buccaneer chief he might have an opportunity of crossing swords with, and probably ridding the world of such a monster, but he was disappointed in this, though at the same time pleasurably surprised that he was appointed to the command of a swift-sailing guarda costa, called the Isolo d'Oro—he, lately a mere midshipman in the British service, and still later a prisoner and companion of pirates—with orders to cruise about, ascertain the approach of the famous buccaneer, and then at once to run back and report thereon.

"I have ascertained from the questions I have put to you, and which you have answered, that you are a thorough sailor, and fully understand the handling of a ship," said the Spanish admiral, to whom our hero had been introduced. "Besides, my friend, the captain-general of New Spain, speaks very highly of you, and has as good as asked me to give you this appointment."

Of course Harry Seaborne was gratified beyond measure, and made abundant promises that the Isolo d'Oro should cover herself with glory if he had the opportunity of putting her alongside any buccaneer that sailed the sea, even were she twice as large and twice as strongly manned.

But the Spanish admiral assured him that this was not required of him, and that at present he must confine himself to merely watching the proceedings of the enemy, and not on any account to engage in conflict with him.

An hour later Harry Seaborne was on board his vessel.

He was highly pleased with her, for she was evidently a fast-sailing craft, though she was not one which resembled the sharp-prowed lateen-sailed guarda costas that in this our present century hover like snowy-sailed sea-gulls around Gibraltar, to pounce down upon and destroy the smuggling craft from Ceuta and Morocco, who are for ever striving to escape them and run their cargo to the Rock.

Though bluff in the bows above the water line she was sharp as a lance below it.

Straight between poop and forecastle, clean in the counter, and bolted with copper, great care and much money had evidently been bestowed upon her build.

Elaborate carving and gorgeous gilding completely covered her hull above the water-line, and amid this flashed the mouths of twenty-four brass culverins and falconets, tier above tier.

The port lids were painted of the brightest crimson, and above her towering poop rose three gigantic lanterns, with tops of polished brass.

Around the butt of each mast, which was composed of one entire piece of wood, stood a rack of spears and arquebuses, and into the tube of each of the latter was inserted the haft of a boarding axe.

The vessel was square-rigged, and at each of her tops were clumsy and basket-like enclosures, surrounded by little embrasures, from whence the cross-bowmen and arquebusiers could gall the enemy in security.

At her mizen-peak proudly floated the castle standard of Spain.

Harry Seaborne was, of course, delighted with his ship, and lost no time in getting to sea. By nightfall the town and cliffs of Chargres were sunk below the horizon.

CHAPTER X.

MORGAN HEARS BAD NEWS, BUT MAKES THE BEST OF IT—A STRANGE SAIL.

LET us now return to Morgan and his followers in the great ship Death Cloud. After sinking the Spanish galleon they sailed in a sou'-sou'-westerly direction, still hoping to sight the headlands around Chargres on the following day.

But the hearts both of the officers and sailors were very ill at ease.

The galleon had been attacked because the pirates knew she was gold-laden, and with a sufficient quantity of the precious ore to make every man of their crew rich for life.

When, therefore, they were obliged to run into her, and sink her in self-defence, the shrill cheer of triumph was soon hushed at the thought that the object of that triumph was lost.

The prize for which they had shed their own and their foemen's blood was sunk beneath the bright blue waves, and had slipped for ever from their grasp.

The loss of so much wealth was most tantalising, and the officers and men of the Death Cloud were alike moody and given to grumbling.

Yet two amongst that ship's company seemed neither to grieve nor suffer annoyance.

These immaculate two were Lieutenant Walter Evandale and the black woman Zoabinda.

The former, when interrogated by Morgan as to his imperturbable indifference, replied—

"My captain, 'tis useless to grumble at the fortune of war. So that I am at your side in life and in death I will strive to be content. Nay, I will not only strive, I will be."

And Zoabinda, the beautiful black woman, had replied in a somewhat similar manner—

"Morgan, my beloved, blessed with thy love what are riches? If you could deck my arms and neck with a million diamonds your love would outweigh them all."

Strange that two human beings should so have attached themselves to one man—the one from ardent love, the other from equally ardent and intense hatred.

A mine full of diamonds would have bribed neither to leave him.

. . . .

Early on the following morning the headlands around Chargres were distinctly visible.

Seaward the hull and masts of the Pestilence were also observable.

Rapidly she approached the Death Cloud, which had hove to.

TALES of PIRATES
SMUGGLERS and BUCCANEERS.

No. 4.]   THE SCOURGE OF THE SPANISH MAIN.   [ONE PENNY.

The boats glided away in the direction of Chargres, pursued by the shot of the buccaneer ships.

MORGAN the BUCCANEER; or, the Terror of the Seas.

When she was within half-a-mile, Morgan signalled for her to follow his example, and for Captain Rupert Russel to come aboard and report. A boat was immediately lowered from the Pestilence, but as it drew near Morgan observed that no Captain Rupert Russel was aboard. Presently the boat hove alongside, a young officer ascended the side of the Death Cloud and mounted on to the summit of the towering poop.

"Has Captain Russel risen so high in his own estimation that he must needs send a subordinate officer in his place to confer with me?" demanded Morgan.

"Captain Russel, I fear, we shall never see again, sir," said the young officer, bowing. "I am at present the chief officer of the Pestilence."

"What has become of him; tell me what has become of him?" cried Morgan, showing far more feeling than he was wont to exhibit on such occasions.

The first lieutenant of the Pestilence, Joseph Bradley, then described the duel of the preceding day, in which his vessel had conquered and taken possession of a Spaniard nearly twice its size, and narrated how, at the close of the fight, a gale having sprung up, and the galleon becoming unmanageable, Captain Russel had gone on board and taken command of her, as she was too rich a prize to be lost through bad seamanship.

Shortly after he had boarded the Spanish galleon a mist had arisen, but through it the crew of the Pestilence had fancied they perceived the Spaniard suddenly disappear beneath the foaming and tumultuous billows.

They had cruised about, but never again managed to catch sight of her.

This confirmed their worst suspicions, whilst directly morning dawned, as though no doubt should remain about the matter, they had seen portions of wreck floating about the ocean, and amongst them part of a poop, bearing the name of the ill-fated galleon.

Such was an epitome of the lieutenant's short, unvarnished tale, and at its close Morgan gave vent to a deep sigh.

"I grieve more for the loss of poor Russel than for that of the ship, freighted with gold though it was," said he. "The fates have given me many brave hearts and ready hands, but very few men possessed with sufficient brains ever to become a commander."

Joseph Bradley was then invited by Morgan to descend into his cabin, and there to partake of refreshments—an invitation that was too great a compliment to be refused.

Zoabinda was also sorry for the death of the brave and courtly Captain Russel, but, in her heart, was a great deal more grieved at the loss the pirates had sustained through the foundering of the second treasure ship.

CHAPTER XI.

THE DEATH CLOUD SIGHTS THE ISOLO D'ORO.

THE very fates seemed to be against the success of their enterprise, yet Zoabinda was all kindness and attention, and helped the young lieutenant with her own fair, or rather dark hands, to wine, cake, and fruit, and all the other luxuries of the cabin table.

Joseph Bradley was even more struck by her beauty than by the favours that she heaped upon him, and really there was very much to admire in this sable Venus.

Her bright, laughing face, black as polished ebony, her aquiline, beautifully-chiselled features,

rosy lips, magnificent eyes, and, above all, the exquisite proportions of her form, constituted sufficient charms to win anyone's admiration.

One did not know whether to pay the most attention to her face, to her colossal and majestic neck, to her full and splendidly-rounded bosom, or to her statuesque arms, than which a sculptor could not have chiselled a more beautiful creation from black marble.

She was a queenly woman, and Joseph Bradley could not help pondering, whilst he gazed upon her, at the depth of woman's love, that leads her to brave all perils beside the companion of her choice rather than to enjoy the greatest comforts away from him.

He knew that this black woman had thrice saved Morgan's life at the hazard of her own; he knew, also, that she bore the marks of three wounds upon her comely person, and that in nearly every fight, on board or ashore, she combatted by Morgan's side.

So closely did she take up his attention that he scarcely noticed the proceedings of Morgan, who was engaged in appointing a new captain to the Pestilence.

"Come, Evandale," said he, "you refused the bonnie craft once, but perhaps since then you have thought better of it. If so, the chance occurs once more."

"As before, I reject the appointment, Captain Morgan," said Evandale. "My right place is by your side, and I will not leave you until I lay you in the tomb."

"How know you that you will survive me?" asked Morgan, considerably startled.

"By a dream. Nay, captain, start not, for I believe in dreams," answered Walter Evandale.

"Ah! I do not. But yet most probably you will outlive me, for you are younger and far more abstemious than I am. Nevertheless, if you do, don't give your dream the credit of it. Well, I will appoint someone else in your place, and, depend upon it, you shall not lose by your devotion to me."

"I feel convinced that I shall not," answered Walter Evandale, while his eyes flashed.

"Go on deck, then, my friend, and send down the Dutchman, old Peter Mansveldt."

Evandale departed on his mission.

A minute later Mansveldt entered the cabin.

"Captain of the Pestilence, I salute you," said Morgan, with a laugh.

"Ah! you jest, Mynheer Captain," exclaimed the Dutchman, sorely puzzled.

"Nay, I do not jest—on my soul I do not. I appoint you captain of the Pestilence."

"And Rupert Russel—what has become of him?" asked the Dutchman,

In a few words Morgan told him that, in all probability, he was no more.

Morgan, it must be remembered, knew not, as does the reader, how Rupert Russel was saved by Harry Seaborne, and taken on board Don Guzman's guarda costa, nor of his subsequent fate. And as for our hero himself, if Morgan thought of him at all, it was to picture him by this time a corpse, his body buried perpendicularly in the sand, his head rendered fleshless by the jackal and vulture, his back towards Tortugo, his eyeless sockets glaring seawards.

Ah—ah! Captain Morgan, that same Harry Seaborne has escaped, unknown to thy gang, from his living grave, and is now searching for thee on the high seas, that he may return the sorry compliment you paid him with a few inches of cold steel or a leaden bullet.

Peter Mansveldt expressed no great concern at the presumed fate of his predecessor, Captain Rupert Russel, but showed unqualified joy at being appointed commander of the Pestilence in his stead, and great impatience to enter upon his new duties.

"You will go on board at once," said Morgan; "when there promptly inspect all stores, and get your guns in good order, for to-night I mean to blockade and bombard Chargres. And here is your lieutenant, take him with you, he is a very promising young man."

Morgan pointed towards Joseph Bradley, who, recalled from his study of Zoabinda to the realities of his life and calling, rose and respectfully saluted his new commander.

All three men ascended to the quarter deck.

"Ah! what means this?" suddenly exclaimed Captain Morgan. "Yonder comes a vessel from the east-south-east, bearing at her peak the banner of the buccaneers waving triumphantly above the three-castled standard of Spain. By Heaven! that must be the captured galleon ye all deemed at the bottom of the sea, Lieutenant Bradley, with my brave Rupert Russel on board. My dear Mansveldt, I fear I have been a little too precipitate in your appointment."

Peter Mansveldt bowed, but inwardly cursed the distant ship and all aboard of her.

It would have been well for himself, for Captain Morgan, and for all the buccaneer crew, could that curse have had the desired effect.

Presently Joseph Bradley, who had been regarding the strange and distant sail carefully, said—

"That is not our prize of yesterday. She is a much smaller craft—a mere guarda costa, I should imagine—looking out for such small fry as smugglers."

"Then why does she bear our banner?" exclaimed Morgan, fiercely. "Captain Peter Mansveldt, get thee on board thy vessel, and capture or sink yonder craft—I care not which. If thou failest, I will disgrace thee by appointing L'Olonois in thy place."

"I will do my best, and no man can do more," said Mansveldt. "Lieutenant, is our boat alongside? If so, let us go at once aboard the Pestilence."

"And see that you make that same Pestilence strike as sorely as did your predecessor in office, and in as short a time, too," was Morgan's parting salute.

"I will do my best, and no man can do more," reiterated Mansveldt, as he went over the side.

Morgan watched the boat as it sped through the water and at last reached the Pestilence. He saw her crew ascend the vessel's sides, and then

every sail was crowded on the mast, until the vessel looked like a snowy-plumaged swan.

Then he noted her glide gracefully away, to give the stranger battle.

But the new-comer was not to be caught as easily as old Peter Mansveldt anticipated and Morgan hoped.

She enticed the Pestilence further and further away from her consort, then gave her the slip altogether, tacked, and bore down upon Morgan's own ship.

"By the devil! the dainty gallant is about to attack us," exclaimed Morgan, filled with as intense a surprise as a lion might be supposed to feel were he to see a mouse rushing forward to assail him. "He is coming down straight upon us. Beat to quarters."

The kettle-drums rolled and the trumpets were blown. In three minutes the ports of the Death Cloud were opened, the sails reduced by the watch, the magazine opened by the gunners, while the arquebusiers hastened to man the tops and poop, and five hundred seamen, grasping the rammers and sponges, the linstocks and tackle of the cannon, and all varieties and descriptions of weapons, stood in fighting order on her decks.

"Can'st make out her name?" asked Morgan presently of his lieutenant.

"Scarcely yet. I can distinguish an 'I' and an 'O,' that is all," answered Evandale.

Morgan shrugged his shoulders and impatiently paced the quarter-deck.

"Ah! I have it now," said Evandale, after the lapse of a few minutes, during which his eyes had never been removed from the name on the broad pennant of the stranger. "She is called the Isolo d'Oro, which in English would mean the Isle of Gold."

CHAPTER XII.

WHEN GREEK MEETS GREEK THEN COMES THE TUG OF WAR.

Now, in spite of the Spanish admiral's injunctions to the contrary, no sooner did our hero from the lofty poop of his new guarda costa sight the two piratical craft, whose outline and trim he knew so well, than he longed to attack them, and at last desire got the better of prudence, and he determined to do so.

Well he knew that if he succeeded in capturing or even inflicting material damage on either of the buccaneer vessels he would not only escape reproof, but actually receive commendation for disobeying general orders, and that he could fail in anything he undertook Harry Seaborne did not for an instant believe.

As the reader has been told in the preceding chapter, by a clever ruse, he had drawn the Pestilence away from her consort as far as he could, and then, evading her, had borne down on the Death Cloud, hoping to be able to capture her before her consort could return to her assistance.

In spite of the fact that the buccaneer was twice as large as their own craft, the Spanish officers and sailors were almost as anxious for the combat as our hero.

The officers stood grouped in all their steel harness upon the lofty poop, while the yeomen of the braces hoisted powder up from the magazine; the boatswain and his mates prepared all the culverins on the big and clumsy slides then in use, the arquebusiers put fresh matches to the serpentine cocks of their firearms, then filled their priming horns, and buckled on their bullet bags, which were hung at their sides.

The boarders were also on deck, accoutred in nearly a similar manner, and armed with axes, hand guns, and boarding pikes, that they had taken from their frames around the masts and the bulwarks of the poop.

They were all noisy, loquacious, and enthusiastic for the coming struggle.

"Rig a guy on the spanker boom, sheet home the mizen staysail, and up with the cross-jack-yard," cried our hero. "By Heaven! if we do not carry the Death Cloud before her consort comes up our chances of success are small."

For a moment the staysails began to quiver, then bellied out again, and, like a mettled racehorse, the Isolo d'Oro swept towards her gigantic adversary.

Suddenly a red flash from the high forecastle of the Death Cloud was followed by a gush of pale blue smoke, and then the iron ball of a carthoun howled through the rigging of the guarda costa and plunged into the water afar off.

Harry Seaborne was much annoyed that the enemy had fired the first shot, but raising his silver whistle to his lips he blew it shrilly.

It was the signal for battle.

"Let fly at her top hamper!" he cried, the next minute, and a line of lighted matches glittered along the guarda costa's gun-deck. "Let us see daylight through her sails—cut her cordage and disable her."

A flood of fire and smoke burst from the Isolo d'Oro's bow, waist, and towering fore and aftercastle, and a storm of missiles were hurled at the Death Cloud, which fairly reeled under the stone and iron hail.

The great stone balls from the Isolo d'Oro's demi-carthouns knocked immense splinters from the hull and carved galleries of the Death Cloud, killing and wounding many of her men.

Neither her masts, spars, nor cordage seemed, however, to be injured.

Our hero bit his lips with vexation.

"'Bout ship!" he cried; "helm hard a-lee. Let go all!"

Round swung the graceful guarda costa, like a seagull on the wing, by this rapid manœuvre escaping almost entirely the thundering broadside with which the Death Cloud had intended to annihilate her.

Then, while everything loose rolled to leeward, as she stood off on the opposite tack, the increasing breeze filled her canvas and carried the Isolo d'Oro gracefully over the bright sea, which her bows cleft as an arrow cleaves the air.

The buccaneers deemed that she was flying, and their loud cheers and mocking laughter rang over the sea and reached the ears of Harry Seaborne and his Spanish officers on their own quarter-deck.

"Henry Morgan is but a sorry fool after all, or he would guess that I was only tacking to get the wind of him, in order the better to cross his bows and rake him," muttered our hero, with a laugh.

"Ha! the buccaneer is giving us chase; they are shotting home the falcons on the forecastle," exclaimed the first lieutenant of the Isolo d'Oro. "The gunners are about to apply the matches. May St. Ebro spoil their aim!"

Three puffs of blue smoke, three flashes of fire, three iron balls whistling high overhead, and pitching into the water some distance in front of the guarda costa.

That was all that resulted.

"Steady, helmsman, steady! To your quarters, tenders of the sheets and braces. Yo, ho, boatswain! take in all the small sails, and prepare to wear!" shouted Harry Seaborne again through his trumpet.

A minute later he gave the signal, and once more round swung the guarda costa.

Morgan now perceived the object of the ruse on the part of his adversary, whom he little guessed to be the English youth whom he had so barbarously consigned to death.

He accordingly lay to and began to open fire upon the Isolo d'Oro, seemingly, however, with but little effect.

Then down went the decoy signal, the black buccaneer flag, from the peak of the guarda costa, and the golden castles of sunny Spain alone fluttered in the ambient breeze of the Gulf of Mexico.

Only for a moment, however, for quick as lightning up went the fifty heraldic pennons of the half-hundred gentlemen who served aboard the Isolo d'Oro for glory and honour rather than for pay, and they flaunted right gaily from mast, and bow, and spar, in the bright sunlight.

"Gentlemen," said Harry Seaborne, "on board yonder ship, rightly named the Death Cloud, are the robber hordes who for years have been the terror of your peaceful coasts—men who have waged war upon you with fire and sword, and who, when victorious, have slain and tortured your men, violated your women, burnt your beautiful cities, and pillaged your palaces and churches. I am about to lay his Majesty's guarda costa, the Isolo d'Oro, alongside of that ship, in order that you may avenge all these outrages."

A deafening cheer from the Spanish officers greeted this spirited speech.

"By the help of Heaven and our swords we will avenge them!" they all cried.

"Now, then, every man to his station," returned our hero, advancing to the quarter-rail and addressing the crew. "Charge home, cannoniers, cross-bowmen to the top, pikes and two-handed swords to the fore, down with the bulk-heads and up with the screens. Viva!"

A loud and prolonged cheer was the response. The poops, tops, and forecastles almost instantly bristled with cuirassed and helmeted men, the yeomen of the sheets and braces stood by their stations, the gunners by their guns, and all were armed to the teeth with swords and daggers, pikes, axes, and other weapons.

The sun was clear and the sky brilliant, the crystal waves rolling in long grassy swells, while the bellying canvas gleamed white as snow, and the gaudy pennons waved from masthead and yardarm in long ribbons of many-coloured silk on the gentle morning breeze.

And thus this beautiful Spanish vessel bore down upon her monstrous antagonist, whose towering poops and ponderous quarter galleries were gay with carving and gilding, but at the same time grim with the flashing of sharp weapons and the brass-mouthed tiers of her shotted cannon, which were all reflected in the clear waves, as they rolled past in slow, heaving ridges, that glistened in the sun.

Then those terrible guns commenced firing, and the balls whistled through the rigging of the Isolo d'Oro as she closed up, without replying, though her crew were longing for the signal to fire.

One ball splintered the guarda costa's mizenmast, another killed three Spanish officers.

But when his ship was within musket range of the Death Cloud, Harry Seaborne did blow his silver whistle, and at the long-expected signal the Spanish guns promptly opened fire.

A broadside of carthouns, rakers, and serpentines opened upon the buccaneers, while the crossbowmen and arquebusiers aloft and below fired their missiles as fast as they could bring their weapons into play.

But two could play at this game, and the Death Cloud promptly replied, the hoarser boom of her heavier metal sounding like the deep bay of a mastiff answering the shrill bark of an audacious terrier.

Still Harry Seaborne, by judicious and skilful seamanship, contrived to keep the weather gauge of his foe, the well-trained Spanish gunners cut up the rigging and battered the gay bulwarks of the Death Cloud, whilst the arquebusiers and crossbowmen, from their elevated position in the tops and fore and aftercastles, shot down so great a number of buccaneers that the Death Cloud's scuppers soon ran with blood.

"Tack !" cried Harry Seaborne, suddenly, as the cannon were charged for the fourth broadside. "Tack again, we must range up on her weather quarter, give her a raking fire, and then board."

The manœuvre was well executed. As the Isolo d'Oro passed the towering stern of the Death Cloud within half musket range, she poured in a broadside that almost blew the buccaneers' poop to pieces.

"Now close in and grapple !" roared Harry, in a voice clearly audible above the noise of the firing.

The Isolo d'Oro instantly shortened sail, the helm was jammed hard home, and there was a frightful rasping as the two vessels came together, tearing each other's canvas to pieces—while a multitude of lesser spars on board both ships snapped asunder like willow wands.

"Senor Don Alonzo, you will take charge of the ship and I will head the boarders," exclaimed Harry Seaborne, in accents of strong excitement. "Now, my men, follow me to death or victory."

As he spoke a bullet tore the crest from off his helmet.

"Better there than three inches lower," he exclaimed, gaily. "Now, then—on !"

Then such a cheer ascended to the cloudless heavens as for a moment to completely drown even the booming of the cannon.

Short ladders were brought and placed against the Death Cloud's great black hull, that rose high above their own decks. The pikemen, and those who wielded great two-handed swords, pressed behind our hero to scale the floating rampart, regarding the crossbow bolts and arquebus bullets that were rained down upon them from the Death Cloud's tops and castles no more than if they had been thistledown or feathers.

But scarcely had our hero placed a foot on the first rung of one of the ladders than a wild shriek of rage and horror from his crew caused him to glance hastily round.

A sight met his eyes calculated to strike the stoutest heart with dismay and horror.

Another vessel was bearing down under a cloud of canvas upon the Isolo d'Oro, looming like the shadow of death between them and the glowing southern sun.

"Heavens ! 'tis the Pestilence, and she will cut cut us in two," he exclaimed.

A dead silence ensued. They could hear the blocks creak, the cordage whistle, the sails flap heavily and fill again on board the approaching vessel, as she bore down upon them.

There was no time to fill the yards and forge ahead, nor to back stern formost from their perilous position. The bow of the Pestilence already threw its shadow across the guarda costa's decks, from which a hundred mingled cries of rage, wonder, and defiance arose.

Our hero caught sight of old Peter Mansveldt on the poop, and he heard him shout—"Yeomen of the braces and bowlines let go ! slack off your sheets and tacks—yare, my lads—yare and square the yards." Then he heard the crash as she came thundering down with her sharp prow upon his bonnie guarda costa, striking her right amidships, as she lay in the trough formed by the heaving waves.

The yells of despair that rose from the crowded decks of the Isolo d'Oro were mingled with the shout of triumph from the jubilant buccaneers.

The Spanish vessel was completely rent asunder, and a minute or two later the forecastle sank for ever in the brilliant blue sea, carrying two hundred brave men down with it.

Those on the aftercastle had time to lower two boats, crowd into them, and push off, before that part of the ill-fated ship sank and sucked them down into the vortex with it.

They rowed with might and main in the direction of Chargres, pursued by the shot of the buccaneer ships. Our hero prayed that one of them might strike him, for if ever he reached the shore what could he expect but death for having acted against orders, and with such a disastrous result, too?

CHAPTER XIII.

AN UNCOURTEOUS RECEPTION—CONSIGNED TO A DUNGEON.

SORE and heavy was the heart of our hero as, rowing for their very lives, the survivors of the crew of the ill-fated Isolo d'Oro stretched to their oars and strained every nerve to escape from the buccaneers.

The boats were very full, so full that there was imminent danger of a capsize, and so heavy to propel did this render them, that the long oars bent like willow wands at each desperate pull.

And great need had they for pulling, for the Death Cloud and the Pestilence, becoming locked together after the collision with the Isolo d'Oro, could not follow in pursuit, yet from their bowchasers did they belch forth such lead, stone, and iron missiles as would infallibly have sunk the frail craft had either of them been hit.

But they were low down in the water, and the hopeless fugitives aboard crouched down as much as they could, and luckily the death-fraught messengers sped over and past them without doing any damage.

Some, however, would ricochet along the waves so closely that at a single plunge they would send a cataract of water over the already drenched Spaniards, whilst others, with a sullen boom, would speed by so near overhead as to take away the breath of those they passed over.

The brows of the Spaniards were black and gloomy; they gazed upon our hero with no friendly eyes, for was he not an alien? Had he not been promoted to the command of a Spanish guarda costa over the heads of deserving Spanish officers, and had he not lost that guarda costa foolishly, aye, even recklessly?

Harry Seaborne noticed the glances of clearly-expressed hostility that were bent upon him, and knew that one and all of these men would testify against him at the court-martial which would assuredly be held to try him for the loss of his ship, where he would be arraigned for disobeying orders.

He little cared what became of himself—his doom was sealed. What mattered it whether a cannon-ball from the Death Cloud or the Pestilence terminated his existence, or whether a few hours or a few days later a file of Spanish soldiers despatched him with a score of bullets.

Of the two alternatives would not immediate death be preferable? Aye, in every way, for thereby the disgrace of a trial, the ignominy of a public execution, would be avoided.

Harry Seaborne thought so, and on that account he was the only one in his boat who was self-possessed and calm—the only one who refused to salute with a lowly bow the passing cannon-balls of the buccaneers.

Pale as death he grasped the helm, and with a firm hand guided the frail craft through the troubled waters.

Often by a quick turn of the rudder, thus throwing the boat out of the line of fire, he saved her from destruction and her inmates from a terrible doom; but they seemed unaware of this, for they had not learned sea-craft in the same service as a Drake, a Raleigh, or a Frobisher.

At last, after a thousand hairbreadth escapes, the boats got beyond range of the two buccaneer ships, and then the little masts were stepped and the sails set thereon.

They then sped swiftly over the waves, but the heart of our hero grew gloomier and sadder than ever, for the death he had courted had been denied to him.

In another hour the Death Cloud and the Pestilence were both hull down on the horizon—an hour later still the battlements of the two castles that guarded the port of Chargres rose to view.

Onward sailed the boats, and ere the sun had set behind the green mountains of New Estremadura they had passed the two castles at the entrance and fairly run into the port of Chargres.

'Twas the fashionable hour of evening promenade, and the bright-eyed donnas and senoritas of New Spain were promenading the Alamada with their mantillas and their fans, their pet dogs and their chosen cavaliers, all glittering in gold lace, velvets, and cloth of gold.

The sound of sweet music swelled upon the breeze, and ever and anon came the cadence of sweeter laughter. On the parade there was dancing, too, and from thence came the clash of the castanet, the sweet melody of the guitar, the still softer music of the harp.

Ha! how different the sounds that will pervade that gay city but twenty-four hours hence, when the boom of the cannon, the sharp fusilade of the musketry, the clash of steel on steel, shall be succeeded by the roar of the flames in her gorgeous palaces and churches, the groans of dying and tortured men, the shrieks of violated and agonised beauty, mingled with the shrill treble of crucified and bayonetted children.

Laugh on, gay city while thou mayest, for to-morrow thou shalt weep tears of blood.

Up to the steps of the Government quay Harry Seaborne steered his boat.

The next minute it was secured to a bolt ring, and the second boat was lashed on behind her.

Then its inmates mounted the steps one by one on to the quay, our hero being the last to ascend them—sad, moody, and silent.

He had anticipated the worst and the worst came.

Almost the first person that his eyes fell upon was the Spanish admiral who had appointed him to the guarda costa.

He was recognised in an instant.

The admiral started as he beheld our hero and his crew of haggard, pale, bloodstained-apparelled men, and charging them to halt, he exclaimed—

"Ha, sir, what means this? Your ship where is it? There has been sword-drawing and blood letting I see, but where are the rest of your comrades? Where is the Isolo d'Oro?"

"Lying many fathoms deep beneath the blue waves of the Carribean Sea, our comrades with her," answered Harry Seaborne, sadly. "We alone have escaped to tell the tale, and 'tis a sad one."

"Not if you bring me news that the two buccaneer ships who have dared to threaten our shores lie beside her," said the admiral, bending a keen, searching glance on the young Englishman's face.

"Alas! I bring no such intelligence. Both the buccaneer vessels are still afloat and bearing up for the city, of which Morgan has sworn not to leave one stone standing upon another."

"Ah! what is this I hear?" exclaimed the admiral, his swarthy countenance growing white with rage. "The Isolo d'Oro sunk, and no victory gained to compensate for such a calamity? By Heaven! Don Harry Seaborne, I fear that you have acted the part either of a knave or a fool!"

"The Englishman ran us into a complete trap, your excellency, and, in my opinion, purposely. A more stupid manœuvre was never executed, for he laid the Isolo d'Oro right between the two buccaneer ships, and suffered one of them to cut us clean in two," growled the first lieutenant, who was one of the saved.

This was the man who had expected the command of the guarda costa himself.

Hence a deadly enmity towards our hero had grown up in his heart. He was resolved now to obtain revenge.

He glanced round upon his companions in mute appeal, for them to back up his assertions.

They also detested the young Englishman, and were nowise unwilling to bear evidence against him.

The consequence was that his accusers were many, and the admiral only seemed too ready to place credence in them.

But suddenly a champion sprang up from whence he had least expected it.

A noble-looking young Spanish officer, no other than the third lieutenant of the foundered guarda costa, stepped forward, and, facing the admiral, said, boldly—

"I, for one, entirely disagree with the representations that my brother officers seem too anxious to make against their late commander. I uphold, and I will do so, if needs be, at the sword's point, that he acted the part of a skilful and a brave commander in the late disastrous engagement."

"As junior lieutenant you will act wisely in holding your tongue," said the admiral, tartly.

"I will remain silent now, but when before a lawfully constituted tribunal my testimony will be of some real value, and it will be quite at my captain's service," was the proud reply.

Harry Seaborne grasped the young officer's hand and wrung it warmly.

"Thanks," he said. "One staunch friend in such a case is indeed invaluable."

"However the matter may stand concerning the fight itself," resumed the admiral, "one thing is clear, Captain Harry Seaborne—namely, that you have acted contrary to orders. For that you have to stand your trial by court-martial, and, if found guilty, your doom will be death. 'Tis too late to-day to hold the court; you will, therefore, have to remain in prison until to-morrow."

"Under the circumstances you will surely give me parole?" exclaimed our hero, indignantly.

"Under the circumstances, I shall not," replied the admiral, sternly.

Then, addressing the others, he continued—

"Lieutenants Burmez and Alonzo, select a guard and conduct Captain Seaborne, your late commander, to the Castle of Angelo. Let him occupy one of the casemated cells on the north side."

"Farewell, my brave commander," said the young third lieutenant, as he was being led away. "I will not desert you if the rest do. In Don Diego Lancia de Luzman you will ever find a champion and friend."

Harry Seaborne was then led away, his own first and second lieutenants, with their swords drawn, closing up on his left and his right, and a guard surrounding him in a dense circle.

Along the Prado, where the dancers stopped for an instant their joyous carnival to look at them, down the whole length of the Alamada, where the castanets were stilled and the harp and guitar silenced in order that eager multitudes might rush forward and gaze upon the prisoner, they slowly passed, Harry Seaborne cold, stern, dignified, and silent.

He knew that in his mad eagerness to meet Morgan and avenge upon him a hundred insults he had disobeyed orders.

A brilliant success would have atoned for this, but in lieu of that he had made a most disastrous failure, and that failure would cost him his life.

Well, he had played for a large stake and lost it; he was ready to abide the issue.

At last the prison was reached.

Sentinels presented arms, huge bunches of keys rattled at the waistbelts of gigantic warders, ponderous gates and doors were flung open in succession, and the "tramp, tramp, tramp" of his guard sounded hollowly along paved subterranean passages, until at last an iron-studded postern door was reached.

This being flung open a wretched cell was disclosed within, having one tiny grated window high up in the wall, beyond reach, and two monstrous pillars, from which, at intervals, depended many rusty iron rings.

Harry Seaborne was pushed into this cell, and, to his great indignation, was also chained to one of the pillars.

His guards then left him to his own dreary and sad reflections.

As he heard their receding steps gradually grow fainter and fainter in the distance a kind of lethargic despair fell upon him.

He felt as though he were going mad.

Twenty-four hours ago how bright was his future.

Honour, power, glory, all seemed waiting to obey his mere nod. Now disgrace and dishonour were alone left him. Perhaps, also, a dreadful death on the morrow.

And all this because he had been a little too brave, a little too reckless.

Ah! but ere to-morrow the Spaniards might be powerless to judge him—their city might be in the hands of the buccaneers, who would stamp out the Spanish rule in blood and rapine.

But even then he would not be better off, for the buccaneers, many of whom must have recognised him in the recent terrible sea battle, would as surely slay him as would the Spaniards; but they would torture him first, that would be the sole difference.

Yet the buccaneers might not trouble to search those underground dungeons, and then he would escape both Spaniards and pirates, but only to find starvation as an alternative.

Ah! his position was very terrible no matter in what light he looked at it.

He presently ceased to contemplate it altogether and to gaze upon his dungeon surroundings.

They were not many, and the light was too dim even to note them distinctly.

The two great pillars, the damp, moss-covered walls, the rusty chains, the small iron-barred window—these were all that for several minutes met his gaze.

But presently, his sight becoming habituated to the darkness, he noticed something unnaturally white gleaming against the pillar directly opposite him.

He strained his vision to the utmost. Heavens! he was confronted by a hideous skeleton.

CHAPTER XIV.

REINFORCEMENTS TO A BAD CAUSE—THE ATTACK ON THE FORTS.

LET us now return to the Death Cloud and the Pestilence, who, directly they found that the boats containing the survivors of the Isolo d'Oro had got out of range, hauled up to the wind and lay to, as they did not wish to approach any nearer to Chargres until after nightfall.

No trouble took they to rescue the drowning Spanish sailors, who for a brief while struggled with the waves, on the breaking up and foundering of the ill-fated guarda costa.

It was wonderful that they were merciful enough to suffer the Spaniards merely to drown.

Within a few moments all traces of the guarda costa and her crew had disappeared.

Scarcely had they done so, the ports been triced up, the dead thrown overboard, and the blood swabbed off the decks, than three strange sails were sighted in the distance.

Lieutenant Walter Evandale had first observed them from the forecastle.

He quickly conveyed the intelligence to his commander-in-chief, Morgan, who was commending old Peter Mansveldt, who had just come aboard, upon the brilliant manner in which he had turned the fortunes of the day by his bringing the Pestilence down upon the Isolo d'Oro's broadside.

"'Twas that gained the victory," he was saying. "I scarcely thought that the conception of such a brilliant idea was within your hoary old head."

"Three strange ships are bearing towards us under easy sail," said Evandale at this moment.

"Where away?" asked Morgan, in tones of surprise, not unmixed with chagrin.

"On our weather bow," answered Evandale, with a profound salute.

"Do they seem to be Spaniards?" again demanded Morgan.

"They have not the rig or the build of Spanish ships," replied Evandale. "If they happen to be so then are they prizes captured from other nations; but I take them to be pirates."

"Ah! indeed," snorted Morgan. "I trust that it may be so, for we will enlist them in our cause. At another time we would drive away any brother wolves who snarled at the same prey, but on the present occasion the prey is stronger than ourselves, and brother wolves may make the conquest of it more sure, therefore they are welcome."

Closer and closer drew the strange ships, and they proved to be at last what Walter Evandale had surmised—namely, three piratical craft filled with armed men.

They were the War, Famine, and Devastation, under the general command of the notorious Captain Kydd, who, happening to hear of Morgan's hostile demonstration against Chargres, had determined to join him, making sure that his assistance would be welcome.

And it was welcome, for this sudden accession to their forces was looked upon by the buccaneers as almost miraculous, and Morgan's crew were commensurately exhilarated.

The great buccaneer leader was now in command of a fleet of five sail, the whole containing many hundreds of well-trained and resolute men.

Morgan called all his captains together and held a great council of war.

He quietly told the new allies that he meant to attack and sack Chargres that very night.

An enterprise so very daring surprised and for a few moments appalled even the notorious Kydd; but Morgan met all counter demonstration by picturing the rich plunder of the churches, and the countless treasures of the beautiful city.

It was then decided into what proportions the plunder was to be divided, and a code of laws were formed for extra compensation to those who were injured in the struggle.

Thus it was decided that a right arm or a right leg, if lost, would entitle the sufferer to £150 sterling, or six shares

For a left arm or leg, £100, or four shares.

An eye, £25, or one share.

A finger was valued at the same price as an eye, and other bodily parts in proportion with this scale.

All this smart money, arranged to be paid to their wounded comrades by the piratical horde from the booty derived by the sacking of Chargres, was over and above the proportion of the shares of the wounded, and was to be paid before a dividend was made of the general stock.

When the time for division arrived each person was to make publicly a solemn oath that he had concealed nothing, and this asseveration was to be depended upon as true.

Directly the sun had set and night had drawn her veil over land and sea, the five ships stood in towards the land.

TALES of PIRATES
SMUGGLERS and BUCCANEERS.

No. 5]   **THE SCOURGE OF THE SPANISH MAIN.**   [One Penny.

"What! three to one, and he disarmed and prostrate," cried Walter Evandale.

MORGAN the BUCCANEER; or, the Terror of the Seas.

The great Death Cloud led the way, with the Pestilence a little abaft of her beam, and the War, the Famine, and the Devastation gallantly bringing up the rear.

After about three hours' sail they saw **two round,** massive objects looming before them from out the darkness. Morgan knew that they were the two forts guarding the entrance to the great harbour.

He hoped to be able to pass them by in the dark.

Cautiously and silently the ships fell into line, the Death Cloud still leading the van.

The gentle ripple of the water against their bows, and the occasional creak of the cordage, were the only sounds that attended that silent, stealthy passage.

As much sail as possible had been taken in, so that the snowy expanse of canvas should not be noticed by the sentinels who paced the ramparts, whose heavy steps and the clatter of whose arms could sometimes be heard from the deck of the commodore's ship.

Morgan had begun to congratulate himself that the passage between the two forts would be successfully accomplished, when one of the casemented batteries of St. Angelo was suddenly illuminated by a flash of blood-red flame, followed by a fleecy cloud of white smoke, and ere the momentary glare had died away the crash of falling timber told him that one of his masts was carried away, while loudly rang out the Spanish battle-cry of—

"Viva Alonza nostra, muerta, a ladrones ! Viva ! viva !"

Morgan stood as one spellbound, not on account of his stricken mast, not on account of the Spanish battery, but because the momentary flash of the cannon had revealed to him a face peering out of a narrow grated window in the wall of the fort far below—a face which he knew to be that of Harry Seaborne.

Morgan had soon, however, other matters to pay attention to than the face of Harry Seaborne, late his prisoner on the Isle of Tortugo.

The attempt of his ships to pass the forts unperceived had evidently been discovered, and it was not altogether unlikely but that it might be frustrated.

The crippled topmast had brought the Death Cloud to for a moment, so that she very narrowly escaped being run into by her own consort.

Old Mansveldt avoided the catastrophe, however, by jambing his helm hard up and backing his fore yardarm. By this time every casement in the two forts was lighted up, and stone bullets and iron balls began to rain around the vessels.

Both the Death Cloud and the Pestilence returned the fire, and continued to forge slowly ahead, hoping to escape before much damage had been effected ; and the War, Famine, and Devastation hastened to follow their example.

Harry Seaborne, from his dungeon cell, could see the whole of this.

The chains which bound him to the pillar had been long enough to permit of his reaching the wall of his prison which contained the window.

Up to the narrow aperture he had, with some difficulty, climbed, and peering through he could see clearly the buccaneer war vessels.

This was because the window through which he looked was more on a level with their hulls than were the battlements high above.

He had been terribly afraid that the sentinels who paced the battlements would not discover the ships running by in the dark.

The first cannon shot had soon, however, solved this query. Others quickly followed.

He could see them hurtling through the air and could hear them as with a dull thud they plunged into the woodwork of the ships, or, with a crash, knocked great splinters of stone from the fort.

But the aim of the Spanish artillerymen was not so good as it might have been, for had it been so the ships must all have been sunk in attempting the passage, whereas not one out of ten discharges took effect.

Morgan at last perceived this, and determined to subdue the forts themselves before he proceeded any further.

First of all he signalled to the two commanders to surrender.

Such a summons was, of course, treated with contempt.

The fury of the fire from the forts, indeed, greatly increased, as though they were anxious to prove that they were able to blow him and his five ships out of the water, and would do so unless he sheered quickly off.

No doubt they were willing, but, alas ! they were not able.

The more rapidly they fired the less correct was their aim, whereas the guns from all five pirate ships were most accurate in their aim.

The blood quickly ran out of the casemented batteries, and the dead could easily be perceived lying around their pieces within them.

But fresh gunners took the places of those slain, and the battle still raged.

Morgan, therefore, determined to land a body of troops, and under cover of the darkness to make an attempt upon one of the forts from the rear.

If they carried it, they could direct its cannon against its opposite neighbour, when its subjection would be remarkably easy.

Morgan himself determined to lead the assault. He desired Walter Evandale to remain and take charge of the ship. But Evandale entreated to be allowed to accompany the expedition. His only wish was to fight, and, if needs be, to die beside Morgan.

The buccaneer captain was pleased at such generous devotion.

"Ever the same," he said, with a smile ; "ever my buckler and my barrier."

"I have sworn to be by you living, I have sworn to be by you dying," was the reply.

Then he muttered to himself—

"Aye ! and thou wilt not thank me then."

The preparations for disembarking the men did not take long.

Four boats were lowered, and the buccaneers crowded into them. The rowers stretched to their oars, and away they swept shorewards. But the cannon-balls all the while fell thickly around them.

One of those heavy missiles would be quite sufficient to sink a boat. But they all escaped, and at length reached the shore in safety. Here the boats were drawn up and left in charge of a slender guard.

The main body then pushed on towards the rear of the fort.

Morgan and Evandale marched at their head. They hoped to find this position of the fort indifferently guarded.

Surely it had never been built to stand a siege shorewards; and yet, when they came near unto it, it looked so. The walls were of immense height and thickness.

True, no guns frowned forth from them in this direction; but then how were the walls themselves to be scaled?

And no doubt when the top was won their difficulties would just have begun.

Doubtless the Spaniards still alive in the fort outnumbered them considerably; but that was the contingency that least alarmed them.

At last they came to the very wall itself. Steel caps and halberds were now seen to glitter on the summit.

They had no scaling ladders, and to reach the top seemed an impossible feat; but Morgan, with all the assurance possible, made his trumpeter sound a parley, and then hailing the commandant of the fortress, who approached and looked over the battlement, he ordered him to surrender, or threatened, with an oath, that he and every soldier under his command should be put to the sword.

Scarcely, however, had the words issued from the buccaneer's lips than the clatter of hoof-strokes was clearly audible, and a party of cavalry the next instant debouched from the shelter of a grove of trees close by and made a furious attack on Morgan's band of warriors.

So sudden was it that the buccaneers recoiled before them, and fell into considerable disorder; but the stentorian voice of Morgan quickly rallied them, and a most desperate conflict ensued.

The Spanish horsemen outnumbered the buccaneers, but the latter fought with such desperate energy that they beat them off again and again, though some of their party would sometimes get cut off and surrounded.

It was upon one of these occasions that Walter Evandale suddenly missed Morgan; he had seen him but a moment before heading a rally, so he started in search.

He was not long in finding him, and arrived not a moment to soon.

The redoubtable freebooter was down on his back, his broken sword lying under him, and three Spanish soldiers had their sword-points at his throat.

"Hold!" shouted Evandale, "the first man who strikes dies. What! three to one, and he disarmed and prostrate! Shame on ye for Spanish poltroons."

His long, straight, double-edged sword covered his leader's body, his dark, eagle eyes measured the three soldiers as keenly as did his good weapon, and in his rich raiment, and with his plume floating in the air, he looked a right noble cavalier.

The three Spaniards were for a moment cowed by his resolute bearing, and in the interval Morgan recovered his feet and had picked up his own broken weapon.

This he hurled in the face of one Spaniard, and so heavily that the fellow fell insensible to the ground, whilst at the same time Evandale slew another.

The third turned to flee, but ere he could escape Evandale's sword was plunged into his back up to the very hilt, and he fell dead over the bodies of his companions.

"You arrived just in time, my friend," said Morgan.

"A minute later and I should have forfeited my pledged word," replied Evandale.

"I will not thank you, because I can only do so in the same strain as I have always done."

"It matters not; one day you will requite me for all," answered Evandale.

"Aye, with a dukedom, if I ever live to be a reigning sovereign."

Walter Evandale smiled a smile of strange portent, but said—

"Come, Morgan, pick up one of the dead Spaniard's swords in lieu of thine own broken weapon, and return to the glorious fight, for our friends may have need of us. Yet, what do I see? By every saint in Heaven the Spaniards are flying."

It was indeed the case—they were, and in a wild stampede, too. The horsemen were striking home with their spurs far more zealously than a few minutes before they had done with their swords; those who had been dismounted, and they were many, were relying on their heels.

The buccaneers did not trouble to pursue them—they had a more pressing matter on hand—the subjugation of the fort.

But suddenly a terrible explosion filled the air, clouds of sulphurous smoke, beneath which millions of lambent tongues of flame wreathed and quivered seemed to roll and spout upwards to the very star-spangled heavens.

When it cleared away the Fort of St. Angelo was a pile of ruins.

A red-hot ball from the Death Cloud had penetrated the magazine.

That had been the cause of the explosion.

Several of Morgan's party were slain by the falling debris, which continued to rain downwards for several seconds, mingled with dead bodies and fragments of heads and limbs.

When this ceased they indulged in a tremendous cheer, and, rushing forward, scrambled like tiger cats to the summit of the ruin, and there raised aloft the buccaneer flag, which was no sooner beheld from the shipping than the cheers of their comrades afloat mingled with their own, until they must have been heard even in Chargres itself.

The buccaneers then swarmed all over the fort, searching amidst the ruins for entrances into the few remaining casements, to see whether any cannon yet remained intact and fit to be used against the opposite fort.

Walter Evandale was not less active in this investigation than the rest, and at last he discovered a narrow passage not quite blocked up by fallen masonry.

He penetrated it sufficiently to discover that it was not a gun-chamber, but a prison, and presently he saw an indistinct form and heard the clank of chains.

"Whom have we here?" he exclaimed. "A prisoner it would seem."

"Yes, a prisoner, and one doomed to death," was the reply.

"Ah! that voice," cried Evandale; "why, as I live, 'tis familiar to me."

"He who owns it has no reason to be ashamed of his name. 'Tis Harry Seaborne."

"Harry Seaborne! Why, I am Walter Evandale. I thought I knew thee, my boy."

The two friends were the next moment shaking hands warmly.

"How comes it that these rascally Dons have dared to imprison thee?" asked Evandale at length. 'I fancied that you were high in their good graces."

"I am imprisoned here, and was to have undergone a trial by court-martial to-morrow, for losing my ship—the Isolo d' Oro."

"By Heaven! 'tis a miracle we did not lose ours. The Death Cloud was never more sharply handled than by that little hornet that you had the command of. I knew that there must be an Englishman at the helm, for no Spanish captain would have fought her as you did, and when I recognised you as her commander—you whom I had left buried in the hot sands of Tortugo—I could scarcely believe my senses."

"Ha! the day was an unlucky one for me. I expected to win so much glory and honour, and, instead, have attained only to disgrace and ignominy."

"Tush, my lad; your future is neither made nor marred by such an event. As for the court-martial affair, that ordeal, at all events, you will not have to go through, for to-morrow there will be no Spaniards left in Chargres to hold one on you. Morgan will be its ruler by that time."

"A far less merciful mester, I fear, even than the Spaniards," said Harry.

"If he caught you he would no doubt be," responded Evandale; "but you must not let him catch you. Nor do I think that there is any need that he should. At present our men swarm all over the fort; but the entrance to this cell is very nearly concealed, and no one else will probably find it, whilst, if they did, in the darkness you might elude them."

"But these accursed chains—they clank at every move," said our hero.

"Let us get rid of them, then," laughed Evandale. "I will show you a trick I learned of the Antilleros—a way to pick a lock without the intervention of a key."

As he spoke he drew his sword, and inserting the point between the padlock heft and the wrist manacle, he gave it a dexterous twist and Harry Seaborne was relieved from his fetters.

"Now," said Walter Evandale, "lie here until our troops have moved up to beleaguer the city, until the sun now rising in the east has again sunk behind the western mountains, then steal forth, avoid our outposts, and Heaven prosper you."

"Oh! my friend, how can I express my thanks?

This is the second time that you have saved my life—aye! and you would do it a third time if I have need of your help."

"Perhaps a third time may come yet, Harry, or, instead of that, you may be able to cancel the debt by twice saving mine. But now I must be off, or Morgan will wonder where I am, and be sending his followers in every direction in quest of me."

Farewells were earnestly spoken, and Evandale then quitted the prison chamber.

When Walter Evandale reached the summit of the ruined fort, and rejoined Morgan, he found that the opposite fortress had capitulated.

A white flag waved from its summit.

The buccaneers were already marching in to take possession.

Thither he and Morgan immediately repaired, and the latter, being strongly possessed with his bloody fatalism, placed every man found in the fortress in one room, fired the powder magazine, and blew at once the castle and all the Spaniards that it contained to atoms.

The historian records that the noise of these double explosions was an awful announcement to the wretched inhabitants of the town of the horrors that awaited them.

They began to cast their jewels and money into wells, cisterns, and every place of secrecy that occurred to them.

The buccaneers had but yet begun their dreadful labours. They marched at once towards the town, and arrived by eight in the morning.

The ships remained opposite the ruined forts in the charge of only a few men.

Directly the town was reached a strong party was despatched to the monasteries and nunneries, who seized all the priests and nuns and put them to the torture, to reveal where they had concealed their altar-plate and other treasure.

The governor of the city was not only a man of courage, but one also of talent. After some ineffectual endeavours to rally the townsmen to defend the town, he retired with the bravest of the inhabitants and all the military into the strongest of the remaining castles, and from thence opened an incessant and destructive fire upon the invaders.

But this fire did not in the least intimidate them, for, drawing as near to the embrasures as possible, every gun that the Spaniards fired upon their foes below cost them two or three men, so excellent were the pirates as marksmen.

This sanguinary battle raged all day, the castle thundering forth its artillery, shaking the houses and tearing up the streets with its heavy ordnance, which was unceasingly replied to by the rattling of the musketry and the wild shouts of the buccaneers.

Morgan, always under cover, yet seeming to be present everywhere, attended by a chosen body of guards, commanded by Zoabinda, his beautiful black mistress, calmly directed the whole of the operations, attending to the various details with the collectedness of one playing a game of chess.

And a most difficult game it proved to be.

It was now full moon, and no apparent impression had been made upon any of the outlying castles, and that one defended by the governor was doing dreadful execution upon the assaulters.

It was in vain that the pirates endeavoured to burn the doors of the fortress with combustibles, for the Spaniards showered upon their heads all

main where they were impossible but as dead bodies.

He got his men under cover, however, and the firing ceased for awhile. But the buccaneers were by no means idle. They employed their time by constructing in all haste twelve ladders;

Up the ladders the buccaneers rushed with ruthless fury.

manner of engines of destruction. Even Morgan began to waver, and to deem his position no longer tenable.

Longer to fight seemed but to be a speedy means for the total destruction of all his force, to fly would be equally disastrous, and to re-

these were so broad that four men could mount them abreast.

When this was effected Morgan mustered all the priests, the nuns, and the wives and the daughters of the principal inhabitants, and, placing them before his men, he compelled them by blows and the points of pikes to carry the ladders towards the strongest castle, which the governor still held and so ably defended.

We might exhaust pages in the description of this heartrending scene, but we have so much of strong fact to recite that we have but little space for amplification.

The governor, before the assault commenced, was summoned, but he replied that whilst he lived there should be no surrender.

The priests and women advanced up to the mouths of the guns—pushed forward by the pikes of the buccaneers—and were mercilessly slaughtered.

In vain was the governor abjured by all the holy hosts of Heaven by the priests, in vain were the hands of wives and daughters uplifted.

The greater part of the supplicants were mown down before even half the ladders could be placed in position.

Up these the pirates rushed with ruthless fury, bearing with them fire pots and hand grenades, which, so soon as they had attained the top of the wall, they fired and flung down among the Spaniards below, causing immense slaughter and confusion.

The resistance after this was but feeble.

First the Spaniards threw down their arms by twos and threes, and then they all submitted with the exception of the brave governor.

He was determined to die then and there, and slew some of the pirates when they were in the act of offering him quarter, and some of his own soldiers for advising him to take it.

To all applications and entreaties he replied that he preferred dying with his arms in his hands, like a soldier, to being hung as a traitor and a coward.

Whilst thus he raved and fought a piercing cry was heard, and his wife and daughter, with streaming hair and bitter sobs, flung themselves on their knees before him, and entreated him to spare their lives and his own.

This only seemed the more to exasperate him, and they narrowly escaped death at his hands.

At last his enemies were forced to despatch him, and he received his mortal wound in the presence of his family, dying in their arms, thus proving that the chivalry of Spain was not extinct.

After this the other defences submitted, and the buccaneers saw themselves the undisputed masters of the place and all it contained.

Chargres had fallen, the keystone to the conquest of the New World had been carried, and that night great was the feasting and revelry that commemorated the event.

In the hall of the palace a sumptuous feast had been prepared, and Morgan and his officers sat down to it with gladdened hearts, for great was their joy at having conquered the place at last. They quaffed the red wine out of goblets of solid gold, many of them set with gems.

These were the altar cups and other sacred vessels that had been pillaged from the temples of God.

From many of them the stains of blood had not yet been washed off—the blood of slaughtered priests, murdered on the very steps of the altar.

But what recked the fierce buccaneers of this! They would have drunk the blood of their foes had it then been the fashion to do so as it had been a thousand years before with their predecessors, the fierce sea kings of Scandinavia.

Morgan was, of course, at the head of the board. On his right sat his beautiful mistress, the negress Zoabinda, her naked arms and legs and neck covered with ornaments of solid gold, brighter than any of which glistened the rows of her ivory teeth, every moment revealed by the enraptured smile with which she greeted her conquering lord.

On his left sat old Peter Mansveldt, a bloody bandage swathing half his face as well as his dexter eye, for a Spanish axe had nearly cleft his head in twain.

The other officers occupied places according to their rank; but the stately form and face of Walter Evandale, the ferocious countenance of L'Olonios, and the saturnine yet excessively handsome one of Rupert Russel were absent.

Our readers doubtless imagine that Rupert Russel lies low down in ocean depths; whether they are right or not in their conjecture it is not our province at present to inform them. But as L'Olonios is a character of subordinate interest we may state at once and for all that he was slain in scaling the ramparts of the great castle just an hour previously. As for Walter Evandale, he, having more qualms of mercy than of appetite, had absented himself from the feast on the plea of illness, and was doing what he could to quell the rapine in the city.

Let us follow him and see what good he was able to effect.

Chargres was in flames in a hundred different places, and so it needed not the light of the sickly oil lamps, that were dispersed here and there along the streets, to guide him on his way.

He entered the great gate of Don Carlos and walked down the Puerto del Principe.

Throughout its whole length there existed a complete pandemonium.

The buccaneers were beating in doors and windows with the butt ends of their pikes and lances, and dragging the terrified citizens forth into the street.

Here they would force them down upon their knees and prick them with the points of their swords and daggers until they confessed where they had concealed their riches.

Even beautiful young girls were subjected to this brutal treatment—young girls with skins whiter than the snows of winter.

The brutal buccaneers would laugh as they drew back their heads by their long black hair and pierced their tender flesh, causing the crimson blood to spout forth on their lovely necks and bosoms.

In the churches hundreds of the populace had taken refuge, but they had afforded them but a meagre shelter; great battering rams in the shape of beams of wood had been brought to bear upon the doors, and these had soon been broken in.

The buccaneers then made short work of the terrified wretches inside.

No quarter was given, though in many instances it was piteously prayed for.

Shrieks of agony, curses, and the crash of arms were heard where twenty-four hours ago the strains of the vesper hymn had risen melodiously to Heaven, and writhing limbs, distorted faces, and gashed bodies covered the floors of naves and aisles—aye! even the very altar steps.

Walter Evandale's efforts to stop the carnage that was still going on were as ineffectual as would be an outstretched oarblade to check the roaring St. Lawrence as it dashes over the wild Falls of Niagara, at that time never beheld save by savages.

In vain he commanded, expostulated, petitioned; the men would not listen to him. Inflamed by wine and ardent spirits, their naturally bloodthirsty dispositions would have vent, and it seemed as if they would not be satisfied until every Spaniard was slain.

At last, as Evandale was making his way back towards the castle, very sad at all the scenes he had witnessed, in passing the corner of a street someone clutched convulsively at his cloak.

CHAPTER XV.

A GALLANT RESCUE.

LIEUTENANT EVANDALE turned round and perceived that the person who had clutched him was a young and beautiful girl.

She was on her knees, and a stalwart buccaneer grasped her luxuriant hair with his left hand, whilst the brandished sword in his right showed that he was about to slay her.

Ere it could descend, Walter Evandale's sword-blade was interposed, upon which the ruffian's steel clashed until sparks of fire sparkled from the rasping steel.

"Off with you, she is mine!" roared the buccaneer, glaring upon Evandale with the fury of a baffled wolf, while he glided his sword-blade up towards his adversary's hilt.

"Release her or you die!" cried Evandale. "I am your officer and I command you."

"Command be hanged!" was the courteous retort. "The battle over discipline is relaxed among us jovial buccaneers. We know no officers then, slit my ears if we do."

"You shall know your master anyhow, and have your ears slit into the bargain, if you do not release your grasp on the young lady's hair and suffer her to depart with me unmolested," replied Evandale, and his eyes flashed like those of a baffled tiger.

The man saw the look and cowered before it more than at the threat, but he was too stubborn to give ground, so he quickly disengaged himself and attacked Evandale with great fury.

Walter had to protect both his own person and that of the young girl writhing at his feet, yet in less than five seconds he shred off the buccaneer's left ear.

"I've kept a third of my promise; by taking to your heels you may save me performing the remainder," laughed Walter Evandale, bitterly.

"Run from thee! bah, never!" replied the man. "I'll have ear for ear and wound for wound yet, and the girl shall die into the bargain!" and he fought with renewed determination.

"As you will," answered Evandale, and even while he spoke off was flashed the remaining ear of his ruffian antagonist, who gave a howl of mingled rage and pain.

"Now away with thee, for the next thing I will deprive thee of is thy life. By Heaven! were we not so short of men I would not give thee a chance of preserving it now," cried Walter.

With lightning rapidity he came to the disengage, and then, with a swiftness of feint and lunge impossible to be excelled, he touched the buccaneer thrice in different parts of his body in less than two seconds of time, thus proving that he had held his life all the time in his hands.

The buccaneer was cowed.

Clashing his sharp sword back into its sheath, he, with a sullen bow of unconscious respect to Evandale, turned round and walked away.

"My poor little girl, I hope he has not hurt you?" said Walter, tenderly raising from her knees the damsel whose life he had saved, and gazing into her face.

A very beautiful face it was to gaze into, with its dark violet appealing eyes, half hidden by long fringed lashes—its transparent skin, white as mountain snow—framed by the long raven tresses that draped her slender form even to the waist.

"No, I am not much hurt; but, oh! I am terrified and frightened nearly unto death," replied the lovely girl. "And my poor father, what will he think has become of me?"

"Who is thy father, fair maiden?" asked Walter Evandale.

"Don Pedro de Guzman, Captain-General of New Spain," was the reply.

"Then if I cannot give thy father news of thy safety I can give thee intelligence of his. He is a prisoner, it is true, but not doomed to death. His ransom has been set at seven thousand pieces of eight. But come, we must not stay here, or I may have to fight a hundred battles in thy defence. I must try and bear thee to a place of safety."

"Oh! take me to the presence of my father," cried the beautiful girl.

"I dare not, for he lies in a dungeon of the castle securely guarded. Did I accompany thee thither those guards would pounce upon thee, and carry thee straightway to the presence of Morgan, one of whose objects in landing here is to secure thy person."

"My person—oh! what good should I be to him?" she asked, innocently.

"On some former pillaging expedition to these shores he saw and learned to love thee. I have heard him mention thy name in his dreams. Perchance he would marry thee."

"Marry me? Oh! that would be too dreadful. Oh! preserve me from him at any cost."

"I will," answered Evandale. "And yet only in one place art thou safe, and that is inside the castle, where at this very moment Morgan holds high carnival with all his officers."

"Never mind—I will not be afraid whilst thy true heart and strong arm are by to protect me," she said, looking up trustingly in his face.

Walter Evandale could not reply; the tears sprang to his eyes and a choking sensation came into his throat at the beautiful donna's words—words of trust and confidence from the lips of innocence.

He had not listened to such for years and he felt them keenly now.

From that moment Walter Evandale's very life was at the young girl's service.

He raised her in his arms, for her trembling limbs refused to support her.

She was very light, and he carried her as easily as though she had been a child.

Half-concealed by his cloak, he might bear her to the castle without being recognised.

Down the fire-illumined streets, along the blood-stained pavement, gliding on in the shades where darkness dwelt, and with more hurried strides crossing such squares and thoroughfares as were all red light from the glare of burning buildings, Evandale bore her.

Entirely on one arm, too, for he dared not relinquish his sword from his strong right hand, as he knew not for an instant when his path would be barred.

At last he was molested by a tipsy roysterer, who brandished a halberd in his face.

With one slash the head of the weapon was cleft from its staff, with one thrust its bearer fell prone amongst the blood and dirt of the gutter, and Walter strode over the corpse.

But shortly afterwards Walter Evandale had to deal with three instead of one.

They were encountered in a narrow street, and stretched themselves across it sword in hand.

"Here is a comrade sneaking away with a pretty lass," sang out one.

"Let him stand and deliver up. Knows he not that all pretty lasses are common property in this good city of Chargres?—aye! and ugly ones, too, for that matter," the second one chimed in.

"Well spoken, mon comrade; so stop, sirrah, in the blue and silver, and let us share thy spoil, or, by my sword, 'twill be a case of thirds instead of fourths, for our swords shall be as busy with thee as spits in the king's kitchen," cried the third.

Walter Evandale came to a halt, but it was the halt of a fierce wolf at bay.

"Back!" he cried, hoarsely; "back, if ye value your lives. I have had to shred off two ears in this young lady's defence, and, by Heaven, I will quickly slit three tongues unless they cease their ribaldry within her hearing. As for your toasting-forks, I prithee put them up, unless ye would never wield them more, or would lose them over the housetops."

"Ah, ah! who is the gay cock that crows so loudly?" bawled one of them in response.

"Evandale of the lightning blade, the best swordsman in the buccaneer army," replied Walter, with a scornful laugh. "Now will ye bar his passage?"

No sooner had he announced his name than the three men sheathed their weapons, and, shrinking back into a deep doorway, suffered him to pass.

"Oh! my brave champion and preserver, when shall we be safe?" sobbed the poor girl.

"In a few minutes, my child," answered Evandale. "Yonder is the castle."

They met with no further opposition until they reached it.

By this time Walter Evandale was so exhausted that he had to set his beautiful charge on her feet.

The warders at the entrance demanded the pass-word and countersign, which were readily given, and then Walter was allowed to enter with the pretty donna leaning on his arm.

The place was dimly lighted within, and they attracted little attention as they glided along the deserted passages and corridors, where all was silent but for an occasional burst of rude merriment from the banqueting hall, or the clatter of arms and the gruff-spoken password as the guards were relieved at different parts of the vast building.

"If we but reach my suite of rooms in the southern wing unperceived I can there offer thee shelter and protection, my poor child," said Walter Evandale. "There will be none of thine own sex to tend thee—merely the kindly offices of a rough soldier are at thy command."

"Of a brave soldier, but certainly not a rough one. From what I know of thee, my preserver, I will trust myself with thee as if thou wert my brother," was the sweet response.

But before Walter Evandale could make any reply to this sweet assurance a door just in advance of them was thrown suddenly open, and forth there issued into the corridor, preceded by torch-bearers Morgan and all his followers.

Most of them walked unsteadily and were flushed with wine, but for all that there was no chance of eluding their observation.

Morgan himself was the first to perceive them and bring them to a halt.

"Ha, ha! my sick lieutenant and right trusty friend, hast been seeking a female physician to cure thine ailment? By Heaven! were such always near at hand who would not be ill? Let me look upon the beauty's face," he cried.

As he spoke he advanced and touched Evandale on the arm.

"Pardon me, captain," replied the latter, with a laugh, "but in this case she is not the physician but the patient—a peasant's pretty daughter whom I saved from having her throat cut, and to whom I am going to give shelter till the reign of blood is over."

"Ha, ha! and by whom thou expectest to be well repaid for thy kindness."

"Her gratitude will amply repay me for so trifling a service," replied Evandale, his cheek flushing redly with anger at Morgan's insinuations.

"Gratitude—ha, ha! That virtue is rare amongst buccaneers. But thou callest her a peasant. Certes! dost think me drunk, or that peasants wear kirtles of silk, and golden fringe and point lace? Bah! thou art deceiving me. I will see the jade's countenance."

TALES of PIRATES
SMUGGLERS and BUCCANEERS.

No. 6.]   **THE SCOURGE OF THE SPANISH MAIN.**   [ONE PENNY.

"Release her or you die!" cried Walter Evandale.

MORGAN the BUCCANEER; or, the Terror of the Seas.

Morgan essayed to raise from her face Evandale's sheltering cloak.

"Captain Morgan, I have five times saved thy life, and have never yet accepted of thee a favour. Look not upon this young girl's face, suffer me to bear her hence, and we will cry quits," cried Walter, trying to restrain his passion.

But he spoke too late, for Morgan had already

raised the cloak and caught sight of the fair and beautiful countenance it had hitherto concealed.

"Donna Teresa de Guzman, by every saint in Heaven!" he ejaculated.

Then he turned pale as death and staggered back against a pillar for support.

In an instant, however, he had recovered his composure, for he caught the black, glittering eyes of Zoabinda regarding him like a lynx.

"Lieutenant Evandale," said Morgan, "your prisoner is the daughter of the Captain-General of New Spain, and as such must be placed under safe keeping. I shall set her ransom down at five thousand pieces of eight, and she must be imprisoned in that portion of the castle I myself inhabit, because it is the most secure and at the same time the most comfortable."

"She shall inhabit the room next to that which I occupy myself," said Zoabinda, stepping forward. "I will at once conduct her thereto; no doubt she will be happier with one of her own sex than with rough men."

The object of this very equivocal consideration glanced at the beautiful but yet terrible-looking Amazon, and then up at the face of Walter Evandale, as if she were very unwilling to exchange the one protector for the other.

But Evandale merely smiled kindly upon her, and bid her go and be of good courage, for what objection could he make to such an arrangement?

What objection, even though he saw hatred, malice—aye! murder, as clearly writ in the negress' tawny eyes as they could have been printed in a book.

Morgan looked as ill-pleased at Zoabinda's officious interference as did Walter Evandale, but he also remained silent, and the next instant all their thoughts were turned into another channel by the sudden apparition in their midst of a ghastly death-white figure, clad in funereal black, in whom they all recognised either Rupert Russel or his ghost.

CHAPTER XVI.

WHICH TREATS OF THE ADVENTURES OF HARRY SEABORNE.

LET us now return to the fortunes of our hero, whom we left amid the ruins of the Fort of St. Angelo, waiting for the arrival of night, in order to effect his escape therefrom unperceived.

At last it came, and directly it was quite dark he stole forth through the friendly aperture the lieutenant had made in his dungeon wall, and gained the exterior of the fort.

Even then he had a difficult and a dangerous task, in the darkness, to creep down over the masses of loose stones that in the morning had been a superb fortification, and gain the level country below, for there was no moon and even the stars were clouded.

Sometimes a glare of light from the distant city as some fresh building was given to the flames shed a momentary radiance around, but the fort was too remote therefrom for the lurid glow to linger long around its piles of ruined masonry.

But, brief as were these flashes, they on more than one occasion saved Harry from falling over precipitous escarpments upon the rocks below.

Cautiously he picked his way downwards, by feeling more than by sight, often pausing to discover with his foot whether the next step would be upon a loose stone or a firm one.

On some occasions he could not ascertain this with any certainty, and that which he had taken to be staple matter would roll away from under his feet, and down he would fall amid a chaos of smaller stones, sometimes for several yards.

At last terra firma was reached, if a damp marshy plain deserves such a title, and Harry stopped to gather breath and recover his strength and vigour.

What to do next was the question, and he found it a remarkably difficult one to answer.

He could not flee to the distant city, because it was in the hands of Morgan and his lawless crew, who would assuredly torture and slay him.

His uniform as a Spanish naval officer would, on the other hand, procure him a certainty of arrest, imprisonment, court-martial, and very probably death, did he dare to show himself in any town or village in New Spain.

His position was precarious in the extreme—yet something must be done.

On his left lay the glassy waters of the ocean, on which the lighted battle-lanterns of the buccaneer ships reflected their massive hulls and tapering masts and spars.

On his right, about seven miles distant, was Chargres, weltering in its flame and its blood, and from thence a great Babel of sound still continued to roll.

Behind him rose the ruined fort, from which he had just effected his escape, and in front stretched the swampy plains before mentioned, leading he knew not whither.

He determined upon crossing these plains, feeling a sort of dismal comfort at the thought that they were so extensive that he would have ample time whilst traversing them to determine what he would do when he reached the other side.

He was never destined to reach the other side, however, for scarcely had he got half-a-mile away from the ruined fort when a host of spectral figures rose up in a body around him.

Yet they were not exactly spectres either, for they turned out to be a company of Spanish soldiers who had escaped from Chargres after some hard fighting, and who, nearly worn out and exhausted, had thrown themselves down on the bare damp plain, to obtain some rest and to wait for daybreak, so that they could resume their march.

Harry Seaborne was surrounded in a instant, and eager questions were asked as to who he was and from whence he came, queries which he found it by no means pleasant to answer.

He did answer them, however, straightforwardly and truthfully, for he knew that if he did not tell his name his foreign accent would make his captors take him to be a buccaneer.

In that case they would, of course, kill him without mercy, but did they know who he really was, though they might treat him with scant courtesy, yet they would not surely slay him.

Of two evils 'tis alway best to choose the least, and Harry Seaborne did so.

Having done so, however, he scarcely knew whether it was the least, for the Spaniards—and there certainly were not less than half a hundred of them—assumed a menacing attitude.

Swords were drawn, pikes brandished, and a hundred invectives hurled at his head.

Invectives, even in modern times, do not hurt so much as brickbats, only, unhappily, they are sometimes the antecedents thereto, and so Harry Seaborne came to the conclusion that the opprobrious epithets and the brandishing of weapons would soon be followed by the practical application of the latter to his head or body.

He put on a bold front, however, and unarmed though he was, confronted his accusers as undauntedly as though he had been at the head of a legion and they a vile rabble fleeing before it.

"Whereof do you accuse me? Why do you howl around me like a pack of ravenous wolves?"

"Say rather why do the pack of hounds bay at the wolf that they have hunted down. We know you, Captain Harry Seaborne, and we know the crime wherewith you are charged. What say you that we should not execute a righteous judgment on you with our own hands?"

So exclaimed an officer richly uniformed, who seemed to be chief in command.

Harry Seaborne merely replied—

"I am in your power. You can do with me as you please."

"Mon capitan, he speaks well," exclaimed a junior officer. "He has been approved a traitor, and he should meet a traitor's doom. Yonder stands a tree, and it has tough boughs."

"And Pedro has a rope, and can reeve a noose as well as any man," cried one of the common soldiers.

"Here is a throat ready, then," said Harry Seaborne, casting aside his collar, and looking calm and determined. "Be sure that the hempen collar fits as neatly as the lace one."

This cool hardihood had its due effect—the brave always win respect.

The Spaniards hesitated, and our hero took prompt advantage of their hesitation.

"Hear me for a minute, my friends," he said, "for presently I shall be unable to address you. I am innocent of the charge laid against me. With my little guarda costa I engaged two piratical vessels, the one double, the other treble her size, and inflicted such damage on the latter—the ship of this obnoxious Morgan — that had not her consort, by a clever manœuvre, come down upon me unperceived amidst the smoke, and literally cut my little craft in two, I should infallibly have sunk her. And this demon, Morgan, instead of being, as at present, in Chargres, would have been lying fathoms deep in the bed of the ocean."

He paused for an instant.

The Spaniards were listening to him attentively.

"Well, was I a traitor for acting thus?" he continued. "I might have been incautious and reckless, but untrue to Spain I was not; and at this very moment, if you will postpone my hanging for a couple of hours, I will lead you on a venture in which you may cover yourselves with glory and make for yourselves a lasting name in the pages of history."

"Speak, speak—what is it?" cried a score of eager voices, and Harry Seaborne, instead of standing before them condemned to death, was the hero of the hour.

Even the officers joined in the enthusiasm and begged him to propound his scheme.

"'Tis a simple one," rejoined Harry. "You see yonder, just to the left of the fort, five lights. Well, they are battle-lanterns on the port sides of Morgan's five pirate vessels. They are riding at their anchors within a quarter of a mile from the shore, a very slender complement of men in each. Follow me, comrades, and we will capture those vessels."

The daring nature of the scheme struck the Spaniards with astonishment.

Their minds could scarcely grasp an undertaking of such magnitude.

But Harry Seaborne so lucidly explained to them the feasibility of the plot that they at last fully entered into it, and became almost frantic in their excitement.

He was now a hero, almost a demi-god, in their opinion.

They clamoured for him to lead them on, and he was in no way loth to do so.

'Twas pleasanter far to return with them on a gallant and what promised to be a glorious exploit than for them to conduct him to the gallows.

He enjoined upon them the necessity of silence and caution, and at their head marched back over the bare, swampy plain, in the direction from whence he had so short a time ago come.

How different were his emotions now. Pride, hope, and military ardour again filled his breast.

Here was a chance of retrieving his lost honour and regaining, perhaps, his high appointment.

On through the slush and the darkness they marched. At last the ruined forts were reached, and, crouching down, they obtained a nearer view of the shipping.

The battle-lanterns rendered them distinctly visible, and lighted up the narrow strip of water that intervened between them and the shore.

The question was how that narrow strip of water was to be crossed.

Had the Spanish soldiers been English sailors the thing would have been easy enough.

The swim would have been child's play, and the Jack-tars would have been swarming up the black hulls of the pirate vessels within a quarter-of-an-hour, like flies up a window pane.

But very few of the Spanish soldiers knew how to swim, and so for them the narrow strip of ocean appeared as impenetrable a barrier as the Atlantic Ocean would have been.

Harry Seaborne was very much puzzled how to carry his scheme out.

And yet it must be attempted—for his reputation, perhaps his life, was at stake.

Suddenly it occurred to him that amidst the ruins of the forts there must be a quantity of shattered timber, which, if carried to the shore, would be well calculated to bear towards the ships such men as could not swim.

Those who could swim would guide the uncouth craft containing those who couldn't.

Arrived at the vessels' sides the ascent to their decks would be easy, for Harry could see, by the rays of the battle-lantern that were fixed directly above, that the steps, or, as we should call them now the companion-ladders, which had been lowered to admit of the buccaneers disembarking, had never since been raised.

At Harry's command the soldiery scattered themselves over the fort in every direction, and presently quite enough wood was procured to put his project into execution, in the shape of beams and rafters and great doors.

Some of these were of such heavy wood that they would not float, but there was an ample quantity that would, and all this was borne down to the water's edge and launched.

The night was so dark that there was no chance of their movements being perceived by the buccaneers on board either of the vessels.

On the other hand, owing to the glaring of the great battle-lanterns, every mast, spar, and rope in the five ships was distinctly visible.

At last the Spanish soldiers were all got afloat—a dozen astride on a single beam, half-a-dozen more crouching gingerly on a door, and so on—the swimmers of the party pushing them from behind in the proper direction.

Harry Seaborne determined to make the great ship, the Death Cloud, the first object of attack, and he swam at the head of his little band of volunteers towards her.

Avoiding the line of light cast upon the water from her port lantern, they slowly neared her, and at last beam and door and rafter drifted under her black hull.

Harry Seaborne was the first to put foot on the companion ladder.

In a crouching attitude he crept up a few steps, and then waited for more to join him.

The two Spanish officers quickly did so, and then a few of the men, until at last a good dozen of them stood grouped together.

The command was then passed down for the others to follow as quickly as they could.

Harry Seaborne drew his sword and signalled to those immediately behind to follow him.

A second later he was upon the deck.

It seemed deserted—but no, a sailor was almost touching him, lying across a carronade, either drunk or asleep.

Harry Seaborne, without a moment's hesitation, plunged his sword into the man's heart.

The buccaneer opened his eyes, and for an instant glared stonily at the densely-clouded Heavens; then the lids again closed over them and he lay still in death.

Again our hero glanced around.

Ah! there was a man at the helm, and another keeping watch at the bow—if it can be called keeping watch when a man is sitting nodding under the lee of the bulwarks, far more asleep than awake.

"There is work for Spanish steel," whispered Harry. "I will dispose of the helmsman."

He and his followers were all barefooted. One of them crept stealthily towards the man who should have been on the look-out and was not, whilst Harry glided towards the helmsman.

This latter was wide awake, but he had not seen the Spaniards come aboard in the waist of the ship, which was completely below his line of vision.

Harry Seaborne had to ascend several steps which led to the high poop, and to traverse its entire length before he could reach him.

He could not hope to do this unperceived.

Our hero could see that he was a gigantic and brawny ruffian, and that a sword hung on one side of his belt and a long dagger on the other.

He sprang up the ladder, however, and advanced upon him at a run, his sword shortened for a thrust that should at once run him through and hurl him overboard.

But the giant perceived him, and with a howl of astonishment relinquished the spokes in favour of his sword-hilt, the weapon flashing in the light of the binnacle lamp.

Harry Seaborne rushed upon him with mad impetuosity, with which, however, there was a certain degree of prudence mixed; but the giant was firm of blade and strong of arm, and our hero's onslaught and rush were of no avail.

And yet Harry Seaborne was destined to win the victory, for by a rapid feint and thrust he a minute later pierced the buccaneer's throat, and he fell to the deck weltering in his gore.

The noise of the clashing blades had, however, aroused such of the buccaneers as had been carousing between decks, and they now rushed up to see what was the matter.

The Spaniards quietly felled each man as he gained the deck, and they were bound and thrown overboard, as a propitiatory offering to the fishes.

"Now," exclaimed Harry Seaborne, in clear, exultant tones, "if I have lost his Majesty the King of Spain a guarda costa I have won him a three-decker. Aye! and, by Heaven! I will blow for him a whole pirate fleet out of the water."

Officers and men came forward to congratulate him on the victory.

"But you have still to hang me," he said, with a laugh. "Well, there is a foreyard arm for you, the proper gallows for a sailor who has failed in his duty."

Officers and men stood abashed—they knew not how to answer him.

He quietly put an end to their confusion by shouting out—

"Whoever amongst ye knows how to load, point, and fire a cannon, step forward."

To his great joy and intense surprise all the men held up their hands.

"What! ye belong to the land artillery, and I thought ye were mere musqueteers," he cried.

"Then, by Heaven! I can keep my word handsomely. Man every gun in the ship," he cried, excitedly, a minute later. "I will take the helm, and cause our prize to swing round so that she shall have the Pestilence and the Famine on her port side, and the War and Devastation on her starboard. How

Harry Seaborne sheathed his sword and grasped the spokes of the wheel with an iron clutch.

Slowly the head of the Death Cloud swung round towards the shore.

At last it remained steady.

"Ready, all ready," was passed up from below.

"If yonder flag lies not the Death Cloud is no longer ours!" exclaimed Rupert Russel

astonished will be the four scourges of New Spain when a hurricane of stone and lead is poured into their quivering sides from the ports of their own commodore!"

The men rushed to the guns with joyous enthusiasm.

"Fire, then, in Heaven's name—two broadsides at once—every gun that can bear!"

Then there ensued a roar that seemed to shake earth and sky; clouds of white smoke, from which lambent tongues and flashes of flame quivered, hid the black hull from sight, the ship trembled with the terrible vibration, and when the murky wreaths cleared away the havoc which her leaden messengers had effected amongst her consorts was plainly perceptible even in the semi-darkness.

Great holes had been knocked in their hulls, masts had been shivered, and spars shot clean away—in fact, they were almost wrecks.

The few men on board each vessel had rushed to their respective decks, at a perfect loss to account for this strange conduct on the part of their admiral's ship, but Harry Seaborne had by this time, alone and unaided, hauled down the buccaneer's flag—the grim death's-head and cross-bones—and run up the royal standard of Spain in its place.

Half-an-hour later he had literally performed his promise—the War, Famine, Devastation, and Pestilence had been blown out of the water, and the Death Cloud alone rode the waves, but she had changed hands and had been given a new name—the Avenger of Spain.

CHAPTER XVII.

HARRY SEABORNE BLOCKADES MORGAN IN HIS
CAPTURED CITY—A PLOT.

A MORE successful venture was never planned and carried through than that of Harry Seaborne, described in our last chapter.

The Death Cloud had been converted into a Spanish frigate and all the rest of the pirate fleet sunk beneath the blue waters of the Carribean Sea within the space of an hour.

Harry Seaborne felt very proud at the succcess of his exploit, and his heart swelled high as he received the encomiums and congratulations of the officers and men who had followed and supported him in the daring enterprise.

He had other projects, however, maturing in his brain, projects that would not admit of his resting on his laurels.

The dead were accordingly promptly thrown overboard, the wounded carried to the sick-bay, the decks swabbed clear of blood, and everything made as taut and trim and neat as before the action.

"Is there anyone present who understands the navigation of the river up to the city?" cried our hero, when all this was accomplished.

There was no reply.

What could soldiers be expected to know about such matters?

"Has anyone seen a ship as large as this lying within gun range of the city?" was the next question.

"I have seen the Marie Magdalena, the flag-ship of Admiral La Hacha, lying a long way up the river, swinging at her anchor, and within half-gun range of the city," replied a Spanish officer, confidently.

"Ha—good!" exclaimed our hero, stamping heavily on the deck in the height of his exultation. "Then we will go up and occupy the same position, and with his own ship blockade Morgan in a foreign port."

It was a delicate and perilous operation, taking so large a vessel as the Death Cloud up a river unmarked by buoys, and the channel whereof was unknown to a single soul on board.

Our hero saw the impracticability of the measure almost as soon as he had conceived it, but he was not one to be daunted by difficulties, and so he despatched half-a-dozen soldiers ashore in one of the ship's boats, to scour the country in all directions and bring back as many Spanish sailors and fishermen as they could find, and, if possible, amongst them a pilot, or someone at least who well understood the navigation of the river.

The party took their departure, but they were not gone more than a couple of hours when they returned, bringing with them all that was required, namely, a river pilot and a dozen strong, active sailors.

On questioning the former as to how near the Death Cloud could safely lay up towards the town, Seaborne heard that she could go up the river to within a quarter of a mile of the city, where she could take up a position that would cover with her guns the principal buildings in Chargres, the castle, and the magazine.

This was all he desired to know.

The pilot was put in charge of the wheel, two or three sailors were placed in the bows to heave the lead, and a few of the higher sails were cast loose to the wind.

Slowly the gallant ship glided up the stream; once she scraped a rock, for she was very deep in the water, but her progress was in no degree stayed.

At length a bend in the river was rounded, and then Chargres lay right before them, the whole city extending along the shore for at least a mile—a city, as could be seen at that distance, of ruin and desolation.

The ship's head was now allowed to swing round until she was broadside on to the town, when anchors were cast from her fore and after castles, so as to hold her immovable in that position.

Chargres was under the dominion of her guns. Morgan was blockaded in his conqered city.

* * * * * *

Let us now return to that worthy and to his bloodthirsty crew.

We left them just at the period when the beautiful Spanish donna was borne off to her chamber by the malignant and jealous Amazon, Zoabinda, and when the sudden reappearance of Captain Rupert Russel, whom everyone had thought to be long since dead, had so astonished the buccaneers.

"By Heavens! is it you, Rupert Russel, or is it your ghost?" stammered Morgan.

"By the token that ghosts never hunger nor thirst, and I at present could eat a raw rhinoceros and quaff a whole cask of canary, I presume it is myself," was the curt, satirical reply.

On hearing this highly satisfactory explanation Morgan grasped his old companion warmly by the hand and said—

"Welcome back, my gallant Russel; and though we cannot oblige you with a raw rhinoceros we can with canary *ad libitum*. In the banqueting hall are the remains of a feast sufficient for a score of famished men, and wine enough to float our whole fleet, were they laden above the water-line with Spanish doubles."

The other buccaneer chiefs imitated their leader's

example in welcoming back the comrade they had deemed lost to them for ever, and then they all returned in his company to the room they had just quitted.

Rupert Russel was, indeed, half-famished.

He ate as though he had not eaten for a month, and now, more clearly than in the dimly-lighted passage, his friends could see how pale and haggard he was.

He was still attired from head to heel in sombre black, but the rich materials were worn and rusty, and discoloured with salt water.

The magnificent diamond aigrette was gone from his hat, too, and with it the splendid plume it had fastened.

The hat itself seemed, indeed, to be a different one, though a cocked beaver of the same shape.

There was no getting a word from Rupert Russel until he had fully satisfied his thirst and hunger.

Then he leant back in his chair and indulged in a sigh of content and relief.

"Having satisfied the inner man, perhaps you will now inform us how you have so strangely returned to find us here, and what you have been doing since we last were together?" said Morgan.

"Not to-night—I cannot, I cannot!" replied Rupert Russel, while his keen, dark eyes seemed to flash fire. "I have endured the torments of hell, and this is not the time or place to picture them."

At these words some of the buccaneers recoiled from him aghast, deeming that he had indeed returned from the other world; but he laughed at their fears and assured them that he had only been speaking figuratively.

But his laughter was hollow and harsh and hardly removed their fears.

Presently Morgan intimated that he wished to be left alone with Rupert Russel, Walter Evandale, Peter Mansveldt, and Captain Kydd, his very good friends and allies, to discuss important affairs.

His half-expressed wish was instantly complied with.

The other buccaneers arose and withdrew.

"My friends," said Morgan, when the lesser chiefs and leaders had taken their departure, "we have this day won a most glorious victory. It is the first of many that must secure our dominion in the new world."

"Has, then, this enterprise a further object than the plunder of coast cities?" asked Kydd.

"Yes, redoubtable captain and world-famed pirate," answered Morgan, exultingly. "I have obtained this small holding on the Spanish Main in order to form a new empire in this part of the world. I can defend what I have won, and extend it, too—yes, from shore to shore, and from north to south.

The four listeners were perfectly carried away by his enthusiasm.

Their eyes flashed, their hands played convulsively with their sword hilts, as though they longed to be up and doing again.

"What is the next move in the expedition? I am with you hand and glove," said Captain Kydd.

"My next descent will be on Panama," replied Morgan, bringing his clenched fist down with a crash on the table, that made goblets and drinking cups, platters and silver trays, clatter and dance again.

"On Panama?" responded Kydd, starting with astonishment. "Can our ships navigate the air, or are you so mad as to think that any vessel built by man could double the Horn—that grim Cape of Storms?"

"Neither—and yet, trust me, I know a way to get to Panama for all that," replied Morgan.

"But consider the number of places to be reduced *en route*, the length of the hostile and unknown country to be traversed, and the impossibility of conveying artillery such a distance," put in Walter Evandale.

"And the general unhealthiness of the climate, that will destroy three men for every one slain by the sword," added Rupert Russel, with a shrug of the shoulders.

But Morgan, with his specious powers of argument, at length bore down all opposition, and brought all four surbordinate chieftains over to his way of thinking, though not without much trouble.

"I know the expedition will destroy, as nearly as I can calculate, seven-eighths of our lads, but what a prodigious booty will remain for the survivors—if they get it," he said.

Goblets were then refilled, and success quaffed to the expedition.

Day had now begun to dawn in the east and the crimson hues of morning increased apace.

Suddenly Morgan looked forth from the window of what might now more appropriately have been called a hall of carousal than a banqueting chamber.

He had no sooner done so than he started back aghast.

"Saints of Heaven!" he ejaculated, "the Death Cloud is coming up the river towards the city. Now, what may that portend? The few men in charge of her had instructions to let her lie quietly at her anchors near the mouth. And now they are warping her broadside on to the stream."

"By the Saints of Heaven you may well say, Captain Morgan!" exclaimed Russel, fiercely, "for if yonder flag lies not the Death Cloud is no longer ours. See, the three golden castles of Spain float above the death's-head and cross-bones of the buccaneers. While you have been taking their city the Spaniards have been capturing your ships. Take my word for it, such are the facts of the case."

"I do not see how it can be so," stammered Morgan. "The ships were left secure and under competent charge. We have scoured the country and cleared it of every foe. Who can have taken them?"

The buccaneers shrugged their shoulders.

It was a query very difficult to answer.

Walter Evandale had, however, answered it quite satisfactorily to himself, though he spoke not his convictions aloud.

He felt convinced that Harry Seaborne was at the bottom of it all, and, as the reader is aware, he was right.

Had a hundred-ton bombshell fallen at their feet the other buccaneer chiefs could not, however, have been more astounded than at the appearance of the Death Cloud flaunting the gorgeous banner of Spain.

And now signal flags began to flutter from her mizen mast and the ends of her spars.

"For Heaven's sake tell me what the fellow says!" roared Morgan, addressing Walter Evandale, "for my rage and chagrin are too great to permit of my thinking or to ascertain what he is talking about by means of his accursed flags."

Evandale peered earnestly towards the distant ship, and presently made reply as follows—

"The vessel is commanded by one Don Harry Seaborne, Captain Morgan."

"What! by that young limb of Satan whom we left buried in the sands of Tortugo?"

"By the same—but, as you are aware, we have met him since then."

"Yes, when with his cockle-shell of a guarda costa he attacked the Death Cloud, and engaged her so hotly that had not the Pestilence come up he had to a surety carried her," growled Morgan between his teeth.

"He is a noble and a gallant youth," said Walter Evandale, musingly, "a very noble and a very gallant youth."

"I wish the noble and gallant youth were at the bottom of the sea," retorted Morgan, fiercely. "I believe that that boy was born to be my evil genius and that I shall meet my death at his hands."

"You will not meet your death at his hands, Captain Morgan, of that never fear," was Evandale's reply.

The reply was so fiercely, so vehemently spoken, that everyone regarded the handsome young lieutenant with surprise.

None more so than did Morgan, who seemed suddenly to quail before his curling lip and flashing eyes.

"How know you that?" he asked. "By St. Christopher! you speak with the air of a prophet or seer of old."

"Never mind how I know; perhaps I am a seer, perhaps a fatalist, perhaps merely a believer in dreams and visions. Be that as it may, this is no time for discussing the matter. Let us interpret those flaunting signals."

"Ah! the signals—the signals! What does the presumptuous dog dare to demand of us?" cried Morgan.

"He demands that we send every Spaniard of gentle blood, both male and female, whom we hold as prisoners, at once on board the Death Cloud—safe, uninjured, and without ransom."

"A moderate request, truly; and what more does he require?" sneered Morgan.

"He offers a reward of ten thousand pieces of eight for your head, and refuses to treat, save with myself."

"Ha—ha! this presumption pleases me," laughed Morgan. "What else is he pleased to communicate?"

"He states that he has the exact range both of this castle and of the powder magazine, and that if his commands are not complied with within half an hour he will send every buccaneer in Chargres nearer Heaven than he would ever have a chance of getting but for his amiable intervention in their behalf."

"Lieutenant Evandale, you are pleased to be loquacious," said Morgan, bitterly. "Such rigmarole as that could not be communicated by signal. Tell us what he really says and no more."

"I was merely putting the message into as soft and courteous language as possible," laughed Evandale. "In plain Anglo-Saxon he says that if we obey not his demands he will blow us into the clouds."

"Let him try—let him do his worst; but two can play at that game. We have the shore batteries in our hands. Let them be manned. We will sink him and our poor Death Cloud together."

"Captain Morgan, this Don Harry Seaborne, as he designates himself, has so artfully moored his ship that not a single gun from the forts or batteries can be trained on her," said Mansveldt.

"The deuce he has!" roared Morgan, springing to his feet and angrily pacing up and down the room; "and what think you of his assertion that he has this castle and the powder magazine within range of his guns?"

"I think the probabilities are that he has," said Walter Evandale, who was now very grave. "You must remember that doubtless he knows Chargres well, and that, furthermore, he must have captured the Death Cloud by the assistance of Spanish soldiers and sailors, who must be many of them good gunners and well acquainted with the place."

"Ha!" exclaimed Morgan, "you speak sensibly now, Evandale. Who present knows anything of this magazine?"

"I do, captain," answered old Peter Mansveldt. "I visited it but two hours since."

"Well, what sort of place is it? What powder does it contain? Is it ball proof?" asked Morgan.

"It's a rum sort of a place, roofed only with sheet lead. It contains a great many tons of gunpowder, I don't know how many, but certainly sufficient to sweep every living thing from off the earth for a circuit of many miles, and to hurl every structure into ruins for the same distance. Added to which, a red-hot shot from one of the Death Cloud's carthouns could reach it with ease, and either penetrate one of its many casements or drop through its roof."

"Then we are absolutely at this fellow's mercy," groaned Morgan.

"Might not the magazine be flooded?" suggested Rupert Russel, who had not spoken for some time.

"The water would have to be conveyed thither in buckets, which would be a work of great labour, and the leaden roof would have to be ripped off to allow of its being poured into the magazine in a sufficient volume It would take a good nine hours to render the powder innocuous for harm," replied Peter Mansveldt.

"And Don Harry Seaborne only allows us half an hour," remarked Walter Evandale, quietly.

"By Heavens! lieutenant mine, you seem almost to sympathise with this daring rascal," said Morgan, fiercely; "whereas I would fain see him boiled in oil and thereafter grilled upon the devil's gridiron."

TALES of PIRATES
SMUGGLERS and BUCCANEERS.

No. 7.]   **THE SCOURGE OF THE SPANISH MAIN.**   [One Penny.

Harry Seaborne started with surprise on beholding the lovely vision.

MORGAN the BUCCANEER; or, the Terror of the Seas.

"I appreciate bravery and valour even in a foe," answered Evandale, stoutly; "but the signals are still flying, and no more are being hoisted. How do you propose to answer them, Captain Morgan?"

"I mean to leave them unanswered. Let the villain do his worst," answered the buccaneer.

"But something must be done," said Rupert Russel, "or we are lost."

"And something shall be done," rejoined Morgan, an idea seeming suddenly to strike him. "The execution thereof I will leave unto Lieutenant Evandale and yourself. We have still half an hour left to act in before the judgment of the avenger can fall upon us, and during that time we can, perchance, prevent its falling at all. Take all the cannon you can, and with relays of horses, mules, men, anything you can press into the service, drag them, unperceived by the foe, down to the water's edge, so that the Death Cloud may be the centre of a crown of fire directly she dares discharge her first cannon at this our city. Do you comprehend?"

"Perfectly," answered Walter Evandale, bowing, and tapping the hilt of his sword significantly.

"And do you, Peter Mansveldt, see that the magazine is flooded in as short a time as possible, for even a dozen buckets of water may be of some service. But that is of secondary importance, for I think our friends Evandale and Russel will lay a trap from which this Don Harry Seaborne will have enough to do to escape, without troubling himself any further about us."

"And yourself, Captain Morgan—what do you intend doing?" inquired Evandale.

"I intend to soothe the fears of a certain fair captive," answered the buccaneer chief, with a hideous leer, "who, perchance, will be terrified at the renewed firing of cannon and sounds of desperate conflict."

Walter Evandale bit his nether lip till the blood flowed, and his eyes flashed fire as his hand involuntarily sought his sword-hilt; but in an instant he had recovered his outward equanimity and composure, and was once more himself.

This was not the time to baffle Morgan in his villainy, and to bring him to a deadly reckoning; he had not yet reached to the zenith of his power, and not even to save the purity of Donna Guzman would he sacrifice the life of his enemy until that life was to him far more precious than at present.

He, therefore, turned impatiently on his heel, and, followed by Rupert Russel and Captain Kydd, strode rapidly in one direction, whilst old Peter Mansveldt strolled more leisurely in another.

Then Morgan himself quitted the banqueting hall with flushed face and unsteady gait, muttering to himself as he did so—

"She shall be mine! Have I ventured and dared so much to be baffled at the last? No, she shall be mine, I say, and this infernal Harry Seaborne may blow all Chargres about our ears if he will. Aye! I will betake myself to her presence forthwith."

CHAPTER XVIII.

DEAD OR SLEEPING, WHICH?—A NOISY INTERCEDER—TO ARMS! TO ARMS!

ALONG the gloomy corridors, up the wide flights of stone stairs, then along several passages, went Morgan, his long steel spurs clanking as he strode, while his sword scabbard clattered in harsh unison.

He knew the suite of rooms in one of which the jealous Zoabinda had confined her younger and more beautiful rival. Would he be able to find it without arousing Zoabinda herself?

This was the question which he anxiously asked himself, and which he could not very satisfactorily answer, for Zoabinda, even if already asleep, slumbered lightly, and was very easily aroused.

Pondering on this, Morgan thought it best to divest himself of his boots and sword, which he accomplished with some difficulty, and, as he was slightly inebriated, not without making considerable noise.

He heard it not, however, and doubtless thought he had accomplished the operation very successfully, for he proceeded on his way with considerable assurance and a certain jaunty manner that was highly ludicrous.

At length he reached the last great flight of stairs which led to the suite of rooms that he was in search of, and at their foot he paused for awhile to listen.

No sound broke the stillness of the early morn save the distant tramp of armed sentries and the wind as it howled fitfully around the towers and turrets of the old Spanish castle.

Cautiously he crept up the steep stone steps, and at last he reached the landing.

As he did so the clock of some distant church struck the hour of six.

He started at the sound, for he did not imagine it had been so late.

In a second, however, he had recovered his presence of mind, and proceeded on his way, silent, stern, and determined, trying and noiselessly opening door after door, and peering into the interior of the rooms, but withdrawing his head upon finding one after another empty.

At last, however, he paused for a moment inside one of them, for there, at full length on a couch, reclined Zoabinda in all her dusky loveliness of perfect form and faultless features, her long, black hair streaming over her neck and shoulders in inky ripples, with the fringed lashes drooping over her rounded cheeks.

She was a beautiful sight to gaze upon, and Morgan, though bound on fresh conquests, could not help pausing a minute to admire her.

Then he noiselessly closed that door also, and continued on his tour of discovery.

In the very next room he entered a widely different sight presented itself.

Through the half-open door he here gazed upon a vision of loveliness such as, sleeping, he had never beheld before.

Upon a couch of the darkest crimson velvet reclined a fairylike form of extreme grace and beauty, in all that unconscious abandon which sleep alone could have produced.

Her hair, dishevelled, strayed not like Zoabinda's sable tresses, but like rivulets of molten gold, over neck and shoulders that might have been hewn from the purest alabaster, so white were they.

The hue of the rose dwelt, however, on her damask cheeks, and over them drooped her sunny lashes, not entirely concealing the orbs of azure hue beneath, which seemed as though opening to renewed wakefulness.

Morgan crossed the room on tiptoe, and softly approached the object of his adoration.

Having reached the sofa he knelt down beside it and softly took her hand in his.

She resisted not nor awakened even, though Morgan pressed it firmly in his great palm.

At last he ventured to bend over and to press his lips to hers.

The tiny coral bow that his lips had violated returned not the pressure. They were cold as death.

A dread suspicion seized upon Morgan, and he gazed anxiously at the face so calmly upturned towards his own.

Then he again bent forward and placed his cheek close to the half-parted lips, but there was no response.

The expression of dread upon his face deepened, and he gently raised her left hand and placed his fingers on her pulse.

For a moment he retained it in his grasp, but then he let it fall with a groan.

"Good Heavens !" he shrieked ; "she is dead—she has been murdered."

He stood contemplating her for a brief space, with his arms folded on his chest, then between his clenched teeth he muttered—

"This is Zoabinda's work. In her jealousy she hath slain her. Well, one day she will have to give me a reckoning for this."

"Why not now ?" whispered a voice in his ear.

He looked round. Zoabinda was by his side.

He turned upon her like the tiger upon the hunter who has slain one of its cubs.

His clenched fist was raised to strike, but his wrist was caught in the subtle grasp of the negress, the muscles of whose sable arms swelled out like those of a Roman gladiator as she held it firm.

"Henry Morgan," she said, "you have never until now raised hand against me. Have you ceased to love me ?"

In reply he gazed fixedly at the unconscious Spanish girl and then at Zoabinda, saying—

"Before I reply to that question I must have an answer to another. Did you do this ?"

"I did not slay the maiden, and whoever accuses me of the crime lies," was the answer.

"Ah ! say you so ?—then I believe you, Zoabinda. Who, then, has dared to take her life ?"

A strange smile flitted over Zoabinda's countenance, but ere she could reply a heavy booming roar from the distance was followed by the rattle of fallen masonry, and then a cannon-ball came rushing into the very room in which they stood in colloquy with the unconscious dead lying beside them.

"A leaden pill from one of the Death Cloud's carthouns. By every saint in Heaven ! her new cannoniers know their craft, and Don Harry Seaborne allows us little grace beyond the half-hour," exclaimed Morgan.

Zoabinda's eyes at the unexpected sound of battle began to kindle and flash like those of a lioness, but she could not account for the Death Cloud's firing at a castle tenanted by her captain, therefore she asked—

"Are the men left on board the ships mad or drunk that they fire upon us thus ?"

"The men we left on board the ships sleep at the bottom of the sea. Whilst we have been conquering their city the Spaniards have been capturing our vessels. What they have done with the other four I know not, but with the Death Cloud Captain Harry Seaborne is blockading us, and has sworn that within the hour he will blow us nearer unto Heaven than we could ever have attained without his assistance."

Crash ! bang ! rattle !

Another cannon-ball entered the room, and piercing the wall beyond, dashed into the second apartment, where, its force being expended, they could hear it roll along the floor.

The wind of the passing ball had nearly knocked Morgan over, and a splinter of stone had cut his face.

"This is becoming serious !" he exclaimed as he recovered himself, "we must beat a retreat, and, what is more, carry this poor dead girl with us, so that her body may not be violated by shot or splintered stone."

Zoabinda smiled grimly, but made no reply. Then Morgan raised the Spanish girl by the shoulders, while the negress took her by the feet, and thus they bore her out of the room and down the stairs without.

They carried her from thence to the basement floor of the castle, and laid her on a rich couch in a chamber where there was no danger of either iron bullet or stone ball coming near her corpse.

"Now for sword and helm !" cried Morgan, "and thou, Zoabinda, get thee thy weapons also, for mayhap this is the last occasion upon which we shall ever fight side by side."

"Then I trust it will be our fate to fall side by side," was the reply of the negress as she grasped his hand.

He returned the pressure, and then they hurried off to attire themselves for the field.

They were not long in doing so, for Morgan was quite sober, calm, and collected now. Five minutes after quitting the side of the dead girl they left the castle side by side and gained the street.

It was full of half-drunken and wholly riotous buccaneers, who knew not how to act.

A stately figure approached Morgan and the negress. It was Rupert Russel.

"I bring bad tidings," he said, gloomily. "Evandale has been unable to get these drunken brutes to drag any cannon down to the water's edge and open fire upon the Death Cloud as you commanded, and Peter Mansveldt has given up all hopes of being able to flood the magazine."

"This is sorry news," replied Morgan ; "and these Spanish devils, is their fire telling ?"

"Unhappily they have just obtained the range of the magazine, and the great stone balls are penetrating it above powder mark, till its walls begin to show as many holes as a kitchen cullender. If they once begin to use red-hot shot ourselves and Chargres vanish from off the face of the earth together."

"And, by Heaven ! they have begun to use them,"

cried Morgan, excitedly. "Look at that ruddy globe even now speeding through the heavens, 'tis like a ball of fire. It is aimed at the magazine, by Heaven it is !"

"Then 'tis time that we evacuate the city," ejaculated Rupert Russel. "Ah ! here come Evandale, Kydd, and Mansveldt."

It was indeed the redoubtable trio who now approached, their faces blackened by powder—terror, rage, and bitter chagrin writ in every feature of their countenances.

It was evident they were in great haste.

"Morgan," cried Evandale, as he drew near, "if we would escape utter annihilation we must leave the city at once behind us. The Death Cloud has the range of the magazine, and is firing red-hot shot point-blank thereat."

"Let us fly—let us fly ! To the interior—to the interior !" cried Captain Kydd. "Pray Heaven there be yet time !"

"Let trumpets sound and drums beat. To the western gate—on to Panama !" roared Morgan.

"Ay ! on to Panama ; we must push forward now for we dare not turn back," cried the negress, in her shrill treble.

Five minutes later, above the angry boom of the Death Cloud's cannon, sounded the gallant blare of the trumpet and the rattle of the drum, calling the buccaneers together for the performance of a duty they had never before contemplated—namely, to retreat from a city they had captured and pillaged only a few hours before.

They were most of them sober by this time, and fell into rank with that mathematical precision common to all well drilled troops even in moments of the most imminent danger.

These begrimed, blood-stained warriors were heavily laden, for the pockets of their hose and gaberdines were well filled with golden doubloons and broad pieces of eight, and as they moved or turned their heads more gold pieces would rattle against the interior of their caps of steel or of their glaring cuirasses.

Many of them also carried in their hands gold and silver plate of great value, fairly staggering under its weight as they moved.

This was the spoil of churches, convents, and other religious houses.

Such booty was calculated to hinder and impede their retreat, but to have endeavoured to make them relinquish it would have led to a mutiny, and this Morgan knew full well.

The men understood by this time the imminency of the danger that threatened them, and were as agile and active as they could be weighted as they were.

"Now, then—march !" cried Morgan. "Standard bearer, fall in the rear—think you the skull and cross-bones are as anxious to be in the van during a retreat as during an advance ? And yet, on second thoughts, stay where you are, for we do not retreat, we are advancing on Panama."

"Panama ! Panama ! Onward to Panama !" shouted Evandale, Russel, Kydd, Mansveldt, and several others.

They did so to encourage their followers, but the feeble cheer that ensued was not exactly such as they could have wished.

It betokened that the men were not in much heart for such an enterprise.

But the flag was unfurled, the word of command given, and again the trumpets blared and the little brass drums rolled as the buccaneers got into motion and began their march.

They bent their steps towards the great western gate, and as they passed down the wide streets, still cumbered with the dead slain in the preceding night's contest, the cannon-balls of the Death Cloud hurtled over their heads, all speeding towards the awful powder reservoir. If one of them should plunge into the magazine then city and buccaneers would be swept instantly from the face of the earth together.

Morgan and Zoabinda marched at the rear of the pirate host.

The former ever insisted upon occupying the supreme point of danger as his peculiar privilege, and Zoabinda quite as strongly persisted in sharing his peril with him.

Hers was indeed a faithful, loving, and tender heart—but to him alone.

Tramp, tramp, tramp down the empty streets, with scowling brows and sullen mien, swept the mighty buccaneers, many with bare blades in their hands, so that they might vent their ill-will and find some satisfaction in piercing now and then the dead bodies of their yesternight foes as they strode across them.

Sometimes, too, one of the buccaneers would draw a pistol from his belt and discharge it at some pale and ghastly face that peered at them from behind a window or a half-open door, and then a loud, reckless laugh would echo through the deserted streets as a groan or the sound of a heavy fall would proclaim that the marksman had made good his aim and the world had been rid of yet another Spaniard.

Ah ! they were stony-hearted men, those gallant buccaneers, but their very trade was blood.

At last the suburbs of the city were reached, and the great western gate rose darkly before them. They greeted it with a cheer, for, once outside the city, their position would not be so perilous.

There would be no danger then of gigantic buildings toppling over on them and burying them beneath their ruins, or of their being torn to pieces by flying stones and particles of masonry.

Soon they defiled through the gate and left Chargres in their rear. Then a cheer broke from their ranks, and they marched more blithely forward.

Danger was in their rear—conquest, glory, and pillage in their van. Hey for Panama !

CHAPTER XIX.

WHEREIN HARRY SEABORNE HALF FALLS IN LOVE.

LET us now return to our friends on board the Death Cloud, and follow their adventures. The trained gunners, acting under Don Harry Seaborne's command, could have exploded the magazine, had he willed it so, with ease, but our hero did not so will it.

His only wish was to drive the buccaneers out of Chargres as quickly as possible, in order that they should no longer be able to torture and plunder the wretched inhabitants.

This he could only do by intimidation, and the threat he had used answered admirably.

Thus his gunners kept throwing red-hot shot as close to the magazine as they could without exploding it, for they knew that if they did blow it up many thousands of the citizens would be involved in one common destruction.

From the topmasts of the frigate the look-outs could see Morgan's force leaving the city, and directly the last stragglers passed through the western gate Harry was duly informed of the event.

The firing at the magazine was, however, still kept up for an hour or more, for our hero rightly guessed that the buccaneers would not pause until they had put themselves out of danger as long as the firing was maintained, but if it ceased they might immediately halt.

He did not desire their presence within some miles of the city, for while they were in close proximity it would not be wise of him to land his men to see to the wants of the wretched inhabitants, a mission of mercy he was most anxious to engage in as soon as possible.

At last, however, the buccaneers were distinguishable as they crossed a spur of the mountains many miles away, and then the command was quickly given to disembark, and the whole party, with the exception of about a dozen men left in charge of the ship, landed. Headed by Harry Seaborne, they made their way into the city.

Sad sights met their eyes at every step—pillaged churches, desecrated houses, sacked and plundered warehouses and shops, with hundreds of dead bodies, many of them powder-scorched or fire-blackened, lying in all directions—old age and youth, manhood in its strength, womanhood in its beauty, childhood in its innocence.

Ever and anon one of Don Harry Seaborne's little band would spring out of the ranks and, with a cry, run and embrace the dead body of a parent, a wife, or a sweetheart, thereafter returning amongst his comrades with lowering brow and compressed lips, breathing between them bitter curses on the buccaneers.

At last the castle was reached, and this great and gloomy structure Harry commanded to be closely searched, for he expected to find therein the Spanish captives that had been held up to ransom.

The greatest dignitaries of the State, with their wives and daughters, were undoubtedly there, but would he find them alive or dead?

Might not the buccaneers, forced to leave the city, have murdered them ere they did so?

They were quite capable of such villainy—Harry knew that very well.

The interior of the vast fortalice reached, the soldiers scattered themselves in different directions to commence their search, and our hero found himself alone.

He did not mind this, however, for he knew that a blast on the little horn that he carried at his belt would assemble them round him again in the space of a very few seconds.

He strolled about and passed through room after room on the basement floor, glacing from right to left and left to right, expecting every moment to behold some horrible sight, though he knew not what.

At last he entered a chamber richly furnished, and started with surprise on beholding, reclining on a sofa almost in its centre, a young and very beautiful girl.

He advanced on tip-toe towards the couch, and bent over it. How sound she seemed to sleep !

Her snowy chest never heaved ; her beautiful bosom never throbbed ; her long-fringed eyelids never quivered.

Could she be dead?

He took her little hand in his, and his fingers glided up until they reached her pulse, then he uttered a cry of horror, dismay, and agony, for it had ceased to beat.

"Dead—dead—dead !" he sobbed. "The only girl I have ever beheld whom I could have loved !"

He bent his head over her, and with lingering fondness, yet with due reverence and respect, he kissed her cherry lips and her little white hands.

"Would that I knew thy destroyer's name, in order that I might avenge thee," he muttered.

He had scarcely spoken when a terrible crash was audible in the room immediately above.

So loud was it that even Harry started like a frightened steed and laid his hand on his sword.

But the next instant he uttered a cry not of terror, but of astonishment and delight, for surely the beautiful being whom he had deemed dead had made an almost imperceptible movement.

He sprang to the side of the sofa again, and again he took her hand and laid a finger on her pulse.

It beat now with sharp, irregular throbs.

Harry uttered a cry of joy, and with caresses and terms of endearment he strove to recall her to herself.

Presently her beautiful chest heaved—her breath returned, and he felt the fragrant vapour on his cheek.

Then her eyes opened, and she gazed upon him with a mingled glance of terror and curiosity.

" Morgan !" she exclaimed, faintly. "Oh ! then the negress has betrayed me after all !"

"You are not betrayed, beautiful lady," replied our hero. "I am not Morgan, but Harry Seaborne, an English officer in the service of New Spain, who rescued you not long ago. Morgan and his followers have left the city."

"Don Harry Seaborne ! I have heard my father speak of thee," said the beautiful Spaniard.

"Ah ! say you so, lady ? Well, your father saved my life. I was buried alive in the burning sands of Tortugo, and he rescued me from my terrible fate. Since then that life has been devoted to him and to Spain. Presently we will try and find him, so that mine may be the pleasurable office of returning to him his child."

"You told me that he is a prisoner in this very castle," said the fair girl. " Let us at once go to him."

She essayed to rise, but her strength was not equal to the task, and so she sank back again upon the couch.

"The opiate must have been a strong one," she said, faintly. "It has entirely bereft me of strength."

"What opiate?" asked our hero, puzzled at her remark; "your words bewilder me, dear girl."

"The negress, Zoabinda, gave me a sleeping-draught, which she said would cast me into a trance, and so, perchance, save me from becoming the victim of Morgan," was the reply.

"Noble, generous woman!" exclaimed Harry; "and I all the while have regarded her as a she-tiger, without one good quality to condone her many bad ones. Oh! I have wronged her indeed."

"You have, I fear. True, she terrified me very much at first, for she played with a dagger which hung at her belt, and seemed half inclined to thrust it into my heart; but then her demeanour suddenly underwent an entire change, and muttering, ' Poor child, it is not her fault,' she gave me some decoction instead."

"And I have no doubt that it saved you from worse than death," said our hero. "And this Zoabinda, whom I have hitherto ever despised and hated, shall henceforth find in me a firm friend when she needs one.

"But come," he added a minute later, "if you cannot go to your father I must bring him to you. You will not mind being left alone for a little while, will you?"

"No, no—I am not entirely unpossessed of courage. Besides, there can now be nothing to fear."

"There is naught to fear, for Morgan and his band of cut-throats are by this time far away. When I return a few minutes hence I will bring your father with me."

With a bow he quitted the room and set out in search of the captain-general.

He had not far to go in quest of him.

Even as he quitted the chamber occupied by the Spanish girl he heard voices, many and animated, on the floor above.

He sprang up the broad stairs and entered a huge door which was standing open.

The vast room to which it gave admittance was very nearly half full of people.

These were the grandees of Chargres and its vicinity, the prisoners Morgan had held to ransom.

Most of the dons were attired in very gorgeous and brilliant uniforms.

Amongst them our hero recognised the admiral who had passed on him not more than twenty-four hours previously so severe and unjust a sentence.

He recognised, also, the governors of the castles of St. Euphemio and St. Mary Magdalen, the general of the army of reserve, the three alcaldes of the city, some brilliantly-garbed officers of the staff, and last, but not least, his old protector, the captain-general.

Some of the officers who had just landed with him from the captured Death Cloud were conversing with these grandees, and Harry could see immediately on entering that full accounts had already been rendered of how the city had been recovered and Morgan driven out of it.

No sooner had he entered the room than he was surrounded, and had he possessed a score of hands they would all have been nearly wrung off, so warm was the reception accorded him.

He was thanked as the preserver of the city and the avenger of Spanish honour until he at length became so thoroughly abashed that he knew not where he stood.

But he at last remembered the lovely young girl he had left all alone in the dark, gloomy room below and of his promise to bring her father.

He succeeded in drawing the captain-general aside and in communicating to him the joyful tidings.

" Come !" said the latter, when he had heard all, "let us return together to her. Henceforth I shall regard you as a son, and Donna Theresa must look upon you as a brother." Grasping our hero's arm, they quitted the room together.

CHAPTER XX.
THE BUCCANEERS BEGIN THEIR PERILOUS MARCH UPON PANAMA.

AFTER leaving Chargres some three miles in their rear, and crossing a spur of the mountain range that looked down upon the city, the buccaneers came to a river called the Garona.

For a long time they looked for a ford, but looked in vain.

At last, however, they thought they had found one, but it was commanded by the guns of a neighbouring fortress, whose towers rose not a quarter of a mile distant.

The garrison had evidently guessed Morgan's followers to be foes, though he had hoped that they would have passed muster as a Spanish corps of irregulars.

But this hope proved delusive, for the guns of the fortress opened upon them, and had it not been for the inaccuracy of the aim of the Spanish gunners the ford would have been impracticable.

Morgan determined to attempt it, however, and was about to spur his horse into the stream, for he was ever the first to risk his life when necessity or expediency called for it, when a large flat-bottomed boat, or rather barge, was found concealed beneath the bushes on the near bank of the river.

It was capable of holding three or four horsemen at a time, and so Morgan, Walter Evandale, and Rupert Russel rode boldly into it, and a dozen sturdy buccaneers, with the long poles that they found lying in the bottom of the barge, pushed them across the stream.

Before, however, they had got to the middle thereof the cannon opened upon them with renewed energy, and a moment later they stuck hard and fast upon a mud-flat.

Their position now was most precarious.

The gunners were getting a better range at every discharge, whilst escape from their present dilemma seemed impossible, for the long poles when thrust in the mud found no bottom, clearly proving that if they sprang overboard, either mounted or on foot, they would sink and quickly disappear therein, a death to which annihilation by a cannon-ball was a hundred times preferable.

In vain the buccaneers strove to get the clumsy craft off the mud-flat—all their efforts were unavailing, and at last they desisted in sheer despair.

But Captain Kydd and Captain Peter Mansveldt saw their dilemma, and saw also that they could only be extricated therefrom by the guns of the castle being silenced.

The only feasible way to effect this was to take the castle itself by a *coup de main.*

Captain Kydd, as though by tacit consent, assumed the chief command of the expedition.

He addressed a few spirit-stirring words to the buccaneers, who responded with a genuine English cheer, and with a sword in one hand and fireballs in the other they advanced close up to the palisades under a tremendous fire from the Spanish soldiers on the ramparts.

But though they made several attempts to climb the palisades they were much too lofty to be scaled, and, after much loss and fatigue, they were forced to retreat—fairly beaten back.

But Morgan, from the boat in the centre of the river, signalled to them not to be discouraged and to renew the assault, for again the Spanish gunners had begun to fire upon him and his companions.

In obedience to his mute signal, once more the buccaneers pressed forward, and while some laboured to pull down the palisades the others fired into the loopholes and embrasures of the fortress, conspicuous amongst them being Zoabinda, the beautiful negress.

She regarded the arrows and bullets that rained around her no more than if they had been descending hailstones or snowflakes. But at length she paused with a sudden gasp for breath, and would have fallen had she not staggered against a tree-trunk.

An arrow had passed right through her body, and the point of the weapon appeared some inches from her back, having entered between her breasts.

Notwithstanding this, with great coolness she drew the arrow from her body, and, in order to make it fill up the bore of her musket, she wound a good portion of cotton around the feathered part of it—then thrust it down upon the powder and discharged it back into the fort.

The powder fired the cotton, and the arrow sticking in the dried palm-leaves with which one of the houses in the fortress was thatched, a violent conflagration immediately ensued.

Poor Zoabinda had the satisfaction of seeing the Spanish stronghold one universal blaze when she fell back into the arms of Captain Kydd in a dead faint from loss of blood.

The next instant the powder magazine blew up with a loud crash.

This threw the garrison into great consternation, but they busied themselves to the utmost in endeavouring to extinguish the flames, which, however, in spite of all their efforts, continued rapidly to gain upon them from the want of a sufficient supply of water.

Whilst their attention was thus diverted the assaulters contrived to fire the palisades, and thus the Spaniards were still more terrified as they saw the flames not only in their own quarter but gradually spreading all around them.

As the woodwork of the palisades was consumed the earth that was contained between them fell into the ditch, which became so much filled up in many places as to form over it a practicable ootway.

Of this the buccaneers eagerly availed themselves, and thus they were soon hand to hand with the Spaniards in the first enclosure of the fortress.

The struggle was desperate.

For long neither party thought of giving or receiving quarter, and each man stood and fought until one or both fell, for the inveterate spirit of slaughter was fired in every breast.

They no longer fought for honour or for victory, but to glut their savage thirst for blood.

In this terrible conflict the buccaneers had an immeasurable advantage, for there was no one amongst them who was not an old and experienced swordsman, who knew every guard and feint, and where to direct the thrust most fatally.

The most fearful struggle took place partly in the half-filled ditch and partly on the platform on which the burning houses and stores of the fortress were situated.

The red glare of the conflagration made everything terribly visible.

On those of the assaulters who still remained below in the ditch flaming pots of combustibles, that emitted the most suffocating stenches, were poured down copiously, and these proved to be the most destructive of weapons.

Notwithstanding the resolute resistance of the Spaniards, within an hour the whole of the palisades were burned, and the ditch completely filled, rendering the ground nearly level up to the castle walls, which remained as yet unharmed.

But the flames of the burning stores behind the castle threw its embrasures into strong relief, so that every Spaniard who showed the least part of his person on the wall was immediately struck down by the unerring shot of the besiegers, who, creeping on their hands and knees, placed themselves close under the fortifications and, even in contact with the walls which they were endeavouring to take.

In this way the fight continued—a succession of single combats often taking place, and indiscriminate death from the aim of the musketeers being fast and frequent; but when another hour had passed away the buccaneers discovered that they had still a very difficulty work to perform before they could make themselves masters of the place.

The flames had extended to the interior of the castle itself, and were slowly feeding upon all that was combustible, but the governor had removed all his cannon to those parts which commanded the passes over the ditch, and he strictly enjoined every man to die at his post.

The beautiful negress, Zoabinda, having recovered from her fainting fit, and again engaged in the deadly strife, had by this time received three more wounds, one by a shot from an arquebus, and two from arrows.

Being thus completely disabled, she was borne from spot to spot on the shoulders of two brawny buccaneers, wherever peril appeared to be the greatest.

Captain Kydd, however, was the real director of the siege, but how to carry the castle he was still sorely puzzled to determine, for he had nothing wherewith to scale it, and the gates were found to be much too strongly constructed to admit of their being forced.

Seeing this, and being determined that himself and his men should rather die under the walls than be repulsed therefrom, he divided his forces into two parts. The one he employed to mark down every Spaniard that should show himself or attempt to load the cannon on the walls, and the other to collect all manner of timber fragments of the half-burnt palisades and earth, wherewith to make a mound against the lowest part of the castle, and where the Spanish governor had placed himself with a score of his best men.

About noon, after five hours of hardly-contested and uninterrupted battle, the buccaneers rushed up this heap of rubbish and met the Spaniards on the walls.

Though many acts of valour had already been achieved, it was here that the most wonderful deeds were performed.

Notwithstanding that every Spaniard died where he had been stationed by his chief, the English found their way over their bodies, and gained the interior of the place.

Those of the Spaniards who were denied the honour of paving the blood-red way with their corpses, with the little remaining strength their wounds had left dragged themselves to the opposite side of the castle, and, leaping from its walls, their bodies bounded from crag to crag down a dreadful precipice, until they were received upon the points of the sharp palisades below.

The commander himself retreated with the *corps de garde* within the castle keep, before which he had placed two cannons, with the intention of prolonging the struggle to the utmost, and of making his enemies dearly rue their conquest.

He answered every offer of quarter by frantic efforts to slay.

At length he was shot through the brain with a musket-ball, and then all further resistance ceased.

The conquerors had now leisure to look around and view the desolation they had caused.

The fort, with the exception of the guard-house, was one mass of blackened and blood-stained ruins.

Out of the three hundred and twenty-three soldiers who six hours before were in vigorous health, laughing to scorn their enemies, only thirty were found alive, with eight unwounded.

The buccaneers had lost in the desperate attack one hundred and nineteen killed outright, including one captain and one lieutanant, and seventy-six wounded, besides poor Zoabinda and two lieutenants. Few indeed of the injured survived many days in that fell climate.

Directly the castle was carried the buccaneers had time to think of Morgan, Evandale, and Rupert Russel, who, in company with the freebooters they had taken to row their clumsy craft, had been stuck in the middle of the river ever since the combat commenced, unable to assist their friends in the slightest degree.

Morgan had beheld Zoabinda receive her first wound; he had seen the long, barbed shaft pierce her tender form and penetrate to her back, and his heart had bled as much as her body.

He had seen her thereafter twice lead the stormers, and though he had longed to be at her side, to protect her with his own life, he was as powerless to aid her as if he had been a thousand miles away.

Terribly long seemed the hours of savage attack and stubborn defence, but when he beheld the fortress carried and the buccaneer flag flying from the highest tower thereof, great was his pride and his satisfaction.

A pride and satisfaction in which Evandale and Rupert Russel jointly shared.

Soon a score of sturdy buccaneers swam off towards the stranded craft, and by their united strength pushed her off the mud-bank and propelled her towards the shore.

It was not long before they reached it, and Morgan was the first to spring to land.

His one thought was of Zoabinda.

He sought her everywhere, but for some time in vain.

At last he found her, and in an instant he was kneeling by her side.

"My own, my dearest girl!" he cried; "and you have suffered all this for the love you bear me!"

"I stood in your place, Henry," she replied, fondly. "You would not have had me disgrace you?"

"No, Zoabinda; but I would have had you protect the form I love with greater care."

"What matters it. If scars are honourable in a man are they less so in a woman?"

"My own dearest one, I will not chide thee," was the reply; "you braved all for my sake—for my safety, for my honour, but methinks I would sooner have died than have seen thee suffering thus."

"The wounds will heal, my beloved—aye! they will heal faster than the one you yourself inflicted on me but a few hours ago," answered the negress, bending upon him a look of deep affection.

"I inflicted a wound on thee?" ejaculated Morgan. "Why I never lifted hand against thee in my life."

"You did not wound me in the body, but in the heart, Henry," said Zoabinda, sorrowfully.

"Ah! you mean the Spanish girl, Donna Theresa de Guzman," replied Morgan, a frown crossing his brow. "You had best not have mentioned that matter, Zoabinda, for you avenged yourself too hastily."

TALES of PIRATES
SMUGGLERS and BUCCANEERS.

A stalwart buccaneer suddenly pushed aside the canvas and issued forth.

MORGAN the BUCCANEER; or, the Terror of the Seas.

"Nay, Henry Morgan, I served my rival better than you give me credit for. I did not kill her."

"Did not kill her? Who did kill her then? Did I not myself gaze upon her corpse?"

"No, for she was living all the while, and has doubtless by this time awakened from her trance."

"Her trance! Not dead!" muttered Morgan in surprise.

"A little scheme I invented to save her honour and thine too. So that I have done her no ill."

The fierce buccaneer stood for a moment gnawing his wiry moustache, a host of conflicting emotions warring in his breast.

Then he threw his arms around Zoabinda and exclaimed, passionately—

"Oh! Zoabinda, can you forgive me my unjust suspicions?"

"When a brave warrior asks forgiveness of a weak woman, hard-hearted must she be if she does not grant his request," replied the negress, embracing him in turn.

In that happy but short-lived state of reconciliation we will leave them, to return to the adventures of the other characters of our tale, in whom our readers we feel assured by no means feel a subordinate interest.

CHAPTER XXI.

THE ABDUCTION OF DONNA THERESA—HARRY SEABORNE TO THE RESCUE.

WHEN Don Pedro de Guzman in the company of Harry Seaborne entered the apartment in which only a few minutes previously our hero had left the beautiful Donna Theresa, in confident anticipation that presently she would be clasped in the embrace of her father, to their alarm and surprise they found it empty.

They both called her name aloud, but there was no response save the echo of their own voices.

A door at the further end of the vast and gloomy chamber was open which had not been so when Harry quitted it.

He fancied he recollected having examined it, and found it secured by a heavy and ponderous lock.

He advanced now to inspect it, but scarcely had he done so closely when he uttered a cry of surprise.

The lock had been blown to fragments either with a pistol or an arquebus bullet.

He examined the flooring of the corridor beyond, and on the soft pistachio wood were the imprints of nailed boots.

The Spaniards wore none such—they were, therefore, the footprints of a buccaneer.

He groped his way down the passage, and when he had nearly reached the further extremity he picked up a delicate pink scarf, such as he remembered not half an hour ago had encircled Donna Theresa's slender waist.

Close beside it something glittered in the gloom of the dimly-lighted vault.

'Twas a dagger, but one of English make, and this confirmed all his prior suspicions.

He at once returned and rejoined Don Pedro de Guzman.

"She has been abducted—carried off by some lingering buccaneer," he cried, fiercely. "We must at once take horse and start in pursuit. He cannot yet have left the city far behind him."

The captain-general was mad with mingled fury and despair.

"Start—yes, start at once!" he exclaimed. "But to think that I dare not accompany you, which is the case, for I have promised to lose no time in raising an army that shall hover on the rear of the buccaneer force, and harass it or cut off its retreat, whichever circumstances may require."

"Mourn not at your inability to accompany me," said our hero, laying his hand on his sword-hilt. "Those who occupy so high a position in the state as yourself must sacrifice much for the sake of their country. With me it is different—my sword and my life are at your daughter's service."

"Noble, generous youth!" exclaimed the captain-general, grasping our hero's hand. "I trust you implicitly. Go, and may Heaven prosper you. If you recover my daughter from these bloodthirsty monsters, notwithstanding her rank she is yours if you can win her affection. Be this your reward."

"A reward more valued by me than would be a waggon-load of diamonds of the first water," cried Harry Seaborne, warmly. "I am off on the wings of the wind. Within a month I hope to claim the fulfilment of your promise."

He left the room as he spoke, and five minutes later he was searching the stables for a horse.

He had some difficulty in finding one, as every available beast in the city had been seized upon by the buccaneers to carry their munition, stores, and the vast amount of their pillage.

At last, however, he discovered a wretched Spanish mustang, and, mounted on this sorry brute, he was fain to set out upon the track of the abducted Spanish girl.

He had scarcely gained the street, however, when three young Spanish officers beset him with an earnest petition that they might be allowed to accompany him on his venture.

They had heard of the abduction of Donna Theresa, and of our hero's being about to set out to rescue her.

For a minute Harry felt annoyed at their importunity.

He wished to effect the beautiful Spanish girl's rescue alone, in order that he solely might be the recipient of her gratitude and eventually, he hoped, of her love. But here were others who wished to share the honours with him, and, for all he knew to the contrary, one of them might win a larger abundance both of gratitude and love than himself.

Such were the selfish and unworthy thoughts that for a minute or two coursed through Harry Seaborne's brain.

Then his better nature prevailed, for he reflected that with three others to aid him the fair Donna's deliverance was far more likely to be effected than by his single arm, so he held out his hand to one and all, exclaiming, in his usual frank and hearty manner—

"Every additional sword is welcome, but for all that we are plenty for the task. Let us set out at once. But what will you do for horses? I had a great difficulty in finding even this miserable brute."

"Oh! we know where some are concealed, and they are in good condition for a journey to boot."

"Well, then, secure them as soon as possible and rejoin me here," cried Harry, impatiently.

They promptly departed at his command, for

he had been tacitly recognised as the leader of the expedition.

In a short space of time the three Spaniards returned, all mounted on good and mettled steeds.

Harry felt chagrined at the sorry condition of his old nag, but he refrained from comment. Perchance on the road he might have an opportunity of changing it for a better one.

The route by which the buccaneers had quitted the city was well known to them.

They pursued it, for naturally the freebooter who had abducted Donna Theresa would follow the track of his comrades.

The silent, dead-strewn streets were traversed quickly, the horses gingerly stepping across the many corpses that strewed the pavement, and a few minutes later the four horsemen were galloping across the open country beyond.

The day was cloudy, raw, and cold, with a southerly wind blowing, which betokened a storm.

Such weather was rare in this latitude. The Spanish officers regretted they had left their espotes behind them.

But Harry Seaborne, who had been reared in the bracing airs of Britain, felt not the damp, humid cold ; on the contrary his blood was at fever heat and his brain seemed on fire.

Unknown even to himself he had fallen in love with Donna Theresa at first sight. It was love which was now urging him on the trail—he deluded himself that it was merely friendship and pity.

He heard not the dead leaves which fell in showers from the trees and crumbled and rattled under the hoofs of the horses. He heard not the conversation of his companions, for his mind was occupied with one soul-absorbing vision, and that was Donna Theresa.

They were following a south-westerly direction, bending their course towards Piqua, a town distant some twenty-five miles from Chargres, for thitherward the tracks of the buccaneer army led.

For several hours they pursued their journey without any occurrence worthy of note, when one of the three Spaniards reined up his horse and placed his finger to his lips in token of silence.

"What is it?" demanded Harry, in a low guarded tone, motioning his friends to halt.

"Methought I heard the rumble of a waggon in the distance," was the reply. "Aye ! and I do hear it distinctly now."

They all listened, and agreed that it was the rumble of a waggon, and in their rear, too.

"I imagine that some of Morgan's luggage waggons must have followed a different route, and that we are between them and the buccaneer army," observed our hero, after a few minutes' pause.

"It would seem like it," answered one of the Spanish officers. "But I cannot guess how."

"Some of the waggons may be travelling by way of Mimia and Carnale," suggested his companion, "and that being a longer way round our having got ahead of them ceases to be extraordinary."

This supposition of the facts of the case was very natural and was accepted as the true one.

CHAPTER XXII.

ON THE TRAIL—CAPTURING A TREASURE WAGGON AND PUTTING IT TO A NEW USE.

"IF it's a waggon in our rear for Heaven's sake let us lie in ambush till it comes up, so that I may have a chance of exchanging this wretched mustang for a beast that will carry me properly," said Harry.

This was agreed to, and the whole party proceeded to plant themselves in ambush.

This was easily done, as the road on either side was fringed with immense trees and a dense undergrowth.

They dismounted and led their horses some way into the wood, so that neither neigh nor whinney might be heard by the drivers or guard of the approaching waggon, which, doubtless, was crammed with the pillage of Chargres.

They then returned and crouched down behind the bushes that lined the roads, looking to the loading of their pistols and musketoons, and shaking the priming into the pans and lighting their slow matches.

They then waited patiently for the approach of the waggon.

Fortunate was it that they had patience, or they would have been wearied out, for nearly half an hour passed before the renewed rumble of the wheels proclaimed that it was still approaching.

The sound during that period must have been intercepted by intervening hills.

However, there it was again now distinct enough, and near by too, for the hoof strokes of the horses could be heard.

With the suddenness peculiar to tropical climates day had by this time changed into night—a night as hot and sultry as the day had been cold, damp, and disagreeable.

The heavens had been suddenly overcast, and the rumble of thunder was presently audible.

"By the blessed saints ! we shall not sight them as they pass, and shall not be able to take aim," growled one of the Spanish officers. "I cannot see the muzzle of my musquetoon as I hold it to my shoulder."

"Nor I !" exclaimed each of his companions as they tested the experiment.

"Then here comes the lightning to aid us," cried Harry Seaborne, exultingly.

'Twas even as he said.

At first two vivid forked flashes quivered out between the heavy rifts of jagged thunder-clouds, then close upon them broke forth several blinding flashes, that rendered the whole country as clearly distinguishable as it would have been at noonday.

At this very juncture an enormous waggon was observable coming round a turn in the road not a hundred yards from the point where Harry and his companions lay concealed.

It was of clumsy build, and was roofed over. A large lamp was affixed to the front, which revealed a portion of the interior, where two or three armed figures were indistinctly visible.

The waggon was drawn by four grey horses, and was approaching at rapid speed.

The near wheeler and the near leader were both mounted, and the cracking of the whips rang out like pistol shots.

"Fire at the horses just as they are well abreast of us," whispered Harry Seaborne, hoarsely. "Even if we only bring down one the onward course of the waggon will be arrested and its occupiers brought to bay."

This proposition was received with a murmur of approval by his companions.

On came the rumbling, bumping, springless vehicle, its occupiers and post riders little anticipating the warm greeting with which they were presently to be received.

In an instant the clear, manly voice of Harry Seaborne was heard to cry "Fire!" and four flashes simultaneously broke from the bushes on the right.

Down went the near leader, and down went its rider, the latter shot through the leg and the former through the body.

The man uttered a groan of pain and fearful anathema.

The horse gave vent to a piercing shriek, for horses can shriek when suffering from intense terror or agony, and the poor animal had received its death-wound

Before the remaining post-rider or the freebooters inside the waggon—which had been brought to an abrupt stop by the fall of its near leader and its rider—could recover from their surprise and dismay, Harry Seaborne and his three companions had sprung from out the bushes and covered them with their musquetoons.

There was no asking for nor offering of quarter.

The man on the near wheeler was shot down by our hero, whilst the three Spaniards fired haphazard into the interior of the waggon.

Their shots evidently told, for one or two heavy falls and more than that number of groans were heard within the cumbrous vehicle, and then a sound as of men jumping to the ground from behind was heard.

Harry and one of the Spaniards dashed to the rear in time to prevent the escape of these worthies.

They found themselves opposed to three stalwart buccaneers, scaled like armadilloes, yet the rascals were panic-stricken and would have flown, three to two though they were.

But Harry and his companion barred the way, sword in hand, and as there was no evading them, the buccaneers perceived that they must fight.

They engaged at once, two attacking our hero and one the Spaniard.

Within an instant one of the robbers had been run through the midrib and laid bleeding on the earth by Harry's invincible sword, and then his companion looked around again for a looophole to escape.

But none presented itself, for Harry dodged and threatened him with point and tierce in such rapid circles that to have evaded him would have been impossible.

The fellow, therefore, fought doggedly and sullenly on—fought with clenched teeth, flashing eyes,

and heavy hand, keenly seeking for an opportunity to thrust over his adversary's guard.

But no such opportunity offered, for Harry was as cautious and self-possessed as though it had been merely a fencing-bout, and presently, with a rapid feint and thrust, he eluded his adversary's guard and thrust his sword through his brawny throat up to the very hilt.

With a sobbing gasp the buccaneer sank backwards, the sword-blade slipping out of the ghastly orifice as he fell to the ground.

Before he touched it life had departed.

Harry very coolly wiped his sword on a tuft of grass and then turned to see how his companion fared with his single opponent.

It was well that he did so, for had he not the young Spanish officer would assuredly have been slain. The gigantic freebooter he had been contending with had beaten him to his knee and broken his sword, the remaining fragment of which he was holding up to guard his head from the descending blade of the buccaneer just as Harry Seaborne beheld his position and hurried to his succour.

That broken sword-blade would have been but a feeble guard against the trenchant steel of the burly buccaneer, but before the steel could perform its fell mission the wielder thereof relinquished it with a shriek of pain and horror, for Harry's sword had sunk deep into his body, between the fourth and fifth ribs.

It was a death-wound, for the giant buccaneer fell to the ground and thereafter neither spoke, groaned, nor stirred.

Our hero assisted the discomfited Spaniard to his feet.

"Are you wounded?" he asked, noticing that he was very pale.

"No, not a scratch even; but what a demon of strength and skill that giant was! He has quite worn me out."

The little sword-play we have described did not take five minutes in its inception and accomplishment, and now the other Spaniards were heard calling them by their names.

They had been busy throwing the bodies of the two dead post-riders and those of the buccaneers from the interior of the waggon amongst the bushes, and harnessing one of their own horses in the place of the late near leader.

They had not noticed the absence of their companions until now, far less did they guess that they had been engaged in a desperate and unequal contest within a few yards of them.

Great was their surprise, therefore, to discover them covered, not with their own but with their foemen's blood, and three dead bodies lying at their feet.

Explanations, however, were speedily given and comprehended, and then the whole difficulty that required solving was—What was next to be done?

This did not take long to determine.

It was decided that the pursuit should be resumed in the waggon, and that the little band of adventurers should discard their own attire for that of four of the slaughtered buccaneers.

They would thus be enabled to follow in the rear of Morgan's army without notice, and even to penetrate his camp of a night without any suspicion attaching to them.

Thus facilities would be offered to them of effecting the release of Donna Theresa if she were, as they had every reason to suppose, by this time a prisoner in the midst of the buccaneer army.

Harry Seaborne was delighted with the plan, which was suggested by two of his Spanish allies, and no time was lost in once more getting under weigh.

The dead horse was dragged out of the track of the waggon by their united efforts, and two of the Spanish officers mounted respectively the near leader and the near wheeler, as the buccaneers had done before them. The other officer and Harry clambered into the interior and gave the signal for the start, their two spare horses having been previously linked on behind, as they might yet be useful in case of an emergency.

Away they dashed at a gallop over the flinty stones, the path being quite easy to follow owing to the almost continuous glare of the lightning.

Away with the speed of the wind, for their great object was to come up with the buccaneer army during the dark hours of the night.

Presently they passed the smouldering ruins of the castle which Morgan's army had captured and subdued not many hours previously, but they halted not here.

Harry Seaborne was anxious to push on to the left bank of the river, for they easily ascertained that the buccaneers had not crossed it until an hour or so before daybreak.

So they gallantly continued their journey although overwhelmed with fatigue, and by-and-bye they were rewarded by discerning numerous camp fires gleaming in the midst of a little plain, which convinced them that they had at last come up with the buccaneer host.

CHAPTER XXIII.

THE CAMP OF THE BUCCANEERS—IN THE TOILS.

WHILST Morgan and Zoabinda were exchanging sympathetic endearments, as recorded in our last chapter but one, the buccaneers were committing the usual excesses and barbarities, which had become a part of their natures.

They made the few surviving prisoners cast the dead of their own party headlong into the deep moat which surrounded three sides of the castle, and compelled them to bury the slain buccaneers in a more decorous manner.

They shut up all the wounded, with the exception of the officers, in the chapel of the castle, thus making of the sacred edifice at once a hospital and a common gaol, where the shrieks of the wounded and the wails of the dying were horribly mingled with the blasphemies and the riot of drunken debauchery.

They took away everything that could be used as food for man, to the extent of leaving the place completely bare, so that there was not even subsistence for a dog, and nothing remained for the wounded and the prisoners but to die a lingering death of starvation.

Morgan ordered the castle to be destroyed with the exception of the tall keep tower, into which the wounded and the prisoners were thrust.

All the ordnance were spiked and thrown into the moat, and then the noble buccaneers took their departure, once more heading towards Panama.

On, on, on, in the burning heat of midday—on, on, on, in the cooler hours of evening, until at last night came, and it was time to think about camping.

The army had by this time reached a small plateau or plain, quite large enough to accommodate the whole force.

They lighted their camp fires and prepared their evening meal, arranging the spoil-laden waggons around the whole camp, thus forming a barrier against surprise either from Spanish or Indian foes, either of which might attack them at any moment.

It was towards this encircling barrier that the waggon containing our little body of four adventurers was deftly steered by the Spanish officers who acted as post-boys, not at too rapid a pace, for that would have attracted suspicion, but at a steady, methodical trot.

At last the cumbrous vehicle was arranged alongside the others, and the horses were unharnessed and turned loose, having been first shoe-hobbled, to render their straying far away a matter of impossibility.

No one would have known the four adventurers from real buccaneers, unless the swarthy visages and coal-black moustaches of the Spaniards had betrayed them.

"Let us now saunter into the camp," said Harry Seaborne; "we need not approach too near any of the fires, and then we shall not attract undue attention."

The proposition was agreed to, and the quartette set out on their voyage of discovery.

The thunderstorm had by this time ceased, but the heavens were still very murky, so that not one ray of moonlight was visible.

The camp fires alone shed a lurid glare over the scene, dimly revealing the forms of the buccaneers who held revelry around them.

They were carding and dicing and smoking tobacco, then a comparatively new luxury, in long clay pipes, uttering anathemas or ribald jokes between each puff.

Sometimes a quarrel would arise, one buccaneer accusing another of having cheated and receiving the "lie" in return, when daggers would be promptly drawn, and if the others did not interfere and separate the angry disputants they would hack and slash at each other until a wound was given, when they would surlily sit down again.

It was very amusing to watch these petty and continual feuds, showing the innate savagery of human nature in its worst form, and yet not altogether divested of a ludicrous aspect.

But Harry Seaborne and his companions were too intent on the fulfilment of their mission to pay much heed to them, far less to take an interest in their details.

At length, however, their attention was attracted and riveted by a scene very similar to the many they had already witnessed, but yet differing somewhat therefrom.

Two buccaneers were fiercely contending with great broadswords, making the camp ring with the din of their clashing blades.

They were evidently quarrelling and fighting about a girl who lay bound and helpless at their feet, her white face upturned to the clouded heavens.

Neither of the four adventurers were near enough to see her distinctly, for her face was only visible by the uncertain and flickering flashes of the fire, and its lambent tongues of flames only darted quiveringly upwards at uncertain intervals, but they all came to the conclusion that she was young and beautiful.

It was sad to see two great brawny ruffians cutting each other's throats to determine who should possess a helpless girl who never wronged either of them ; but these were noble buccaneers, and she was their lawful prize.

The singular duel that was being waged was, however, put an abrupt end to by the sudden and startling appearance of a third person upon the scene.

This third person, though not very tall, was evidently a man of immense bulk and strength.

Unhesitatingly he stepped almost between the two combatants, and with a long, heavy sword, that he held firmly grasped in his right hand, struck down their opposing blades.

With such force did he strike that one fellow dropped his sword with a howl of astonishment and rage, and the point of the other's blade touched the earth before he could recover his guard.

"What ! are there not enough Spanish throats to cut that ye must needs be slashing away at each other's ?" cried the new comer, in stentorian tones. "By Heaven ! our force is already so small that every man is worth his weight in gold-dust—aye ! almost in diamonds. Tell me, what is it ye quarrel over for all the world like two dogs about a bone ?"

" 'Tis a girl, your excellency. I captured her in Chargres after the army had taken its departure, for you must know that I had taken too much wine, and, going to sleep in a cellar of the castle, heard not drum beat or trumpet blare. Well, when I woke up I found this bonnie lass, and, stealing a horse, bore her before me on the crupper to the camp, and now this rascal wants to deprive me of her," exclaimed one ruffian.

" I found her lying by the watch-fire, alone, not an hour ago," growled the other, " and I took possession of her as my lawful prize. I don't believe a word of this fellow's story."

" I only left her for a few minutes to endeavour to procure her some food," said the first speaker.

" Cease this unseemly brawling !" cried the man who, unsolicited, had made himself the arbitrator of their dispute, and in whom Harry Seaborne at this moment recognised Morgan himself. " Or stay ! I will put an end to it by passing my sword through her, and then you can divide the corpse between you."

The men offered no opposition to this proposal, but fell back, one on one side and one on the other, to let him pass.

In a couple of strides he stood over the unhappy girl. She had fainted.

He raised his great sword to strike, but ere it could descend he dashed it to the earth with a cry of astonishment and joy, and took the sylph-like form of the young girl in his arms.

As he did so Harry Seaborne exclaimed, excitedly—

" Good Heavens ! 'tis Theresa de Guzman !"

" Stand back, my men, I will not slay this girl, as I recognise in her one whom I have sworn to befriend and protect, and will ransom her from you at a thousand dollars each !" cried Morgan.

" Hurrah for the noble captain !" cried the two ruffians, highly pleased at the barter of a mere dainty piece of flesh for what was very much more in their line. " Shall we help you to carry her, captain !"

" No, she is a mere feather-weight," replied Morgan. " In my tent she will be safe from all harm. Yes," he muttered to himself, " from all harm, for Zoabinda will not be able to leave her couch for a week."

His stalwart form was soon lost in the darkness, for Harry Seaborne did not care to follow him too closely.

He knew that there would be no difficulty in discovering the tent of Morgan in the morning, so for the present it was best to leave well alone.

CHAPTER XXIV.

AN ATTEMPTED RESCUE—ITS FAILURE—THE CAMP ALARMED.

HARRY SEABORNE was of opinion that enough had been done for that night, as it would be a matter of the greatest difficulty to discover Morgan's tent in the darkness, though with the first break of dawn it would be easy enough.

He and his three companions retired, therefore, to their waggon, and composed themselves to sleep therein. They found, however, that their bed was a hard one—aye, hard as a bed of flint could have been.

Feeling some curiosity to know the cause thereof, and taking up a few sacks that were spread carelessly on the top, they discovered that the waggon was laden with dollars and broad pieces of eight—a fine booty if they could escape with it as well as with the pretty Spanish senorita.

Harry thought very little of the gold, however, for his mind was bent upon Donna Theresa. As for courting slumber, that he might do, but the attaining of it was a feat of sheer impossibility.

His companions were equally unsuccessful in wooing the drowsy god, as he could tell by their restlessness.

At length the silence of the sleeping camp was disturbed by the renewed rumbling of the thunder, and soon after the downfall of a heavy tropical shower caused a noise almost deafening.

The rain soon penetrated the cover of the waggon and drenched our adventurers to the skin.

Of course after that both sleep and comfort were entirely out of the question.

"Comrades," said Harry Seaborne, "an idea has just struck me—namely, that it is a most propitious hour for attempting the rescue of Donna Theresa. This dreadful weather will keep the buccaneers inside their tents, and the very guards will get under cover, for discipline is bad, and the officers are as bad as the men. Well, under such circumstances, if we can but discover the tent in which the donna is imprisoned we may be able to carry her off with impunity."

"A good idea and I second it," exclaimed Don Pero, the youngest of the cavaliers.

"And I, and I !" ejaculated the other two, rising from their recumbent attitudes.

"It will not do for us all to go," said Harry Seaborne, "for if we are all captured Donna Theresa will be left without protection. Don Pero and myself will undertake the enterprise. Should we fail, or meet captivity or death, two champions will still remain. Do I not speak wisely, my friends ?"

His words met with unanimous approval, and it was arranged that he and Pero should go alone.

They started at once, having first looked to their arms, and stepping very cautiously over the dead leaves.

Harry led the way, charging Pero to exercise great caution, and not to make the least noise.

By the aid of the still smouldering watch-fires they could plainly perceive the tents and mia-mias of the buccaneers scattered over the little plain, and occasionally a dusky figure stalking about in the uncertain light, which, together with the neighing and whinnying of the restless horses, which were exposed to all the violence of the tempest, convinced them that their enterprise was more hazardous than they had imagined.

Nevertheless, as Harry Seaborne had predicted, the weather had the effect of keeping most of the buccaneers closely housed, or rather tented, whilst the roaring of the thunder and the sighing and moaning of the wind prevented any ordinary sound from being heard, or if heard, proved a ready means of accounting for it without creating suspicion or alarm, and so the two adventurers proceeded with a certain amount of confidence.

At this juncture the storm came on with renewed fury, and the rain again poured down in torrents, completely drenching our hero and his companion, and this time altogether extinguishing many of the camp-fires.

At the same time it became suddenly so cold that the drops began to freeze as they fell, forming a kind of sleet, which the wind drove with such fury against their faces, hands, and necks as would have rendered their situation almost too uncomfortable to be borne had not their spirits been cheered by the reflection that the same peltings would drive their enemies under cover, and, consequently, lessen the danger of detection.

"Everything, so far, favours our enterprise," whispered Harry. "Let us on."

Slowly and cautiously they moved about between the tents and mia-mias, gradually nearing the centre of the camp, where three or four tents, larger than the rest, proclaimed them to be those of Morgan and his principal officers.

Most of the tents were dark inside, but occasionally a ray of light gleamed out through the crevices made by the swaying to and fro of the canvas which was hung across the doors to protect the inmates from the inclemency of the weather.

Wherever a light of this kind could be seen Harry or his companion would approach the tent, and cautiously raising the canvas, peer inside. They would generally perceive a few buccaneers either lounging about in careless attitudes, stretched at full length asleep on the bare earth, or engaged in pipeclaying their belts, polishing their armour, or sharpening their weapons.

The interior of some eight or ten of these tents had been examined in this manner without the occurrence of any incident worthy of note, when just as Harry Seaborne approached another a stalwart buccaneer suddenly pushed aside the canvas and issued forth.

Our hero immediately drew back and stood still, and the buccaneer passed close by without perceiving him.

Harry then softly retreated to the rear of the tent, where he remained in deep shadow till the buccaneer re-entered, when he heard him comment with many others upon the rough state of the weather.

Then he drew a long breath of relief, for he had been in great fear lest his companion, Don Pero, should be discovered, but fortunately the latter had seen the buccaneer also, and had exercised sufficient presence of mind to throw himself on the ground and lie motionless as a log until the danger was past.

Some three or four more tents were now examined in the same manner as those described, which brought our adventurers almost to the centre of the encampment, but still no traces of the beautiful Spanish girl could be found, and they had begun to debate whether is was best for them to look farther that night, or retrace their steps to the waggon and wait until daylight, when a cry and a long deep moan, followed by a sharp reproof, proceeding from a darkened tent close by, reached their ears.

One voice was the shrill treble of a woman, the other the gruff voice of a man, and the former, in the breast of Harry Seaborne at least, excited emotions both strange and indescribable.

Without speaking a word, and scarcely venturing a natural respiration, our two spies slowly and silently drew near the tent whence the sounds proceeded.

They listened, but for some moments all was still.

Then several low moans succeeded, and another sharp and angry reproof was given, which evidently came from the lips of a half-tipsy buccaneer. From the tenor of the language it left no doubt in the minds of our friends that it was addressed to a female captive.

Oh ! how wildly beat the heart of Harry Seaborne, and what strange, almost unaccountable feelings were excited in his breast, as the following threat reached his ears—

" You calm down, nor dare to make a noise, or I will brain you with the butt-end of my musquetoon."

What would he not have given to know to whom those words were addressed?

Could it be that he was so near to the beautiful donna, and that it was her groans, wrung from an agonised soul, that had sounded in his ears and caused those harsh threatenings in return?

Oh! if such were the case, how gladly would he take her place and endure all the horrors of imprisonment if by this means she could be restored to liberty and happiness.

CHAPTER XXV.

A FRIEND IN NEED—AFTER MANY PERILS.

HARRY SEABORNE loved, and loved truly, and there was no sacrifice too great for him to make for the object of his affection.

All within had once more become still, but without the storm was raging as fiercely as ever, and the wind moaned and whistled among the tents and flapped the canvas and drove the rain and sleet against them with a loud pattering sound.

Taking Don Pero aside, Harry Seaborne, in low, hurried tones, informed him that he had resolved upon the bold experiment of entering the tent and endeavouring to ascertain whether the prisoner confined therein was the young lady of whom they were in search.

"It is a great risk, and I fear that very little good will come of it," said Don Pero.

"At all events I can ascertain whether my hopes have any foundation," answered Harry.

"And if they have what will you do then?" queried Don Pero.

"Why, rescue the captive, though a hundred buccaneers barred the way," responded Harry.

"One, if he is wide awake, will be enough to alarm the camp, and in five minutes we shall have a pretty swarm of hornets around our ears, through which it will be impossible to escape."

"I hope your courage does not fail you, Don Pero?" said Harry Seaborne, rather bitterly.

"No, but I have thrown my prudence into the opposite scale, and the balance is thus upset."

"Notwithstanding which I will rescue Donna Theresa at all risks, or die trying. I know that it is she who is a captive in this tent, for I am certain that I recognise her voice."

"Then you are determined upon the desperate expedient of entering, even though the guard is awake?"

"I am, for doubtless the sentinels have the strictest injunctions not to slumber. Once get her outside in this murky gloom our retreat will be easy, and we shall stand every chance of escaping detection," urged our hero.

"I will fall in with your view on condition that you allow me instead of yourself to enter the tent," said Don Pero.

"Ah! why that strange request? I had thought you half a coward, and now—"

"And now you find out your mistake," said Don Pero, finishing the sentence for him. "Well, I would enter the tent, since it must be done, instead of you, because the guard must be disposed of silently, before he can utter an alarm, and I flatter myself that a Spaniard knows how to handle a poniard better than an Englishman."

"Go, then, in Heaven's name! My mind revolts at the deed, but better that than fail in our enterprise."

"Stand still and don't move, then," said Don Pero, putting his mouth close to Harry Seaborne's ear and speaking in a whisper. "I'll just slip round the tent and see if there's any other opening about."

The next moment his dusky figure was lost in the darkness.

Something like a minute elapsed, when he again made his appearance on the opposite side of the tent, and added—

"It's all right—be careful and keep your powder dry. I'm going to enter now."

With these words he dropped quietly to the earth, extended himself at full length on the wet ground, then cautiously raising the flap of the tent he put his head under and slowly and silently drew his body after him.

The moment of Don Pero's final disappearance was one of the most mentally and physically painful to Harry Seaborne that he had ever experienced.

It seemed to him as if his blood had all rushed to his heart, and his heart to his throat, producing a strange species of suffocation and strangulation.

For some time, as he stood and listened, he could not breathe, then, with a degree of pain that almost forced him to cry aloud, his heart seemed to leap back to its proper place, and began a series of palpitations that to him really appeared audible, and threatened to force a passage through his breast.

Gradually he grew calmer, and he approached closer to the tent, so as to place his ear against the canvas. Then he listened with every faculty of hearing exerted to the last degree his will could give it.

For a time all remained still within, and no sound save that caused by the driving storm without was heard.

Suddenly, however, a quick, sharp cry, followed by a stifled groan, smote upon his ear, and then he could distinguish sounds indicating a struggle where one is endeavouring to strangle another.

Next he heard a voice, that sent a thrill of joy and fear through every fibre of his frame, exclaim—

"Oh! Heaven, he will be slain, and my cords prevent me offering the least aid to my chivalrous preserver."

This was said in Spanish, and not only did Harry Seaborne gather from it that the speaker was, indeed, Donna Theresa de Guzman, but also that his comrade Don Pero was in imminent danger of his life.

Without pausing to reflect he at once bounded into the tent, his pistol firmly clutched in his hand.

TALES of PIRATES
SMUGGLERS and BUCCANEERS.

No. 9.]   **THE SCOURGE OF THE SPANISH MAIN.**   [One Penny.

Harry Seaborne saw that not a moment was to be lost if he would save the don's life.

MORGAN the BUCCANEER; or, the Terror of the Seas.

Don Pero was struggling desperately with a burly buccaneer, into whose mouth he had thrust the pommel of his poniard up to the hilt, smashing in his teeth and rendering him incapable of uttering a sound.

But for all this the ruffian had got the upper hand of the young Spaniard, and having come to the ground together he had seized his bare throat with both hands and was rapidly and surely strangling him.

Harry Seaborne saw that not a moment was to be lost if he would save the young don's life.

Grasping the barrel of the pistol he swung the stock round with all his strength, until it came in contact with the buccaneer's head.

The next instant his fingers had relaxed their clutch on the young don's throat, and he had rolled off his body on to the ground, stunned and to all appearance lifeless.

Not staying to satisfy himself which was the case, Harry Seaborne cut loose Donna Theresa's bonds, raised her in his arms, and made towards the door of the tent, bidding Don Pero to follow.

"Stay, stay!" cried the latter, "really I—"

The unfinished sentence was drowned by deafening cries, and Harry Seaborne, who had just gained the outside of the tent, with Donna Theresa in his arms, was laid senseless upon the earth by a blow from a clubbed arquebus.

At the same instant three or four buccaneers, one of them bearing a lighted torch, sprang over his body, and, bursting into the tent, made Don Pero also a prisoner.

CHAPTER XXVI.

PRISONERS—A FRIEND IN DISGUISE.

IT is of course impossible for us to convey anything more than a general idea of the rage and indignation excited throughout the buccaneer army by the daring attempt of our hero and Don Pero to rescue a prisoner.

To such a degree of vindictive fury were the passions of the mighty buccaneers excited that for a time it seemed probable that the two prisoners would be torn to pieces in spite of the efforts of a more calculating few to reserve them for a more cruel fate.

But at last, by entreaty and menace, their guards succeeded in restraining the mob from violence, and then gradually the tumult subsided.

Our hero and his companion were conducted to a large tent, bound hand foot, and put under a strong guard, to await Morgan's will concerning them, which could not be learnt until the following day.

Order at length being restored, the recently-alarmed and exasperated buccaneers quietly withdrew to their tents, all more or less elated at the prospect of shortly being both spectators and actors in the amusement of human torture.

Silence, as concerning the human storm of passion, again reigned throughout the camp, but the storm of the elements still raged as fiercely as ever, and the wind sighed, and moaned, and whistled amongst the tents, and the rain and hail pattered against the tightly-drawn canvas as before, rendering the night pitchy dark and gloomy.

And doubly gloomy was it to our two friends, whose last hopes had expired, and who could look forward to nothing better than a horrible death on the morrow.

As for Harry Seaborne, on first coming to himself and perceiving at a glance what had transpired, his anguish of soul knew no bounds, and he repeatedly groaned aloud and rolled to and fro in his fetters as one in mortal agony.

On the point of liberating her he loved he had been struck down, she had been torn from him, and now there was little hope that he would ever behold her sweet face again.

And more than this, he had involved another in his ruin, and brought upon him a doom at which he shuddered and grew sick at heart to think of.

Oh! he thought, if he could but die alone, and thus atone for his incautious act, how gladly would he do so.

But this could not be—the chivalrous young Spaniard would also be a victim. Perhaps also the other two, who had so nobly consented to risk their lives to rescue the girl so dear to him, would be discovered and receive the same horrible tortures and death.

And then, alas! what would become of poor Theresa, without a single protector left?

The prisoners, though near each other throughout the night, were not permitted to speak, but as the day dawned it revealed the pale countenances of the prisoners, with their blood-shot eyes, which clearly showed that the night had been passed in intense mental agony, devoid of all hope.

The positions of Harry Seaborne and Don Pero were such that, though tightly bound and extended at full length on the damp ground, they could look into each other's face, and as they did so they almost read each other's thoughts.

Don Pero was unhurt, but Harry's head was somewhat bloody from the wound he had received at the time of his capture, although the contusion was not a dangerous one and he experienced very little pain.

About dawn the guard over the captives was changed, but nothing else worthy of note took place until a short time after, when, to our hero's joy, Walter Evandale entered the tent.

But his first emotions of pleasure soon vanished as Evandale rested his dark eyes coldly, almost savagely upon him and his fellow captive, without the least sign of recognition.

He was splendidly apparelled, and the plume in his hat was fastened by an immense ruby.

Previous to his appearance there had been a faint hope in the mind of our hero that the brave buccaneer lieutenant, who had befriended him on so many former occasions, might in some unknown and unexpected way assist them in their present difficulties, but the moment he looked upon Evandale that hope fled, and he closed his eyes and shuddered.

All this the buccaneer lieutenant evidently noticed as his keen black eyes glanced from one to another, and when he had finished his survey a smile, which seemed one of fiendish triumph and delight, rested on his handsome countenance.

He had read Harry's thoughts, and they seemed to give him intense inward satisfaction.

"Dog of a spy!" he said, addressing himself to our hero, "your time and that of your companion has come. Ere the sun has risen you will be condemned—ere he has set you will be tortured and executed."

"Begone!" exclaimed Harry, vehemently, his indignation raised to a pitch he could not control. " Begone ! false friend and atrocious buccaneer, and may my blood be upon your head !"

" Ha, ha ! You see I only smile now, but I will laugh at the stake as I invent tortures wherewith to make you groan anew. Let me tell you one of those tortures now that you may ponder on it—let me whisper in your ear," and he bent down his head apparently for the purpose, but instead of hearing the language he expected, the following words sent a mad revulsion of feeling to Harry's heart—

" Courage ! I am true, but Morgan suspects me, and I must play a part. Outwardly I am your bitterest foe, inwardly your staunchest friend. Aid you I can and will, but not yet."

Then he added, aloud—

" Ha, ha, ha ! how like you the invention? That, methinks, will put your bravado and courage to the test," and, turning abruptly on his heel, he strode to the door of the tent, exchanged a few words with the guard, exhorting them to the greatest vigilance, and then disappeared.

About a quarter of an hour later several of the buccaneer officers made their appearance, and after walking around the prisoners and examining them, occasionally turning them over with their feet in a careless manner, they gathered themselves together in a group near the tent door, and a very animated discussion took place, of the nature of which both Harry Seaborne and Don Pero were ignorant, the conversation being carried on in a tone too low to reach their ears.

Presently, however, their voices assumed a somewhat higher pitch, and then Harry Seaborne gathered enough of the discussion to know that his own doom, as well as that of his companion, was sealed.

By-and-bye, a handsome young buccaneer from the party near the door came up to them and proceeded to cut their bonds.

When this had been effected he told the two captives to get up and follow him.

After repeated trials, during which the buccaneer exhibited his haste and a small portion of his hatred by repeated kicks on their bodies, Harry Seaborne and Don Pero succeeded in regaining their feet.

Harry was the last to rise, and when he finally did so it was only by a great effort that he could stand.

He felt stiff, numb, and weak, with occasionally sharp, darting pains through his body, and a slight dizziness in his head, but their bonds had been very tight, and they had not tasted food for many hours, so their condition was not to be wondered at.

" Cheer up, comrade—all may yet be well," Harry, however, managed to say to Don Pero.

They were the first words he had ventured to address to him since being taken prisoner, and he was now warned against repeating the offence by receiving a back-handed blow across the face from a buccaneer, which caused blood to flow profusely from his mouth and nostrils.

Our hero started, his eyes flashed, and he instinctively placed his hand to his side, as if to draw his sword, but instantly recollecting that it was gone, his countenance fell. Turning a hopeless,

mournful look upon the young Spaniard, he bowed his head upon his bosom, and quietly walked out alongside the young buccaneer who had him in charge.

As they emerged from the tent and gazed around, Harry Seaborne and Don Pero beheld a sight that made them shudder and involuntarily recoil, but we must describe what it is in another chapter.

CHAPTER XXVII.
RUNNING THE GAUNTLET.

THE morning was cold and disagreeable—a rare thing in such a latitude, but then it was the depth of winter, if such a term may be applied to a country all but tropical.

It had ceased raining, but heavy, dreary-looking clouds were floating through the atmosphere, and the ground was covered with a kind of sleet, that made it very slippery.

The two prisoners remarked all this, but only in relation to the chances which were offered for an escape from death, just as the sailor scrutinises each object on the coast against which he knows his vessel is about to strike.

The nature of their initiatory punishment was apparent at a glance.

They were to be made to run the gauntlet, and preparations had already been made therefore.

About a dozen or twenty yards distant from the tent in which they had been confined, and extending down nearly to the bank of a small river on the northern boundary of the camp, forming two parallel lines of something like a quarter of a mile in length, were drawn up at least a third of the mighty buccaneer army, armed with musquetoons, bill-hooks, pikes, daggers and halberds.

They were indiscriminately mixed, as regarded age, regiment, and size, but the lines were very straight, the distance between them being about ten feet.

The moment Harry Seaborne and Don Pero neared this terrible assemblage, accompanied by their savage guard, who by this time numbered at least half-a-dozen men, they were greeted with one universal yell of ferocious delight, and as they were led down the lines several buccaneers stepped forward and indignantly saluted them with foul epithets, pinching them with their fingers, striking them with their hands and fists, and sometimes with the weapons they carried, so that long ere they reached the other end they were considerably bruised and injured, though providentially no bones were broken.

Harry knew there existed a great uncertainty that either would be able to run the gauntlet successfully ; indeed, he felt that the chances were greatly against their being able to do so.

" This is terrible !" exclaimed Don Pero. " Oh ! that I had died upon the field of battle."

" Could I but see Theresa de Guzman in safety, how willingly would I purchase the boon, even by dying in this manner," sighed our hero, for even at that moment he thought not of himself but of her he loved.

Harry was the first selected to make the trial, and

as he prepared to start he turned his eyes for a moment upon Don Pero and breathed a half-uttered farewell.

We have said that when brought to the ground he was very weak and exhausted, but looking upon him now it seemed as if his strength had been suddenly restored on seeing the dreadful task before him, and when at length he bounded forward it was with such swiftness that for a time he escaped the blows aimed at him on both sides.

But he had not run more than twenty yards when a stroke on the head from a halberd in the hands of a drummer-boy made him reel and almost fall to the ground.

He recovered himself, however, and redoubled his efforts, but the blows now unfortunately fell fast and heavy, and he was on the point of sinking under them when he heard a voice shout—

" Break the lines !—break the lines !—and escape outside.   That is buccaneer law !"

Harry could have sworn, though the voice sounded like an assumed one, that it was in reality Walter Evandale's, and he determined to take advantage of the counsel thus offered.

Turning suddenly upon the right line, therefore, he exerted his remaining strength, and burst through.

He now knew that if he could only reach the flagstaff that formed the centre of the encampment he would, by buccaneer law, for the time be safe ; but this required another almost superhuman effort, for a hundred savage yells and shouts in his rear assured him he was followed, while the way before him was blocked up by a large crowd of freebooters, who had forsaken the lines to bar his progress.

With no time for thought, but acting rather by instinct or impulse, he bounded away to make a half circuit, while the most active of his enemies darted forward to intercept him.

By this means his chances of escape were reduced to the very smallest number, and already looking upon himself as lost, he was upon the point of yielding to their mercy when a guardian Providence again interposed in his favour, for Don Pero, seeing the lines broken, thought it a favourable moment for himself to gain the place of refuge or buccaneer sanctuary, and immediately set out to do so.

The cry that the other prisoner was escaping drew the attention of the whole assemblage upon the latter, and left our hero's course unobstructed, Instantly profiting by his good fortune he reached the flagstaff, but so exhausted that he fell down overcome beside it.

As to Don Pero, for some time he bid fair to outrun his pursuers, but chancing at last to slip on the sleety grass, he was struck on the head with an axe and instantly killed, much to the regret of the buccaneers, who mourned the loss of witnessing another victim's agonies at the stake.

The running of the gauntle over, our hero was again bound, but this time with his hands at liberty.

He was then offered food, which he eagerly devoured, after which water was given him, and anon he was informed that his trial would immediately take place.

An hour later Harry Seaborne was marched, his hands bound securely to his sides, to the tent of Morgan, where his trial, and, as a matter of course, his condemnation, were to take place.

Scarcely had he reached it when two buccaneers, who had evidently been sent out as scouts, came in and reported something in a low tone to the buccaneer chief.

On hearing it he seemed to question them with a great degree of interest, and to receive their replies with satisfaction.

Presently he nodded his head in token of approval, and then dismissed them from his presence.

There was a pause of several minutes' duration, and just as Harry had begun to wonder why it was that his trial was not proceeded with, the two buccaneers re-entered the tent, dragging between them the young Spaniards whom our hero and Don Pero had, a few hours previously, left in the baggage waggon.

At this sight the young Englishman felt the icy chill of despair enter his heart, not on his own account, but on that of her he loved, for there was now no champion left either to save or to avenge her.

There were about a dozen of the buccaneer chiefs present.

The handsome Walter Evandale, sitting next to Morgan, as was his wont ; the cynical Rupert Russel, clad as usual in black velvet ; the taciturn, one-eyed Dutchman, Peter Mansveldt ; and the brutal-looking Captain Kydd, being the most conspicuous of the number.

A large crowd, however, had surrounded the tent on the outside, all eager to hear the sentence.

For some moments a deep and solemn silence prevailed, during which the eyes of the buccaneers were fixed with savage sternness upon the captives, while here and there a sudden gleam of vindictive malice, which some of the judges could not wholly restrain, warned the prisoners that all hope of mercy must be abandoned.

At length Morgan arose, and after looking upon the prisoners for a short time, during which his malignant eyes seemed to burn with a deep-seated, unconquerable hatred, he slowly turned towards his officers, and raising his right hand, delivered an oration.

Of course all that he said was strongly against the prisoners, and when his discourse ceased several speeches were made in quick succession by the other chiefs and warriors, but all were in the same strain.

All voted for the death of the prisoners, all were for having them burnt at the stake.

Walter Evandale came last, but he spoke more bitterly, more resentfully than any of them.

As he finished speaking a fierce, universal yell of delight from those around, and also from the listeners without, attested the popularity of his language, and the great power he had of working up the feelings of his auditory to the highest degree.

Morgan even lost his habitual taciturnity, and grasped him warmly by the hand.

The time was now come for deciding the fate of the prisoners by vote.

'Twas done in the following manner.

Whoever was in favour of putting the prisoners to death held his drawn sword aloft; whoever was opposed to the measure plunged its point into the ground.

The motion was carried with only one solitary dissentient vote.

A short discussion now followed with regard to the time and locale for the execution of the horrible sentence, and it was finally settled to take place on the following day at sunrise, on an open piece of ground just below the southern limit of the camp.

The council then broke up, and a guard was set over the prisoners.

They had just fifteen hours to prepare for death —the terrible death of the stake.

But the night that was shortly to ensue was to be one of strange, startling, and thrilling events, and it was fated that many wonderful things were to happen in the buccaneers' camp before the dawn of another day.

CHAPTER XXVIII.

A CLEVER RUSE—HOPE OF ESCAPE.

FOUR buccaneers, selected for their keen watchfulness and tried courage, were set as guards over the prisoners doomed to die on the morrow.

They were armed with daggers, swords, and musquetoons, and were so placed that the slightest movement of either of the captives could be seen.

But all these precautions seemed unnecessary, for the latter were so tightly and securely bound that to move at all was next to an impossibility.

They were placed in a row, and every man was bound hand and foot with a strong ligament attached to a stake near his head.

Two torches stuck in the ground on either side cast a ruddy gleam over their dark figures and the cuirassed and gaudily-attired guards standing over them with untiring vigilance.

Some hours had already passed away since they first entered this, their last prison-house, when a noise outside attracted the attention of the guard.

As the noise was close to the entrance of the tent one of the guards levelled his piece and challenged.

But at the same moment the door of the tent was pushed rudely aside, and a burly buccaneer staggered into the interior, holding in one hand a huge leathern bottle, which he seemed in vain to be trying to get to his lips, with a drunken gravity truly ludicrous.

The buccaneer who had pointed his musquetoon at the intruder elevated the muzzle and indulged in a silent laugh, a proceeding in which his companions also joined.

The drunken buccaneer, apparently not aware where he was, but winking visibly from the effect of the light in his eyes, continued to stagger forward, still trying to bring the bottle to his lips, but from the unsteadiness of hand and body not being able to succeed in his purpose.

At length he came to a sudden halt—that is to say, a drunken man's halt—and, balancing himself as best he could, stared curiously upon the guard, whom he now seemingly beheld for the first time.

"What are you doing here?" he exclaimed, accompanying his remark with a number of hiccups, and flourishing his leather bottle with the comical gesture of an intoxicated man endeavouring to appear very wise and dignified. "I say, what are you doing here all drunk as beasts? Go home and get sober, and take a sensible friend's advice— don't ever taste liquor again."

Again the guards laughed, and one of them said—

"What have you got in that bottle, jovial comrade?"

"Poison!" answered the other, fumbling about his dress for a place to hide it, as if afraid it would be taken from him. "Yes, poison," he repeated, beginning to stagger back, as if with the intention of making his escape. "It wouldn't be good for you, but would make you sick, and so I will drink it instead."

"Let us try if it will make us sick," laughed one of the guards, approaching the drunken man, and extending his hand as if to seize it.

"No, no, no!" returned the drunken buccaneer, with great eagerness, fumbling more than ever for a sufficiently capacious pocket in his garments, and retreating all the while towards the door of the tent.

"No, no, no!" he repeated, dropping the leather bottle to the ground, apparently unconscious of the fact, and continuing his retreat with quickened but still unsteady steps. "It isn't good for ye—it's poison—it would kill ye."

And as the last words were uttered he made a sudden lurch towards the door, missed it, and fell sprawling on the earth, where he lay as if stunned.

The buccaneers laughed heartily as they passed the leather bottle round, each taking some three or four deep draughts, and smacking their lips with true relish, for the poison was unmistakably rum.

This emptied the bottle, which they then shied at the head of its inebrated owner with good-humoured derision, and then resumed their guard over the persons of their prisoners.

Then it was that a near observer might have seen in the dark eyes of the apparently-intoxicated man, as he still lay extended where he fell, a gleam of intelligence and of triumph, such as the eyes of no really drunken man could by any possibility express.

The explanation was soon apparent, for after the lapse of a few minutes the heads of the guards, in spite of their efforts to the contrary, began to nod and droop, and in the course of five minutes more they themselves sunk down to the ground, unconscious of everything around them.

The moment he perceived this, the intruder sprang to his feet, and, gliding forward with the stealthy tread of a panther, he approached the prostrate buccaneers. Bending over them, he examined each closely, and then carefully deprived him of his weapon.

All this, or as much as their peculiar positions would allow, was witnessed by Harry Seaborne and his fellow captives—witnessed with emotions of hope and joy impossible to be described, but with a cautious silence that spoke volumes in favour of their presence of mind.

The hope of liberty and the fear of failure caused their blood to alternate between head and heart, and they experienced an acute sense of suffocation so intense were their feelings.

The friendly buccaneer having satisfied himself that the guards were safe and deprived of all their weapons, he drew his dagger, and, with a rapidity that threatened injury to the captives, severed their bonds.

"Now, then, up and follow me," he whispered, "but if you speak or make the least noise all will be lost. I will go before and lead the way, but the moment I halt let all sink to the earth, and remain so until they hear my signal."

The force of his words were felt, but unfortunately it was impossible to comply with his request, owing to a want of circulation of blood in their limbs, particularly their legs, which were paralysed from being so tightly corded.

By quick and vigorous rubbing, however, added to the desperation of men straining every nerve for life, our friends soon had the satisfaction of finding themselves able to stand, and even to walk.

The arms of the guards were then distributed amongst them, and, extinguishing the torches, the whole party followed their deliverer out through the door of the tent. A minute later they once more breathed the open air of freedom, though surrounded by dangers the most imminent.

With a quick, but stealthy step, their guide led the way through the least frequented and most thinly-settled portion of the camp.

For something like ten minutes they carefully followed their guide among the clustering tents, which could just be discerned in time to be avoided, and then, with a degree of joy amounting almost to wildness, but which they were forced to restrain, the prisoners found themselves on the outskirts of the camp and on the borders of a mighty forest.

The guide continued to pick his way among the trees as he had done among the tents, and as well as they could the escaped prisoners followed his movements.

It was of course impossible to prevent their feet from causing the dead leaves to rattle, while here and there the sharp snapping of a dry twig made their hearts beat furiously.

For several minutes all went well, and they were just congratulating themselves mentally upon having passed all immediate danger, when the guide suddenly stopped, and in the lowest possible whisper said—

"Hist !"

As soon as the guide had uttered his warning exclamation he dropped upon his knees, applied his ear to the ground, and listened.

Then rising to his feet he made signs to the one nearest to him, which happened to be Harry Seaborne, not to speak nor stir, and Harry communicated it to the two Spaniards.

The guide presently strode forward, and in a single moment lost his friends in the pitchy darkness, but the unavoidable crushing of the dry leaves

could be heard some time longer, indicating the course he had taken.

At last all became still, and a short but painful suspense succeeded.

Suddenly they were startled by an exclamation like the challenge of a sentinel.

There was a reply in another voice, and then a conversation in low tones followed.

This lasted only for a few seconds, and was apparently broken off by the commission of some deed of violence, for a sentence seemingly only half completed was ended by a sharp groan, and then was heard a dull sound, as of the fall of some heavy body.

Then a voice close to them briefly, and in hollow tones, ejaculated one word—-

"Follow !"

It was the voice of their liberator, and in a great measure it reassured them.

They asked no questions of their guide and no explanation was made by him, but all continued to move forward in Indian file, silently and steadily.

At length they came to a small stream, one of the tributaries of the Carona, which the guide entered, followed in turn by Harry Seaborne and the two Spaniards.

The stream was not deep but rapid, and it was with no little difficulty that they succeeded in maintaining a foothold on the slippery stones that formed its bed.

The water, too, was so cold as to be painful, and the crossing was undoubtedly a physical feat of a severe nature.

After continuing up the stream for some forty or fifty yards the guide waded out on the opposite shore, and held the same course on the land for a similar distance, when he suddenly came to an abrupt halt.

The clash of steel was heard within the woods, and the guide parted the branches of the undergrowth as he and our three friends peered through them upon a strange and interesting scene.

In a little open glade a mortal combat was being waged between two swordsmen.

A single glance revealed the fact that the combatants were Rupert Russel and Peter Mansveldt, and in his right hand each duellist grasped a sword, in his left a dagger.

Each duellist also had a second, who stood behind his principal with sword drawn, ready to interpose his blade in case any unfairness was observed on the part of the principals.

CHAPTER XXIX.

A PERILOUS ADVENTURE—THE ESCAPE.

LOOKING calmly upon this strange scene stood two other men. The one of gigantic stature was unmistakably Captain Kydd. The other was attired as a monk, and his cowl was drawn so far over his face that not a single feature was distinguishable, so that his identity could not even be guessed at.

The scene was illumined by the rays of half-a-dozen flickering lanthorns, that were hung from the tree branches, and shed a dubious and uncertain light upon the conflict.

Aided by this light, Harry Seaborne and his companions turned instinctively to gaze upon the countenance of their deliverer, for our hero possessed a vague idea that he was not unknown to him.

Judge of his astonishment, however, when, upon glancing round, he perceived that the great red nose, the shaggy eyebrows, and the blotched face that had distinguished the roystering buccaneer who had entered the tent to effect their rescue half an hour previously, had all vanished, leaving in their place the handsome countenance of Walter Evandale.

Just as our hero was about to grasp his hand and tender his heartfelt and hearty thanks for all he had done for him and his companions, a sharp cry from one of the combatants distracted his attention, and Peter Mansveldt was observed to fall, with Rupert Russel's sword thrust through his body up to the hilt.

At the same moment the lamps were all extinguished, and a rush as of many feet seemed to be coming directly towards them.

Evandale clutched our hero's arm and drew him hastily on through the bushes.

He again entered the stream, when he retraced his steps, Harry and the two Spaniards following, the latter greatly wondering what would be the result of this apparent change of purpose on the part of their guide, not having had enough experience in buccaneer cunning to know that the object of their conductor was to break the trail, and, if possible, thereby to baffle any parties that might be sent out in pursuit of them.

Continuing adown the bed of the stream, Evandale passed the place where they had at first entered the water, and as the river ran close to the northern extremity of the camp the tents were presently again in sight.

"Why do we return, my kind and generous friend?" asked Harry Seaborne of Evandale.

"Hush! do not speak," was the warning whisper. "A sentry should be posted hereabouts, and can't be far off."

Again a long silence followed, during which nothing could be heard but the rippling murmur of the stream as it dashed along its rocky bed, with occasionally a splash as now and then a foot slipped in the water. These slips were rendered more frequent in consequence of their feet being benumbed with cold.

At last they came directly opposite the camp, and the stream, which thus far had run swift and shallow, now began to grow deep and still.

Evandale came to a halt, merely whispering—

"Not a sound now, as you value your lives!" he continued to move forward some eight or ten yards, in which distance the water deepened from one to three feet.

Approaching the bank farthest from the camp, he loosened three long, narrow boats, shaped like canoes, and then waded back, drawing them after him.

These boats were securely lashed together, side by side, with strips of deerskin, and in consequence of this they were rendered almost secure against upsetting even in a rapid and serpentine current.

Evandale now informed Harry and his two friends that they must enter these boats, and in no case allow the slightest exclamation to escape them, no matter what migh· happen, nor how severely their nerves might be tried by perceptible dangers.

One of the adventurers being seated in each of the boats, Evandale entered the centre one, which held Harry Seaborne, and standing erect in the bow with a paddle in his hand he made a few vigorous but silent sweeps, and then allowed his singular craft to float quietly down the stream.

For a time all went smoothly, and the camp was safely passed, when the musical sound of running water began to be audible, gradually growing louder, till presently the adventurers became aware that they were approaching either a cascade or some rapids.

Had there been light sufficient for the purpose, there might have been seen frowning brows and compressed lips in that triple barge, as it slowly but surely floated down towards the rushing waters, whose first low distant murmurs were now changed to a solemn, heavy roar.

"Hist!" whispered Evandale, and his words were uttered with that fearful distinctness which more than louder tones impress one with something awful and mysterious. "Hist! don't move a hair's breadth now."

Scarcely was the warning given when a slight shock was felt underneath, and the boats were sent forward with a velocity that showed they had entered the rapids.

Now to this side, now to that, were they suddenly shifted by the winding current—dipping here and dipping there—jerking and rocking, and obeying every undulation and impulse of the water, but still floating onward as airy and buoyant as a feather or cork.

Swifter and more swift now speed the boats, and louder and more loud comes up the roar of the foaming waves from below, giving them the impression that there is a fearful chasm adown which they are about to plunge and be for ever engulfed in a whirling pool.

On, on speed the boats, and every breath is held and every heart has ceased to beat in fearful expectation.

Now the last dread moment has come.

The boats are suddenly lifted as if by giant hands, and flung forward into the boiling, hissing, foaming surge.

Round, round, round—here and there, right and left, up and down—they go, and the flashing of the furious element and its thunderous roar are all that can be seen and heard by their helpless inmates, as they cling tenaciously to their frail sides and breathlessly await the eventualities.

Suddenly a fearful shock and a downward lightning plunge are felt, but just at the moment when all hope seems lost the boats glide into still water and the roar of the rapids is heard behind.

"Thank God the danger is past!" said Evandale, drawing a long breath of relief, and with his paddle he gave one vigorous stroke, which sent them farther from the hissing waters.

"Now we are safe if we make not too much noise."

And still skilfully using his paddle on either side he kept the boats in position.

Presently a slight grating underneath, and the stoppage of the boats, together with a dark mass of something looming up above them, assured the trembling captives that they had gained land at last.

Evandale now bade them remain quiet where they were, and, stepping ashore, he made the boats fast, then he strode away along the beach and beside the rocky cliff, that rose almost perpendicularly upwards to the height of fifty feet.

Suddenly he disappeared in a narrow fissure of the rocks, and was absent some five or ten minutes, when he reappeared, and again approached our friends.

"Follow me once more," he said, in a low, guarded tone.

And immediately retracing his steps he led his wondering followers in between gigantic rocks, where all was total darkness.

The density of the atmosphere convinced our hero that they were entering a cavern, while the two Spaniards, completely bewildered with their already strange adventures, hardly knew whether the things around them were real or whether they were being made the sport of some wild, fantastic dream.

At length, after following their guide for a considerable distance through a winding, zigzag passage, which apparently had no outlet or termination, they were agreeably surprised to find themselves entering a large, dry cave, in the central part of which was burning a fire, whose ruddy blaze formed a cheerful contrast to the cold, dreary night without.

Near the fire were several large pitch-pine knots, to serve them both for fuel and light, and Evandale showed them a quantity of hominy and Indian corn, which had apparently been conveyed thither expressly for their use, in the event of their being obliged to remain there for any length of time.

Our hero would fain now have inundated his brave and generous buccaneer friend with thanks for all he had done for him and his companions, but Walter Evandale nipped the demonstration in the bud.

Nor would he stop to converse, save to warn Harry Seaborne and his companions that they must on no account leave the cavern for four-and-twenty hours, by which time the buccaneer army would be far on its march to Panama.

Giving them some other advice, unnecessary for us to repeat, he then left them to themselves and rethreaded his way through the narrow passage leading to the water's edge.

On reaching the canoes he cut the thongs that bound them together, and proceeded to secrete two of them.

This done he jumped into the third.

For a moment or two his dark figure, standing erect in the boat, could be faintly traced in the dim light, then it blended with the gloom, and was presently lost in the darkness.

CHAPTER XXX.
ANOTHER ESCAPE—THE FLIGHT ON HORSEBACK —THE SPANISH CAVALRY.

IT was long past midnight, and silence reigned profound in the buccaneer camp. Chief, captains, soldiers—all save the sentries were locked in deep repose.

Even these kept loose watch

The buccaneers had sunk to sleep, looking forward to the morrow as a day of fiendish amusement and savage delight, for they none of them knew that the objects of their hatred had escaped.

In one of the largest tents the beautiful Donna Theresa de Guzman was confined as an honorary prisoner.

A hideous old hag, the only female with the exception of Zoabinda in camp, had been instructed to keep watch over her, and had received strict injunctions not to let her eyes close in sleep for the whole night.

This old woman, with a warm skin thrown over her shoulders and wrapped round her scraggy person, was squatted upon the bare earth near the door of the tent.

Outside was audible the tramp of a sentry.

The night was cold, and still cloudy and dark, but the delicately-nurtured Spanish girl had no other bed than the damp ground, and naught to cover her but the thin raiment in which she had been clad when abducted from the city—a low-necked short-sleeved, evening dress, that showed her superb beauty of form to advantage.

Hour after hour the old woman set to watch over her smoked a short, black pipe, and muttered strange things, but at last she became silent and began to doze and nod.

Suffice it to say that half-an-hour later from nodding and dozing in a dreamy state, she glided into the utter forgetfulness of heavy sleep; whilst even Donna Theresa, with all the painful incidents of the past day fresh in her memory, and with all the horrors of the coming one staring her in the face, began to doze also, for so weak is poor human nature that long fatigue and excitement will cause us to sleep upon the very brink of death—the awful threshold of eternity.

No sooner had the lovely Spanish donna fallen into that state which can neither properly be called sleeping nor waking, but which partakes very strongly of both, when an object—which might well have been taken in the dim and uncertain light for a log of wood, a stone, a slight elevation of the ground, or anything in short but what it really was—might have been observable just inside the tent.

But had either Donna Theresa or the old hag, her guard, been capable of watching it closely for a few minutes, they would have been undeceived as to its being a collection of mere inanimate matter, for though they might not have seen or heard it move, they could not have failed to become aware that its length gradually shortened, as if it were being drawn out of the tent.

Three minutes later they would have found it had entirely vanished, without being much the wiser as to what it really was.

TALES of PIRATES

SMUGGLERS and BUCCANEERS.

No. 10.]   **THE SCOURGE OF THE SPANISH MAIN.**   [One Penny.

The steed struggled gallantly across the stream with Evandale and Donna Theresa on his back.

MORGAN the BUCCANEER; or, the Terror of the Seas.

In another five minutes, had they waited patiently, they might have seen the same object reappear, but much quicker than it had disappeared, and by .ts suddenly rising to an erect position would have pro-nounced it a human being. Yes, it was a human being—a man—and if not a buccaneer, it at least had all the appearance of one, even to the gorgeous armour and the superabundance of gems and jewellery.

As this mysterious nocturnal visitant rose to his feet he moved softly around the tent, and at the point opposite to that where the old woman lay crouched in sleep, with her black pipe still clutched between her teeth, he began to cut away the canvas, as if to effect another entrance.

In this proceeding he was not long engaged, and then he glided to the side of Donna Theresa and touched her.

She awoke, and was about to scream, but he made a sign of silence by placing his finger on his lips, and warned her of the danger of discovery by rapidly going through a series of pantomimic gestures.

"I am a friend," he said. "Get up quickly and follow me."

He then glided away in the darkness, apparently without touching the earth, and Donna Theresa, acting more in obedience to instinct than following the dictates of reason, got up and followed him in the same stealthy manner.

Gliding between the tents they soon reached the confines of the camp, but had hardly done so when drums began to rattle and trumpets to blare, making it very evident that some kind of alarm had been given.

But by this time they were close upon an enclosure which contained some of the baggage horses.

Seeing that the beautiful girl clung in alarm and terror to his cloak, her deliverer said, kindly—

"Fear not, maiden, I am a friend of the chivalrous young Englishman, Harry Seaborne, and though by calling a buccaneer I am not all bad. I will save you from Morgan and his vile crew or perish in the attempt."

As he spoke he entered the enclosure, leading Donna Theresa by the hand.

More than a dozen horses were grazing therein.

From a tent near the hastily constructed gateway he abstracted a halter, and catching the nearest horse he threw it over its head and led it forth.

There was a fire in the eye of the proud animal as he arched his neck, champed his teeth, and pawed the earth, that seemed to bespeak safety from all pursuit provided his rider could manage him without saddle and with no other guide but the halter, which was all he would have to depend upon.

Evandale—for our readers will already have guessed that he it was who had set himself the task of delivering Donna Theresa, even as he had done Harry Seaborne and his companions—lifted the beautiful Spanish girl upon the horse, and then sprang on its broad back behind her.

He did not immediately urge his steed out of the enclosure, however, but making it gallop in a mad circle around it drove the other horses out first, so that the buccaneers should find none whereon to pursue them.

A minute later the snorting, whinnying, and prancing hoof-strokes of the half-tamed beasts created a noise that was almost deafening, and the horse whereon Evandale and his fair companion were mounted, seeing its companions loose, became impatient to join them in their frolic, and reared and plunged and pulled upon its halter, becoming for the time wholly unmanageable.

Suddenly a shrill cheer came borne upon the still night air, making the heart of the chivalrous Evandale bound with apprehension, and that of the beauteous Spanish donna sink with fear.

This was immediately succeeded by the desultory discharge of arquebuses and musquetoons, and then by a succession of whoops and halloes from different parts of the camp, betokening that the alarm had spread.

Evandale drew his dagger from its sheath and plunged its point into the horse's flank.

Directly the animal felt the stab he made a spring from the earth, nearly throwing both his riders, and finding himself free at last, dashed away like a meteor, bearing directly back for the camp, in spite of all Walter Evandale's efforts to change his course.

Already the first two or three tents on the outskirts of the camp were passed with a velocity that left its riders no time for other reflection than that they were being borne with lightning speed into the very hands of their enemies, whose yells and shouts of fury made a horrible din in their ears.

But presently the horse of its own accord turned off to the left, and a few minutes later it again became answerable to the rein.

Evandale now guided it in a course that lay over an undulating country, partially cleared and in some places very stony, and the line of flight, if not deviated from, he knew would strike the river about half a mile above the camp, at a point where the hill forming the eastern bank of the stream sloped down into the water.

As they neared this place, however, a succession of shouts, oaths, and execrations, apparently from a party of buccaneers at no great distance, led Evandale to believe that they were hotly pursued by mounted foes who had anticipated their purpose, and coming directly up the bank of the river from the camp were striving to cut them off or engage them in deadly strife.

And the supposition was correct, for presently at least a score of hostile riders, all armed and ferociously eager to overtake the fugitives, were observable in their rear.

Knowing that flight alone would save them, Evandale pricked his fiery steed again with the dagger, goading it into a state of perfect fury, and it sped on with frightful velocity.

As they gained the sloping bank they espied another band away to their right, and it scarcely needed the furious yells which came borne to their ears to inform them that this was also so many mounted and ferocious enemies.

Down the bank, however, they plunged, and the next moment the cold water splashing in their faces and over their persons told them that their gallant steed was struggling across the river, swimming against the current.

A brief and vigorous floundering in the watery element, which occasionally dashed over horse and riders, and they gained the opposite bank, up which Evandale urged the now panting and foaming beast with many probes of the long Spanish dagger.

But ere they gained the summit of the bank and disappeared in the undergrowth, which here and there came down to the water's edge, loud yells and splashes behind warned them of the close proximity of their enemies, and that they had still desperate efforts to make to render their escape possible.

Up the acclivity they pressed, and soon the height was gained, when they found themselves upon a small level opening, across which they urged their steed with the speed of fear and desperation.

They had not ridden many hundred yards, however, and had only begun to emerge from the thick copse fringing the plain, when Evandale thought he heard the gallop of horses far ahead.

They had no choice but to proceed.

So again the dagger was had recourse to in lieu of spurs, and onwards once more dashed the swift-footed animal—down into a deep dingle, through a small patch of wood, then into a dense copse, over a rough stony tract, and still Walter Evandale maintained an erect position on its back, grasping the single rein of the halter in one hand, with the other arm thrown around the slender form of his beautiful companion.

Presently however, they discovered to their great horror, by the yells of the buccaneers both in front and rear, that they were surrounded by the foe. Certain destruction seemed inevitable.

What was to be done?

Set off in what direction he might the result was almost certain to be the same—death, or what was even more to be dreaded, captivity and torture.

Oh! it was an agonising reflection, and Walter Evandale shuddered and grew sick at heart, whilst beads of cold perspiration, wrung forth by mental anguish, stood upon his pallid features, not at the dangers that threatened himself, but at those which surrounded his beautiful companion, whose heart was throbbing so wildly against his breast.

But while there was life he knew that there was hope, and again urging the horse forward he sought not to guide him, but, offering up a short prayer for deliverance, consigned himself and his companion to the will of Providence.

The horse, finding himself at liberty to choose his own course, no longer followed the one he had been pursuing, but, turning more to the left, bore straight down towards a distant bend of the river, and soon gained its bank.

A party of buccaneers had already passed this place, as could be seen by the many hoof-prints in the soft turf, and their shouts of fury and demoniac yells gradually growing less and less distinct relieved Evandale of any apprehension concerning them; but unfortunately there was still another party thundering close in their rear, whose wild, discordant cries, together with the loud clatter of their horses' hoofs, and the snorting of the spirited animals, put poor Donna Theresa in mortal terror.

True, she could not see them, owing to an intervening ridge, but she felt that they were close upon them, and that the chances of escape were now reduced to the very smallest number, more especially as their steed, eager to rejoin his companions, began to evince a strong inclination to wheel round and bear them amongst the ranks of their enemies.

In vain Evandale tried to check him or change his course; every moment he was becoming more completely unmanageable, and he was about, as a last resource, in company with his companion, to fling himself off its back, when suddenly, as if they had touched enchanted ground, a troop of horsemen broke through the cover in their van and bore down upon them, while a loud voice shouted—

"Amigos ou inarnigos? Are you friends or foes?"

"Thank Heaven we are saved!" cried Donna Theresa, in an ecstacy of joy, as she half-sprang out of Walter Evandale's embrace. "These are Spanish troops, and it is my father's voice who is addressing us."

Her own voice was now recognised in turn, and a moment later they were surrounded by Spanish horsemen, while the leader, springing to his feet, revealed himself as no other than Don Pedro de Guzman, Captain-General of New Spain.

"Who is this cavalier who accompanies you?" asked Don Pedro de Guzman of his daughter.

"He is one who has saved me from captivity and worse than death," answered Donna Theresa.

"Then he must look upon us as friends, even though he is in the uniform of our foes," said the captain-general.

Walter Evandale grasped the hand that was so frankly extended to him, and said—

"We have little time for exchanging courtesies or congratulations, for the buccaneers are close at our heels, and in less than five minutes your men will have plenty of work cut out for them."

At that moment the blast of a trumpet went echoing through the surrounding forest.

Then a confused mob of buccaneers burst through the copse into the opening, to the number of a hundred or more, but their yells of ferocious delight were suddenly changed to terror and dismay when all unexpectedly they found themselves confronted by a body of horsemen, who instead of flying greeted them with yells as appalling as their own, at the same time pouring in upon them a murderous fire, and charging along the whole line.

Down went some four or five horses, and twice the number of riders fell to rise no more, while of those who turned to fly only about a score escaped without injury.

Wild were the yells of terror of those who had so late been pursuers, but who were now in turn pursued, as they rushed down the bank of the river and sought to avoid their foes, who with Spanish "vivas!" pressed close upon their heels and slew without mercy all the buccaneers who were so unfortunate as to be overtaken.

Maddened with the desire for blood and vengeance, and smarting under the disgrace which the defeat at Chargres had so recently brought upon them, the Spanish horsemen, once let loose upon the flying foe, could not be restrained by the trumpet blast of their commander, but giving rein to their worst passions, as well as to their steeds, they dashed pell-mell across the ford, up the opposite slope, and down along the stream towards the buccaneers' camp, vowing to wash out the stain of ignominy that was upon them in the life blood of their enemies.

But the buccaneers were by this time prepared to receive them, for a party of mounted freebooters who had been following in the rear of those closest in pursuit of Evandale and Donna Theresa, and who had just reached the ford as the affray began on the opposite side, had hurriedly returned to the camp and reported that a large body of Spaniards had killed their friends and were fast coming down upon the camp.

Great was the alarm and confusion this intelligence created, and amidst the universal and appalling cry of " The Spaniards are upon us !" the freebooters rallied, and inspired with renewed confidence by Morgan, formed an ambuscade just above the camp, at a point where it was most likely the attack would be made.

Into this ambuscade the foremost of the daring Spanish cavalry directly ran, but the hot valour of those behind suddenly cooling at this unlooked-for reception, they were wise enough to show the buccaneers the tails of their horses, and make the heels of the latter save them.

Fast as they had ridden towards the camp, they now rode as fast away from it, and it was not until the river rolled between them and their foes that they began to feel their safety regained and their courage revived.

The continued blast of a trumpet summoned them around their commander, who, with most of his officers and a prudent few of the cavalry, together with a regiment of foot soldiers, had not been rash enough to follow them.

The captain-general gave them such a severe reprimand for their disobedience and foolhardiness that the most forgetful one amongst them remembered it to the day of his death.

"And now, Don Evandale," said the captain-general, turning to the handsome lieutenant, " with the hope that yon buccaneers and myself together have succeeded in beating a little hard sense into heads where it recently was so sadly wanting, I must, I suppose, permit you to return to your comrades."

"Don Pedro de Guzman," said Walter Evandale, " it is many years since I drew my sword on the side of justice and right, but I have a strong inclination to do so to-day. Let me fight on your side, therefore."

"Your proffered sword is accepted as frankly as it is given," exclaimed the captain-general, as he shook the buccaneer lieutenant warmly by the hand.

CHAPTER XXXI.

MYSTERIOUS DISAPPEARANCE OF THE DONNA—DON GUZMAN'S ALARM.

"AND now, my men," Don Pedro de Guzman continued, raising his voice and addressing the discomfited cavalry, " you see what a calamity your rashness has brought upon us. Henceforth you must obey me, and the first who disobeys I will bring before a court-martial. Come, we must be on the move, or morning will break ere our purpose be accomplished."

The horse and foot again got into motion, and moved slowly down the western bank of the river, or that opposite to the buccaneer camp, Evandale riding beside the captain-general.

A Spanish hat had supplied the place of his own, and his buccaneer uniform was concealed by a red cloak.

The buccaneers, however, were not to be caught napping.

The Spanish infantry made the first attack, but before the impetuous dash of the buccaneers they gave way and rushed back upon their supports, throwing the Spanish front into a state of disorder from which it could not be recovered, as the buccaneers followed close upon their heels.

The buccaneers were, however, checked for a short time by the fire of the supports, but immediately a very heavy fire was concentrated on them, and in a few minutes they fell back on to the second line.

The great weight of the buccaneer's fire was directed to the Spanish centre, where five light field-pieces had by this time been wheeled up, from which the men were repeatedly driven back with great slaughter.

In this emergency resort was had to the pike, and Don Alberto Burmez was ordered to make a charge with a part of the second line, which order was executed with great spirit.

The buccaneers instantly gave way, and were driven back several hundred yards, but for want of a sufficient number of arquebusiers to preserve the advantage gained, the freebooters soon renewed their attack, and the Spanish troops in turn were forced to give way.

At that instant a party of buccaneers, under Rupert Russel, attacked the Spanish forces on the left, and forced back the troops stationed at that point.

Another Spanish charge was then ordered and made, but with a very heavy loss of men and particularly officers.

In this charge the colonel of the first regiment fell with a bullet through his body.

The artillery being by this time silenced, and all the officers belonging to it killed, half the army fell back and tried to regain the road to make good their retreat.

For that purpose a successful charge was made on the buccaneers by the Spanish horse, as if to turn their right flank but in reality to gain the road, which was effected.

But as it is not with the general feature of the battle that we have especially to do, but rather with a certain train of incidents arising therefrom, we shall leave the former in the hands of the historians while we proceed to narrate the latter in the best manner consonant with our humble abilities.

It was, then, while the battle was raging at its greatest height, and on all sides the dead and dying were mingled in bloody confusion, and heaped one upon another, over which the living forces were trampling as they alternatively rushed to and fro in their advance and retreat, that a tall veteran officer was conspicuous riding up and down the lines and encouraging his men—by look, gesture, speech, and action—to press on the foe and sell their lives as dearly as possible.

It was Don Pedro Guzman, the Captain-General of New Spain, mounted on a coal black charger, sitting erect, with his head bared to the breeze, and his long iron-grey hair streaming out behind.

In one hand he held a bloody sword, the point of which was broken, showing that its owner had been no idle spectator, and as he swung it to and fro and shouted words of encouragement to his men, his lips compressed and his dark eyes flashed a fire that would have become one who had not lived half his years.

Wherever the battle raged fiercest and the danger was most imminent there this gallant man could be seen doing his duty like a true hero.

So prominent a mark could not of course escape the quick eyes of the buccaneers, and more than a hundred freebooters made him a target.

But in vain they burnt their powder and spent their bullets.

All failed to bring down their intended victim, or even check the progress of his fiery charger.

Surely a watchful Providence preserved him for another destiny.

So for more than an hour he remained in the thick of the fight, encouraging his men, now reduced to a small number, to hold out to the last and die like Spartans, when Walter Evandale, still wearing the Spanish beaver and scarlet cloak, came dashing up to him on a horse as fiery as his own, and cried out—

"For Heaven's sake save yourself, Don Pedro, whilst there is yet time. Already your men are flying in every direction, and you will soon be surrounded and cut off."

The captain-general reined his horse up directly in front of the speaker, and eyed him with almost savage sternness, while his immediate followers, catching the word retreat, and seeing their comrades flying, turned and rushed after them, leaving him and Evandale for a moment alone.

"What's this?" shouted the captain-general, as soon as his astonishment would permit him to speak. "Retreat, say you?"

The young buccaneer lieutenant made no reply, but with a gesture of impatience and alarm he caught the bit of Don Pedro de Guzman's horse with one hand, struck the animal on the flank with the sword he carried in the other, and at the same time buried the rowels in the sides of his own gallant charger.

Both horses reared and plunged, and the next moment were rushing away with the speed of the wind, guided by the bold, strong arm of the young and daring Evandale.

At first the captain-general was so astonished that he offered no resistance, and it was well he did not, for a large party of buccaneers had nearly surrounded them, and another moment's delay would have been fatal to their escape.

As it was they had barely time to dart through the nearly closed circle, and many a crossbow bolt and arquebuse ball came whizzing past them, too close for comfort, though fortunately both remained unharmed.

"This is sheer cowardice," cried the captain-general at length, tightening his grasp upon the rein and making an effort to check his horse.

"Remember your daughter," shouted Evandale, in reply.

"True; but is she not in safety?"

"Nothing is safe here, Don Pedro de Guzman; but I trust she will escape, for directly I found the tide of battle was setting against your troops I sent her with an escort back toward Chargres."

"We must overtake them, then, with all speed," said Don Guzman, now really anxious.

"So I thought, and thus ventured upon doing what I did."

"You did right, my friend, and I was at fault; but still I cannot but think it is cowardly to fly and leave these poor wretches here to the mercy of the buccaneers. Oh! woeful day. How will it sound at home in Spain to say that a few hundred buccaneers defeated two thousand of her regular troops in a pitched battle, and that, too, one of her own seeking."

Evandale could offer no consolation in this sore strait, and so he remained silent.

"Look!" continued the captain-general. "Behold the poor wretches lying on every side of us, and some of them entreating us with looks, gestures, and supplications to save them. Oh! it is heart-rending, and were it not for my daughter I would dismount and die with them, for the shame of this day is worse than death."

Such were the remarks of Don Pedro de Guzman as side by side he and Walter Evandale dashed along the road, past the dead and dying and wounded, and overtaking parties of flying fugitives, who were straining every nerve to escape the horrible fate which awaited them if caught by the pursuing buccaneers.

Parties on foot and on horseback, all doing their utmost to escape, and alike regardless of every life but their own, were alternately passed by the unusually swift-footed steeds of the captain-general and Evandale.

But the road ahead was still lined with fugitives, and the shrieks and fierce oaths behind proclaimed that the terrible work of human butchery was still going fearfully on in their rear.

"Oh! woeful day—oh! woeful day!" groaned the captain-general. "That I should live to witness such a terrible defeat as this. Ah! I should have died on the field of battle along with my poor soldiers!"

"Then what would have become of her who so much needs your protection?" asked Evandale.

"True, true—my dear little daughter. But, oh! where can she be?"

"I think that she may be ahead of us," said Evandale.

"You think! But suppose we have passed her?"

"Do not say that, Don Pedro. It makes me shudder," said the young buccaneer, turning deadly pale.

"You sent her with an escort, you say?"

"I did, and the escort consisted of six well-mounted men."

"Where did you direct them to stop?"

"Nowhere short of Chargres."

"That was right. Heaven grant that they may have escaped," said Don Pedro, fervently.

"Amen! I trust we shall soon overtake them. Remember they have had half an hour's start."

"Spur on, then—our poor beasts must do double duty now," replied the captain-general.

For some twenty minutes more Don Pedro de Guzman and his strange ally rode as fast as their gallant steeds would carry them, by which time they had passed all the fugitives on foot and nearly all those that were mounted.

Not less than five or six miles now interposed between them and the battle-ground, and yet they had not overtaken those for whom they were in search.

"This is strange," observed the captain-general, reining in his foaming and panting steed, and looking eagerly around on every side. "Brave friend, they have either escaped faster than I should have deemed it possible for them to do, or something serious, if not alarming, has happened."

"Heaven forbid the latter!" cried Walter Evandale, turning deadly pale, and checking his horse so fiercely as almost to throw him on his haunches. "It does seem strange, Don Pedro, I admit. And yet it cannot be possible that we have unwittingly passed them if they kept the road; they may have turned off it to take a shorter or a safer course. Ah! what is that yonder?"

"Where—where?" eagerly demanded the captain-general.

"Yonder—ahead—beside the road! As I live! I do believe it is a dead soldier, and if my eyes do not deceive me—oh! the thought is too horrible."

Burying his spurs in his horse's sides as he spoke, Walter Evandale sped away like a meteor, followed instantly by the now really alarmed father.

A ride of less than a minute brought the buccaneer lieutenant to the object he had espied, and again reining his horse up, he uttered a cry of horror, placed both his hands before his eyes, and bowed his head in silence towards the saddle-bow, while his whole frame shook with heartrending emotion.

"What is it, my friend, what is it?" cried the captain-general, riding up to his side.

Walter Evandale raised his head slowly, withdrew his hands from a face which bore the ghastly hue of death, and, pointing to the awful scene before him, at length gasped forth—

"Behold!"

"I see—I see!" returned Don Pedro de Guzman, quickly. "Six soldiers all dead—well?"

"They are the escort!" again faintly gasped Walter Evandale.

"Merciful Heaven! the escort!" groaned the captain-general. "Then my daughter is lost."

"Lost!" echoed Evandale, in a hollow tone.

They both remained silent for a moment, gazing shudderingly upon the bloody scene, and both experienced such feelings as alone could be felt by a father and a true man in such a case.

"My daughter, my dear little daughter!—death and defeat. Oh! it is too much," groaned the captain-general.

At this moment several horsemen passed our friends, but they merely glanced at the two officers with inquiring looks, and rode on without speaking.

"Ha! the sergeant; see, he moves!" cried Evandale, and instantly dismounting he sprang to the poor fellow's aid and raised him in his arms.

In doing this he exposed a deep wound in his left side, some two inches below the heart, from which the blood was slowly oozing.

He had been lying on his face helpless, and was apparently nigh unto death, but changing his position seemed to revive him, and, opening his parched and livid lips, he gasped faintly—

"Water, water— oh! give me water."

By this time the captain-general was dismounted and standing by his side.

"We must save him if possible," said the latter. "There is a small stream about a mile ahead— we must place him on one of our horses and bear him to it with all speed."

As Don Pedro de Guzman spoke he tore off the scarf which he wore around his waist and bound it about the wounded man, in order to staunch the blood.

Then, placing him upon his own horse, both he and Evandale remounted and set off at as fast a pace as was deemed prudent for one to be carried in a situation so critical.

In a short time the party gained the stream, and having bathed the brow and temples of the sergeant, they scooped up water with their hands and placed it to his lips, which he drank eagerly. Soon he revived sufficiently to be able to open his eyes, look around, and speak distinctly.

"Who are you?" was his first question; "and why am I here? Ah! I remember now. These are the captain-general and the strange officer in the scarlet cloak who ordered me to carry the young lady to Chargres in safety. Ah! do not blame me, noble signor, I did my best to save her."

"And what has happened to her? Where is she now?" cried the two officers in a breath.

"Heaven knows! I cannot answer either of your questions. Oh! my side pains so."

"Be thankful for that, for it shows that your wound is not mortal," rejoined Walter Evandale. "But now tell us all you know about this affair with as little delay as possible?"

"Give me more water. There, I thank you. Ah! I feel somewhat revived again."

"Would that we had a surgeon here," said Walter Evandale, putting his hand upon the sergeant's side, and finding that it still continued to bleed profusely.

"A surgeon would do me very little good," muttered the wounded man, "for I am dying."

"Tell me, before you become too weak to do so, what has become of my daughter!" exclaimed Don Guzman.

"All I know, sir, is that we were overtaken and set upon by about twenty mounted buccaneers, and were dispatched as fast as musquetoons, swords, and daggers could do it. I saw two or three of the enemy fall before I fell myself, and I also saw the young lady hurried away, and that's all I know of it."

"Then we must ride on in search of her, and rescue her at all hazards," said Walter Evandale.

" I think, sir," said the wounded man, " it will be useless to search for her now. She is undoubtedly a prisoner, and her recovery will not be an easy matter. If you attempt anything rashly you will be likely to lose your own lives without rendering the young lady any service whatever."

" Alas ! I fear that he speaks the truth," said the heart-broken father. " We must wait for a happier moment."

" At all events we must be off at once," returned Walter Evandale, " for the infantry are coming up rapidly, and the buccaneers may be close behind. We must take care of our own lives now in order one day to be able to save her who is very dear to us both. We can manage to take the sergeant with us."

" Right, my friend—right. Let us mount and away," echoed the captain-general.

A minute or two later Don Pedro de Guzman and Walter Evandale were dashing down the road, bearing the sergeant across the front of the latter's saddle, while hundreds behind in wild disorder came panting after, straining every nerve to escape the horrors they had so recently witnessed.

CHAPTER XXXII.

WHICH TREATS OF THE FURTHER ADVENTURES OF OUR HERO AND HIS COMPANIONS.

SCARCELY had our hero and his two Spanish allies lain concealed in the cavern whither they had been conducted and hidden by Walter Evandale more than a couple of hours, when strange sounds reached their ears.

The noise of a battle, evidently, for they could hear the rattle of musketry, the deeper boom of cannon, the clash of steel on steel, and the fierce cries of the combatants.

" The captain-general at the head of an army has overtaken Morgan and his robber horde, and is giving him battle," Harry Seaborne cried, in wild excitement. We must issue forth, my boys, and take part in the fray."

The two young Spaniards were by no means loth to fall in with his views.

In fact they ardently seconded them, and voted for quitting the cave that very moment.

" Come, then," said our hero. " It is hardly probable that Evandale took with him to the other side of the river all three of the canoes in which he brought us hither, and if not, two, or even one, will suffice for us."

They hastened towards the mouth of the cave through the narrow, tortuous passages, and at length reached it.

A brief search proved the correctness of Harry Seaborne's conjectures.

One of the canoes was gone, and another was damaged, but the third was found and drawn forth from its hiding-place.

It was soon launched into the water, and the three adventurers seated themselves in it.

An unexpected difficulty now, however, arose.

There was no paddle, for Evandale had to take away with him the only one wherewith he had guided and propelled the boats hither.

This threw a heavy damper on their spirits, which had already begun to feel comparatively buoyant. As there was nothing to be done but to make the best of their circumstances, however, the canoe was pushed from the shore, and allowed to float down the current with no other guide and propelling power than the hands of its crew.

Fortunately the bend of the river was such as to drift them towards the western shore, but the stream ran so slowly that the best part of an hour was consumed ere the canoe touched land, which it finally did at the first projecting point in the river above the falls.

As the canoe touched the shore Harry Seaborne bade his companions not to speak or move until he had first landed and discovered that no foes were lurking in ambush in the vicinity.

It did not take him long to satisfy himself on this point, and he then quickly returned to the water's side. But to his surprise and dismay the canoe no longer lay alongside the bank.

Its inmates had paddled it a little way off the shore, and had been caught in a rapid. They were now drifting broadside on towards a waterfall more stupendous than the one Evandale had already guided them safely through.

Without oar or paddle their fate was sealed. They would be carried over the falls and dashed to pieces on the scattered and foaming waters at its base.

Harry ran alongside of the river's bank to see the catastrophe, too awe-struck to speak or halloa.

The ground grew steep and the level shore soon changed into cliffs.

Our hero presently stood on the summit of one, and the river glided by at least a hundred feet below him.

He could still see the boat.

It was close to the falls, and its inmates seemed to be too much overcome by horror and dismay to make any attempt to avoid the dread catastrophe.

And yet, though his every faculty was riveted upon them and the destruction that was so soon to overwhelm them, his attention was in an instant distracted altogether.

A terrible cry—evidently that of a brute, not of a human being—issued from the dark wood in his rear, which was succeeded by angry growls.

The tramp of hurrying feet and the crackling and snapping of parting underwood followed, and a minute later a magnificent stag dashed close past Harry, hotly pursued by two bears.

Almost as soon as our hero beheld them the stag had, in its wild terror, leapt over the cliff into the river that flowed so rapidly a hundred feet below, and the foremost bear, unable to check its onward course in time, went over after it, falling like a vast lump of lead.

The second bear, however, brought himself to a halt on the very edge of the cliff, and after savagely contemplating for a minute or two the fate of his companion and their intended victim, he turned round, and catching sight of Harry, seemed to think there might yet be a supper in store for him.

Our hero, in contemplating his own danger, forgot that of his late comrades.

He turned and ran, upon seeing which the bear quickened his pace and started in pursuit of him.

Harry ran quickly, but the bear ran quicker, and he would infallibly have been caught and devoured had he not unexpectedly come upon a horse that was tied to a tree-stump.

It was with the greatest difficulty that he succeeded in unfastening and mounting the animal, and when he had done so he found that he had no control over him whatever.

Fortunately, however, the fiery animal sighted the approaching bear, and had sense sufficient to run from instead of towards the great ungainly brute.

It dashed madly across a narrow stream, and made for the open country beyond.

Suddenly, however, the horse shied, and threw Harry, but he had the forethought to grasp the halter with both hands, and by this means, although swung to a considerable distance, alighted on his feet without injury.

The impatient animal, once clear of its rider, now sought to be free from all incumbrance, and in its efforts to get away he dragged Harry several yards through bushes and over stones, which tore his clothes and skin, and bruised him not a little.

But, with the tenacity of a drowning man clinging to a rope, he stuck to the halter-rein, and at last had the good fortune to find his beast approachable.

It was very fortunate that he did so, for the bear was approaching too.

When he had succeeded in mounting him, however, he found to his horror, by yells and cries that seemed to come from every direction at once, that he was surrounded by buccaneers.

Their yells had one good effect, however, for they frightened away the bear.

What was to be done?

Set off in what direction he might the result was almost certain to be the same—death, or what was even more to be dreaded, captivity and torture.

He shuddered at the thought and grew sick at heart, and beads of cold perspiration, wrung by mental anguish, stood upon his pallid features.

"But while there is life there is hope," he argued, so he again urged the horse onward.

But now his steed, hearing the neighs, the whinnies, and the hoof-strokes of other horses, became eager to join its companions, and presently wheeling suddenly, plunged forward in an opposite direction to that in which Harry wished to proceed.

Harry knew that it was now bearing him right into the hands of his foes, but in vain he tried to check him or to change his course.

He was completely unmanageable, and beyond all control. Reckless of what might be the consequences, since he now believed himself irrevocably doomed, Harry leaped from his back, and was thrown violently upon the ground, being rendered almost senseless by the shock.

The next moment the riderless steed came into fearful collision with the foremost one of the approaching party, and both horses went down as if struck by a cannon-ball, crushing in their fall the leg of the stalwart buccaneer who bestrode one of

them, who, uttering one loud yell of agony, called piteously upon his friends for help.

Great was the confusion this accident occasioned, for several of the buccaneers instantly stopped their horses and, springing to the ground, ran forward to ascertain what had happened.

But as soon as the truth was known the majority mounted and rode on, so accustomed were they to wounds, bloodshed, and death.

Some three or four, however, remained to assist their injured companion, and getting him from under the two animals they carefully placed him on the back of another.

Then a buccaneer mounted behind, to return with him to the camp, and they rode slowly away in that direction while the others prepared to continue their course in pursuit of the discomfited Spaniards.

All this was witnessed by our hero, who, not more than twenty paces distant, remained on the ground exactly where he had fallen, scarcely daring to breathe lest he should be discovered.

He was already congratulating himself upon his fortunate but very narrow escape when a loud ejaculation, as if the speaker had suddenly made some new and important discovery, caused a thrill of terror to run through his whole system.

And Harry had good reason to tremble at that ejaculation, for an important discovery had been made and one which would have transpired much sooner had the buccaneers been a little more observing.

The presence of the horse at such a time and place did not excite suspicion, for there were many riderless and ownerless horses running about in every direction ; but when, by the merest accident, the truth was discovered that on this steed was a halter, they immediately remembered that Donna Theresa de Guzman had been carried away on a horse thus scantily harnessed, and that it was one of their own horses too.

A hurried consultation ensued, for might not the liberator and the liberated be even now skulking amongst the undergrowth close by ?

Such was the opinion of the greater part of them, and they presently commenced searching among the bushes in every direction.

Scarcely had a minute elapsed after the search began ere one of the party approached so close to Harry that he felt certain exposure must follow.

Resolved to make one more desperate effort for his life, he firmly grasped the hilt of his dagger—that dagger given him by Evandale—and springing suddenly to his feet buried it to the hilt in the breast of the astonished buccaneer, who, in the very act of uttering a cry of surprise, quickly changed it to a shriek of agony and sank down at his feet.

There was no time to be lost now, and leaping over the prostrate body Harry made for the nearest horse.

He reached the animal a few yards in advance of the other buccaneers, who, hearing the cry of their companion, and at once divining the cause, bounded after him, making the woods ring with their yells of fury.

TALES of PIRATES

SMUGGLERS and BUCCANEERS.

No. 11.]   **THE SCOURGE OF THE SPANISH MAIN.**   [ONE PENNY.

For a single instant only Harry Seaborne remained suspended from the cliff.

MORGAN the BUCCANEER; or, the Terror of the Seas.

Catching the bridle in his hand, Harry vaulted upon the back of the animal, and struck him a mad blow with the end of the reins.

With a fearful plunge forward away rushed the terrified quadruped, and in less time than it takes us to tell it some fifty yards intervened between our hero and his pursuers.

But short space had our hero for congratulation,

for the next moment, as it were, the agile buccaneers were themselves mounted and thundering after him, uttering the most terrible cries and yells.

As if Fortune, too, had determined to see how long she could toss him about between life and death, the horse he bestrode now shaped his course towards the buccaneer camp again, in spite of all he could do to turn him aside, for the animal had got its bit between its teeth, and bore him with frightful velocity right into the very hands of his enemies, who, afoot and on horseback, were swarming about in every direction, like bees when their hive is improperly disturbed.

On he dashed, however, lashing his horse, since he could not control him, in unutterable fury—and on came his bloodthirsty pursuers, still yelling as wildly as ever, but unable to gain upon him a foot.

"Oh!" thought Harry, "if this was not such a hard-mouthed brute, and if he had not got that infernal bit between his teeth, I might even yet escape."

The horse was too headstrong to obey anything but his own will, and the consequence was that our hero was borne right in among the yelling and howling crew of sick, wounded, and camp followers, who were all wide awake and anxious to gather the earliest news connected with the battle just fought.

Suddenly these sighted him, and more than a dozen sprang forward to intercept horse and rider.

Knowing his doom would be death in its most terrible form if taken prisoner again, Harry, with not a single hope beyond that of provoking by his daring a speedy termination to his life, lashed his horse furiously forward, reckless of the blows aimed at his person on all sides, and actually rode down several of his opposers.

But this triumph over numbers was necessarily of short duration, and the grasping of the halter by a tremendous buccaneer, who immediately raised his sword for the purpose of severing with it the head of our hero, seemed likely to put an end to all further strife.

But here again capricious fortune changed in Harry's favour, for the horse, mistaking the intention of the buccaneer, and thinking the blow was meant for him, reared and wheeled so suddenly as to loose the hold of the freebooter just as the sword was brandished to cut its rider down, which thereby missed its aim by a bare inch.

By this sudden turn of the horse its head was brought in the direction of the mia-mia, distant not more than eight or ten rods, and the thought suddenly occurred to Harry of making his last desperate effort for speedy death or speedy liberation, by forcing the maddened beast to leap the steep cliff which overhung the dark waters rolling slowly and quietly along many feet below.

For this purpose he gave him several rapid blows with the slack of the reins, and the next moment the bank was gained, but the animal recoiled with a snort of horror, and at the same instant a bullet pierced his brain and he fell dead in his tracks.

As he went down Harry gathered all his remaining strength, placed his hands upon the neck of the sinking beast, and vaulted clean over its head.

For a single instant he remained suspended from the cliff.

The report of a dozen musquetoons and arquebuses was heard, a dozen balls went whizzing through the air, and then down—down went our hero, a single sullen splash as the cold dark waters opened to receive him and then closed over his head denoting his fall.

Rushing to the brink of the cliff, several of the buccaneers now threw themselves flat upon the earth, and, placing their ears over the edge of the precipice, listened for any sound that would indicate human life below.

But no such sound was heard.

All was as still as the grave, save the solemn roar of the rapids a short distance down the stream, and of the falls over which Harry's friends had long since been swept.

Springing to their feet, the buccaneers uttered loud yells of disappointment at the second loss of one they had counted on so surely as a victim at the stake, and then another short silence followed, during which several prepared to descend to the water at points both above and below the steep cliff where Harry went over, in order to make sure that he did not escape alive.

But not one amongst the bravest dared to try the venturesome leap after him.

Their plan of search was, however, frustrated by the blare of trumpets and the rattle of drums.

It was the signal for marching—the camp was being broken up. Once again it was—"On for Panama!"

CHAPTER XXXIII.

HARRY SEABORNE AGAIN AMONGST FRIENDS.

ALTHOUGH the living target at which a dozen musquetoons and arquebuses were discharged, and as many daggers and knives thrown, Harry Seaborne providentially escaped them all, though more than one of them rent his clothes, and he struck the waters uninjured then suddenly found himself buried far below the placid surface of the dark, rolling river.

Being an excellent swimmer and having great presence of mind, he soon rose to the surface. He kept perfectly quiet, floating along on the slow-moving current, well knowing that any sound indicating life would be heard by his enemies above, and bring down a hundred of them, all fierce and eager for his capture. He had a faint hope that if they heard nothing they would believe he had perished and give up the search

He heard their yells of disappointment at his loss, and his heart began to beat with renewed hope.

There was still a chance of escape where a few minutes before he had looked for none, and so from himself his thoughts now reverted to his friends—the hapless death of Don Pero, the sad fate of the other two young Spaniards, and as to whether Donna Theresa had been delivered by Evandale or still remained a captive.

To preserve his own existence without effecting her release was failure in his view, for it was to rescue her that he had imperilled his life, and not to succeed was to render that life valueless.

"Ah!" he said, mentally, as all these thoughts rapidly floated through his brain, "since I have been unable to accomplish my mission may I not as well die where I am, and put an end to this feverish, unquiet existence, so full of vexations, disappointments, and heartrending woe?"

But though Harry reasoned thus with himself Nature gave no sanction to the false logic, but still urged him to live on and hope on, by causing a cold shudder to pass through his frame at the very thought of approaching the confines of that mysterious "beyond" by his own act and with all his senses in full and actual play.

At length the shouts and cries of the buccaneers ceased to be audible, and presently he felt his hand touch the trunk of a drift tree, one end of which was embedded in the sands of the shore.

He grasped it with a firmness and listened with an eagerness that ill-befitted one who, tired of life, was about to throw off this mortal coil and pass the dread portals of eternity.

The fact is the feelings of our hero soon experienced a wonderful change, and he was now as anxious to live as at any moment of his eventful existence.

Chilled to the very bone with his rather long immersion in the water, and in consequence hardly able to use his limbs, he now made vigorous efforts to reach the shore by dragging himself along the trunk of the prostrate tree.

He at length succeeded, but on touching land found it almost impossible to stand, and when the thought flashed across his mind that his only chance of avoiding his enemies was by again taking to the river, his heart sank and for a time hope again gave way to despair.

Then the thought occurred to him that he might creep on under the shadow of the tall bank till he found a ford.

But even then was it not likely that his trail would be discovered when the morning broke, and that, weak and faint, he would then fall an easy prey to his bloodthirsty foes, from whom he could never hope to make a third escape?

But notwithstanding all objections to the course he intended to pursue, one thing was certain— that to remain where he was would not better his condition.

So he went off up the stream, keeping along the edge of the water. A few steps brought him to the base of the cliff from which he had made his leap.

He found it too precipitous to permit of a foothold, and was therefore forced to return.

He now attempted to go down the stream, but some twenty yards below, where he had first emerged from the water, he again found his progress checked, and this time by the rapids already more than once referred to.

The bank here was steep but not precipitous, down which the water dashed with force and fury, and with a much heavier body than usual, owing to recent rains.

To think of crossing this at the point where he was now was wholly out of the question, for no foot, however sure, could stand a single instant in such a current.

To ascend a steep bank to where a crossing could be made was, our hero conceived, a proceeding even more rash and dangerous, as he would thus, he imagined, be certain to reveal himself to his enemies—he knew not that they were already on the march—whilst to remain inactive, with the hope of freedom before him, was little short of madness.

Thus, hemmed in as he was on every side, there was no alternative, and his only means of escape seemed to be to betake himself once more to the water, and either swim around the rapids and come out below them, or cross the river to the shore he was so anxious to reach.

For several reasons he decided on the latter course, and so he dropped quietly into the river at the foot of the rapids and was quickly borne upon its bosom some yards, until the rushing force of the smaller stream was lost in the stillness of the greater.

Then, nerving himself for the tedious task, Harry struck boldly out for the opposite shore.

What was his surprise when he had only swam a short distance to feel his hands touch land.

As he crawled out upon the narrow strand his first impression was that his head had somehow become turned in swimming, and that he had actually swam back to the bank from whence he had started.

But a little reflection and observation put him right in this particular, and he then came to the rightful conclusion that he had landed upon a small island.

This proved a source of much gratification to him, as it would form a resting point on his short voyage, and enable him to gain the western bank with greater safety and ease.

But that he might be ready to set forth again ere too chilled and benumbed by the cold, he began to move along the bank in search of the point projecting farther westward, so as to save as much swimming as possible.

He had not gone many steps, keeping close under the shadows of the rocks on his right hand, when his foot striking a stone caused him to stumble.

He threw out his hands to prevent his head from striking, but to his surprise they touched nothing, and the next moment he found himself prostrated within a deep and narrow fissure.

Feeling carefully around in the dark as he attempted to rise, that he might make no false movement—as for all he knew to the contrary there might be a yawning chasm on one side or the other of him—his hand encountered something smooth and soft, in what appeared to be a small recess.

Judge of his surprise and delight on examining it with the sense of touch to find it to be a regularly-constructed canoe of the largest class.

"Surely," though Harry, as he drew it forth from its hiding-place—"surely I am a lucky dog in all things."

Even while he indulged in this reflection there came to his ear a low, faint, almost inaudible murmur, like the sound of distant human voices, or of far off running water.

He listened and still the faint murmur continued. Under the impression that it could be traced to the latter cause he was about to turn away for the purpose of embarking in his canoe when the sound ceased, and while he was still listening it began again.

"Surely," thought he, "if it were water, as I supposed, there would be no cessation. No! it must be made by human tongues—aye, more than one, for it varies and is not monotonous. Ha! it stops again, and is now again renewed."

A sudden idea now flashed through the brain of our hero, and, springing to his feet, he mentally exclaimed—

"Oh! if only my surmises prove correct."

Then he disappeared into the dark opening of the rocks.

Slowly and cautiously he threaded his way along the narrow, winding, zigzag passage, and at length arrived at its furthest limit, where it enlarged into a spacious cavern.

For the last few yards a faint, soft, lurid light shone into the dark passage, which enabled him to pick his way with greater ease, and as he turned the last sharp angle the bright light of a blazing fire flashed full in his face and revealed to him ten Spanish soldiers seated around it.

For a few moments Harry stood and gazed, whilst his heart beat wildly with many and varied emotions.

Then he bounded forward, exclaiming—

"Amongst friends at last! I am Don Harry Seaborne, a Spanish subject."

Great was the scene of confusion and excitement which followed, but a hearty welcome was given him, and a thousand questions were asked on either side, to more than half of which no answers were given.

Our hero learnt that the ten Spaniards were fugitives from the battle that had just been fought.

They told him that the buccaneers had been the conquerors therein—a fact until then unknown to him.

Then they all lay down and composed themselves to sleep, while the fire burning near threw a flickering light over their recumbent forms, penetrating far into the gloomy recessess of the cavern, and casting strange, fantastic, dancing shadows upon the ground, upon the walls, and upon the ceiling.

There we will leave our hero, and follow for a while the movements of the buccaneer army.

CHAPTER XXXIV.

THE MARCH TO PANAMA—A BATTLE AND AN ASSAULT.

THE buccaneer army recommenced their march in high-spirits, a little eager for glory, and very much for plunder, rapine, and their numerous et cæteras.

During the next twelve hours they made only six leagues, and arrived at a place called Da Evo Bracos, where they expected to have found hostile forces to dispute their further advance, for Morgan had received intelligence that they were to have been impeded here by barricades and arquebuses.

If they found no enemy, neither did they find any provisions.

Parties of troops, however, scoured the plantations around in the hope of procuring some refreshment, but all in vain.

Morgan, depending upon this fertile district for the subsistence of his little army, had neglected to furnish them with provisions, so that the next day they were very nearly starved, having nothing to satisfy a buccaneer's appetite but water and tobacco, either smoked or masticated.

All the next day they continued their march, miserably famished, and, as night fell, arrived at a village called Cruz de Juan Gallags, but found it also deserted and quite void of provisions.

On the next day, receiving the assurance of two guide prisoners that a few miles in advance they would find the country more practicable for rapid marching, Morgan delivered a spirited address to his followers, and at its close enjoined them to bear their hunger as well as they could, and to make their small stock of food last to the utmost, in order that they might all live to reach the land of milk and honey awaiting them.

But when, a few hours later, the army turned into the woods, they found the ground so swampy and miry, and the jungle so thick, that Morgan believed he should make more progress if he transported a part of his army in some roughly-made canoes up a river which ran towards Panama.

The canoes were made in a day, and by their means, in three trips, with those who forced their way through the bush at nightfall, the whole army found themselves as far as Cedro Bueno.

As the little provisions that they had hitherto possessed were now completely exhausted, the army had to undergo another access of hunger, or rather an increase of the same famine that they had now so long endured.

They scoured the country as far as they dared, but could meet with neither Spaniard nor Indian, and they were obliged to venture upon devouring herbs, leaves, and berries, the very nature of which were unknown to them.

On the fourth day of their advance they again fell in with the river, and seized some very slight Indian canoes, into which they placed as many men as they could float with, whilst the rest of the army advanced along the shore by land.

Proceeding in this manner, under the direction of careful guides, both ashore and on the river, about noon they arrived at a place called Perna Cavallos.

Here one of the guides announced an ambuscade, to the great joy of the buccaneers, who looked upon it as announcing a dinner.

But bitter was their disappointment when they found the place deserted and nothing left behind but a number of leather bags, all empty, and a few crumbs of bread scattered on the ground.

Notwithstanding the violence of their anger, and the bitterness of their disappointment, they did the best they could in their famishing condition.

They pulled down the houses and turned them into fuel, then soaked and well boiled the bags, throwing into their kettles as many vegetable matters as appeared edible, and with this mess would have made a very comfortable meal had it not been for the dreadful quarrels that ensued about the division of it.

Morgan and his officers affirmed that the men, so ravenous had they then become, had they caught either Spaniard or Indian they would assuredly have cooked and eaten him.

After this repast they advanced to another place called Torna Munin, where the Spaniards had also formed an ambuscade, but their hearts failed them, guessing, we suppose, the state of their enemies' stomachs.

This strong post was deserted and foodless.

Happy now was he who had secreted a small piece of leather for his supper.

We will now quote the words of one of the sufferers—

"Some persons," says he, "who were never out of their mother's kitchens may ask how these pirates could eat, swallow, and digest those pieces of leather so hard and dry. Unto which I would answer, that could they experience what hunger or famine is, they would certainly find the way to do so by their own necessity, as we did. First we took the leather and sliced it apart, then we beat it between two stones and rubbed it, after dipping it in the water of the river, to render it by these means supple and tender. Lastly we scraped off the hair, and then roasted it, or broiled it on the fire. And being thus cooked, we cut it into small morsels and ate it, helping it down with frequent gulps of water."

What our authority calls "leather" must, however, have been untanned hide, a very nutritious substance, if one can only persuade the digestive organs to assimilate it.

On the fifth day of the march the army arrived at Barbacoa.

Here were also the traces of an encampment, but nothing to eat, not even a leathern bag.

The straits of the buccaneer army had now become desperate, so the strongest of the troops were despatched in all directions in search of food, and it would almost seem that this enterprise was under the especial protection of Providence, for by the merest accident, whilst despair was staring every man in the face, several sacks of meal were discovered, various kinds of provisions, two great jars of wine, and several bunches of that nutritious and cooling fruit called plantains.

A strong guard was immediately placed over this treasure, and refreshment given to those who had nearly fallen victims to famine.

When this was done there still remained enough to give every man a slight meal, and then placing the weakest in the canoes, and the whole army being much refreshed, they started forward with renewed spirits, and in the full confidence of ultimate success.

At night they arrived at a very extensive plantation, which offered every accommodation but supper.

The place had been swept clear for them—of victuals.

The reader will by this time perceive that the greatest enemy Morgan had to contend with was famine.

On the sixth day the invaders advanced but little, the weak from hunger in the canoes, the stronger toiling through the woods.

At this part of their route they found the land tolerably rugged, and they were compelled to eat anything vegetable that they could masticate and swallow.

They must have returned or died here had they not discovered a barn full of Indian corn. They rushed upon it like wild beasts and devoured it dry, beating down the doors and walls.

After the first pangs of hunger had been appeased order was restored, and the remainder of the maize was apportioned through the whole army.

They then advanced again, but had not proceeded far before they met with an ambuscade of about a hundred Indians, and then they foolishly threw away their means of sustenance, trampling it in the mire in pursuit of these fleet-footed enemies.

CHAPTER XXXV.
THE CITY WON.

AFTER all this rash precipitance they could only look at their foes on the other side of a river. However, some of the buccaneers plunged in and waded and swam to the other side, in the hope of making a single prisoner, who might discover where all the food of the country was concealed.

But even this attempt proved fallacious; it was fatal to three of Morgan's men, who were killed by the arrows of the retreating Indians, hooting at their pursuers, and crying out—

"To the plain—to the plain, ye dogs!"

After this—the day being too advanced to cross the river, which it was necessary for them to do in this place—they bivouacked on its northern shore for the night.

Here a part of the troops broke out into open mutiny.

Morgan was bitterly reviled by the starved and worn-out wretches, but, nothing daunted, and accompanied by Rupert Russel, Walter Evandale—who had overtaken and joined the buccaneers—Captain Kydd, and other officers, he went from rank to rank, from group to group, endeavouring to reanimate their courage.

The task was difficult.

They asked for bread and Morgan gave them fine words.

The aspect of things grew almost alarming.

They began to hustle him and his suite, exclaiming that they were willing to be led to die in battle, but not to be starved like rotten vermin in a wilderness.

In this perilous crisis he beat to arms, and placing himself where he was conspicuous and could be heard by all, he addressed them with a very pleasant countenance, thus—

"My brother warriors! my stout hearts! we are a pack of hungry dogs, of a truth. I calculated upon the strength of your courage and forgot the weakness of your stomachs. I was wrong. Let us remedy the matter as well as we can. Let all those who are willing to return file off to the left. Do it merrily, my lads."

About one-third of the host betook themselves to the left, and a very woe-begone troop they looked.

"Very well," resumed Morgan, "these are my pinched foxes who intend to turn tail. All good fortune go with them, but I sha'n't. Now, my brother fire-eaters, who is for crossing the river to-morrow into a land that floweth with milk and honey, and where doubloons are piled up in heaps before the doorways and jewels are measured by the bushel. I won't say much about the fat oxen, the generous vines, the luscious fruits, or the tempting lips of the sweet senorettas. Hey, my lads, who's for Panama with Harry Morgan? Let them stand to the right."

Then a noisy set, amounting to another third, hooting, huzzaing, and laughing, stood aside to the right. There remained another third — body-worn, soul-wearied sufferers, with long visages and feeble frames, in the centre.

"And what's to be done with ye, brothers, who will neither go forward nor back?" continued Morgan. "You look like a set of miserable hang-dogs. What would ye—to the right or left? Speak, ye wind-filled cravens!"

Then a murmur arose among these faint and sick wretches and they intimated that they wished to lie down and die where they were, for they would not go back for very shame, and could not go forward for weakness.

They said that there was some religion still amongst them, and that they would administer its last rites to each other and then expire where they were.

Though he showed it not, Morgan was moved to pity by this last division, for they had been subdued by physical suffering only.

But suppressing all indications of his feelings he jocularly proposed that, as the party who wished to return and those who wished to remain were about equal, they should draw up in battle array against each other and fight whilst a man on either side remained, and thus they would meet honourable deaths, escape being tortured by the Indians while dying lingeringly under bushes or in holes, or insects and reptiles feasting upon them before life was extinct.

He promised to keep the ground with the third division during the combat, and offered to extend his good nature so far as to knock the wounded on either side on the head who seemed likely to die lingeringly.

He then dropped his bantering strain and appealed to their judgment and better feelings, to his fraternal care of their lives and healths, and, lastly, to the manliness of the English character.

To strengthen the effect of his oratory Morgan then produced one of his guides, who assured them that the worst of their journey was over, and that they would soon revel in an abundance of all good th ngs.

The mutineers were thereupon ashamed of themselves, but they were at the same time reassured, and testified by their shouts their return to their duty and their reliance upon their extraordinary commander.

All the forenoon of the seventh day of their progress they were busily employed in examining their arms and making themselves ready for any encounter.

Sleep had somewhat repaired the weakness that want of food had inflicted upon them, and at noon they all crossed the river in canoes in very good spirits.

When they had come in sight of a village called Vera Crux or Cruz, their exultation was great at seeing smoke issuing from all the chimneys.

They fancied that the Spaniards had put down to roast and boil the excellent dinners that they, the hungered ones, were to eat.

Full of this delicious idea they broke their ranks, and set off at full speed, but desolating was their misery when they discovered, as they arrived on the spot panting and perspiring, that the fire was not only in the fireplaces but all over the houses.

The Spaniards had anticipated Moscow on a small scale.

Every house was consumed with the exception of the King of Spain's stables and his storehouse, and nothing eatable save a few cats and dogs were to be found.

These domestic animals were soon cooked and devoured, the fires being ready kindled to cook them.

They had the luck, after this very welcome repast, to find, concealed in the storehouses, sixteen casks of Peru wine, and as a natural consequence nearly every man in camp was drunk that night.

Next morning several leathern sacks of bread were also found, and served out equally, without any distinction of rank, and we may suppose with what avidity it was swallowed.

But for some time the results were most alarming, for almost every man in the army was taken ill, and they all supposed they had been treacherously poisoned.

They did, however, in this instance, their enemies great injustice, for their illness was produced solely by their long fasting and the various kinds of unwholesome trash with which they had endeavoured to alleviate their famine.

The malady attacked the army so grievously that they were forced to stay upon the spot the whole day and take up their quarters there for the second night.

The village of Vera Cruz was distant about twenty-six leagues from Chargres and eight from Panama, and was the last place at which the river was navigable.

Here, then, was the landing place for all the merchandise transported upon the river, that from Panama being brought hither on the backs of mules.

Consequently at times it contained great riches.

On abandoning Vera Cruz the Indians and Spaniards retreated no farther than to the adjacent plantations, so it appeared that henceforth they intended to offer more serious resistance.

Apprehending this, Morgan gave positive orders

than none of the buccaneers should leave the village in parties of less than one hundred each.

But hunger is not obedient, and a small band of freebooters ventured out in search of provisions, but were attacked, beaten back, and a prisoner snatched up from among them.

On the sixteenth of January and the eighth day of the march Morgan formed a forlorn hope of two hundred men, whom he despatched forward to discover the road to Panama, and to clear it of ambuscades.

This was very necessary, as the roads were sometimes diminished to paths and passes, through which only four persons could march abreast.

As this column proceeded, commanded by Rupert Russel, they became aware that they were attended both on the right and the left by the enemy, who, however, only showed themselves at intervals and momentarily.

After marching ten hours they arrived at a place called Quebroda Obscura.

Here they were suddenly assailed by a flight of arrows from unseen hands.

This attack proceeded from a high, rocky mountain, through which there was a cleft that would only admit of one buccaneer passing at a time.

This flight of arrows much alarmed the buccaneers, but not finding it repeated they advanced and entered a wood, where they found the Indians flying before them in great numbers, with the apparent design of securing another place of ambush.

But one troop of them remained and disputed the path, and this they valiantly did until their chieftain fell wounded.

He would receive no quarter, and was therefore pistolled by a buccaneer against whom he had lifted his azagaya.

A great many of the Indians were slain around their leader.

In this engagement Rupert Russel lost three men killed and seven wounded.

During the various skirmishes that ensued almost hourly the buccaneers vainly endeavoured to make a prisoner, the Indians being far too active for them.

In the pass which we have just described, had these natives been more cognisant of military matters, all Morgan's advance guard would have perished.

However, it was won in the manner that we have narrated, and when the buccaneers emerged from the forest a glorious view broke upon them of rich meadows, gardens, and all manner of cultivation, which announced their approach to some large city.

But there was something not quite so pleasant in view—another strong party of Indians posted upon a hill near which they had to pass.

A troop of fifty of the fleetest men were selected to pursue them, and, if possible, to make even a single prisoner, in order to gain intelligence.

But all their efforts were in vain, for the Indians were always too quick for them, fleeing and calling them all manner of opprobrious names.

By this time the main body, under Morgan, had closed up with the forlorn hope, and thus all his army pushed forward in one solid mass, yet not without having his front always cleared before him by skirmishers.

They shortly came to a plain in which a wood lay before them, and on each side a mountain.

Morgan possessed himself of one mountain while the Indians held the other.

The buccaneer chief very naturally feared an ambuscade in the wood, and despatched a body of men thither to clear it, upon seeing which the Indians descended from their post of observation and entered the wood before the buccaneers, but neither they nor a huge body of Spaniards dared to make a stand, for both fled before Morgan's advance guard and disappeared.

After fighting and fasting all day the buccaneers halted for the night, but their miseries were much increased by rain falling with all the violence usual in a tropical climate.

It was in vain that they sought shelter, even for their arms and ammunition, for the Indians had apparently burned every roofed building for miles around.

At length three shepherds' hovels were discovered, to which the arms of the entire army were removed, also the sick and wounded, but all other persons were exposed during the whole night to the rain.

Luckily the morning broke cloudless, and the drenched army immediately recommenced its march.

After two hours' progress they discovered a troop of twenty mounted Spaniards, who hovered about them, observing their motions all day, but every attempt to take any one of them a prisoner proved fruitless.

They were out of sight in a moment, withdrawing themselves to places where the buccaneers dared not follow them.

At length, about noon, on attaining an eminence to their infinite joy the whole army obtained a view of the Pacific Ocean.

They made the hills resound with their acclamations.

From this point they observed that the Spaniards at Panama had already taken the alarm, for one large ship and several smaller vessels were making sail from that place towards the two islands of Tovago and Tovagilla.

All things now wore to the buccaneers a cheerful aspect.

On descending into the vale they found large flocks and herds, and then slaughtering, boiling, and roasting began immediately, and that and feasting were the principal occupations of the rest of the day.

How much they enjoyed this repast may be understood from the evidence of one of the company, who says—

" Thus cutting the flesh of these animals into convenient pieces, they threw them into the fire, and half-carbonised or roasted, they devoured them with incredible haste and appetite. For such was their hunger that they more resembled cannibals than Europeans at this banquet, the blood many times running down from their beards unto the middle of their bodies."

They ate their meat with the gravy in it, and Africans might have envied them their appetites.

Giving his men some hours to enjoy this delicious repast, a little before sunset Morgan again pushed forward, sending before him a body of fifty skirmishers, with orders to do their utmost to make prisoners.

He was now much concerned that in traversing the whole of the isthmus, and during his nine days' march, he had not been able to meet with a single person from whom to obtain any intelligence as to the force and position of the enemy.

A little after sunset a body of several hundred Spaniards appeared in Morgan's front, and commenced shouting, but at too great a distance to be understood.

On pressing forward to overtake these vociferous warriors the steeples of Panama burst upon their sight, and the whole army halted with one accord.

Then ensued the most extravagant demonstrations of joy.

Hats flew into the air, men leaped and shouted, and a hundred different tunes arose on the instant. Then every trumpet brayed forth ts loudest triumphal note, and the drums rolled and thundered in unison.

They looked upon the victory as already won, the city plundered, and the booty shared.

Instead of repressing these undisciplined acts of presumption, Morgan and his officers went from file to file encouraging their enthusiasm, jocularly upbraiding those who had desponded a few days before, and ardently praising those who had never failed in their courage.

In this excellent state of mind they halted themselves before the city, fully intending to attack it early on the following morning.

At the noise of the shoutings, and of the trumpets and drums, fifty well-appointed horsemen came forth from the city to reconnoitre the buccaneers, after they had taken up their ground for the night.

They came almost within musket-shot, being preceded by a trumpeter, who sounded his instrument marvellously well.

Some of these troopers were even so bold as to come within hearing, and then, with horrid grimaces and menacing attitudes, shouted—

" Piratical dogs ! we shall meet you—we shall meet you !"

After performing this feat they rode proudly back into the city, leaving eight of their best mounted companions near the camp to watch the movements of the buccaneers.

The two hundred Spaniards also, whom they had passed on their march, now took up a position in their rear, thus threatening to block up the invaders, whilst the guns from the ramparts of the city opened upon the camp, though luckily without reaching it.

All these things gave the buccaneers no concern, although the fire from the great guns was kept up all night.

The freebooters, in answer to this, began to make themselves comfortable, for though they were actually surrounded they very quietly seated themselves, each man at his ease, and opening their wallets drew forth the remaining pieces of half-roasted beef and mutton which they had reserved from their noon's repast, and fell to eating in such a way that no one would have supposed they had so recently dined.

Having satisfied their appetites they laid themselves down quietly on the grass, notwithstanding the roar of the Spanish guns, and with great satisfaction fell into a sound sleep, made the more delicious by dreams of the plunder and feasting with which the morrow was to bless them.

Early on the morning of the next day " General " Morgan put all his army in motion, and at first marched along the highway, directly upon the town.

Then calling to him one of the guides he took counsel with him, and suddenly broke off to the right, and took to a path through the woods, which was much the safer, though the way was tedious and difficult in the extreme.

Had he been burdened with horses, baggage, or artillery, he could not have forced the passage.

By this detour he escaped a mine and several ambuscades, and the Spaniards were thus compelled to leave their batteries and barricades, also to take up a new position, in order to face the buccaneer army as it debouched from the wood.

Don Balverara, the President of Panama, drew up his army before the lines of the city, consisting of two squadrons of horse and four regiments of foot, with several thousands of a novel kind of auxiliary troops, being herds of wild bulls, driven and directed by a sufficient number of Indians and negroes, who were well versed in such matters.

The Spaniards consisted of two thousand one hundred foot, and six hundred horse, whilst Morgan could bring into line scarcely one thousand men.

When Morgan and his army emerged from the wood, which the Spaniards suffered them to do without molestation, in order that their wild cattle and their cavalry might act on the savannah, the buccaneers, or many of them, suffered a sudden panic at beholding the numerous forces and the strength of the position before them.

Again Morgan had occasion to use all his eloquence, and going from rank to rank he excited in them a spirit of desperation, until every man pledged himself to his neighbour to find death or victory.

When his army was fairly disengaged from the wood, Morgan drew it up in three lines, each line forming a division of itself.

The van was commanded by Walter Evandale.

It consisted only of two hundred men.

The main body counted six hundred, and was commanded by Rupert Russel ; and the rear was only two hundred strong, commanded by Captain Kydd and Morgan's black mistress, Zoabinda.

Morgan did not choose to leave the brow of the hill, with the wood in his rear, nor would the Spanish leader leave the spacious plain in which he was posted, which was so favourable for the operations of his cattle and his cavalry.

TALES of PIRATES
SMUGGLERS and BUCCANEERS.

No. 12.]   THE SCOURGE OF THE SPANISH MAIN.   [One Penny.

At last the steeples of Panama were in view of the buccaneers.

MORGAN the BUCCANEER; or, the Terror of the Seas.

Morgan did all that he could to provoke the enemy to commence the attack by sending forward small bodies of marksmen, but these were never followed in their retreat after having discharged their musquetoons and arquebuses. Seeing this, Morgan began to edge slowly round the wing of the Spaniards, which in modern warfare would be termed outflanking.

This the buccaneers were suffered to do for some time unopposed, and the manœuvre gained them the advantage both of the sun and the wind.

At last Don Belverara was obliged to change his front, but his troops, not being used to military operations on a large scale, got embarrassed with a bog that, before they changed position, lay between them and the buccaneers, and in which they had hoped to have entangled their enemies.

Morgan, seeing this partial disorder, advanced a little way into the plain to take advantage of it, when the leader of the Spanish horse, Francisco Delarro, charged the buccaneer van-guard with loud shouts of "Viva el Rey!"

Although Morgan had no pikes in his army, the vanguard, under Evandale, doubled their ranks, and the first line kneeling with one knee on the ground, gave the cavalry so slaughtering a volley directly in their faces that it brought down nearly the whole front file, and the rear turned and fled immediately.

It is true they attempted to rally, but were unable to make any combined movement, and the buccaneers brought them down at their ease, and with as much certainty as if they had been firing at targets in a review.

As yet the van only of the buccaneer army had been engaged, and they had completely dispersed the Spanish cavalry, killing their gallant leader, Don Francisco Delarro.

The main body of the Spanish foot now advanced, when the buccaneer van opened in its centre to right and left, wheeling backwards, and thus forming, with Russel's troops at the base, three sides of a hollow square.

When the Spanish foot were thus enclosed on three sides their position was much worse than that of their horse had been.

They did not at all like it, and after losing a vast number of men, for they fought courageously, endeavoured by slowly retreating to extricate themselves.

But whilst they were thus giving ground Morgan advanced his rear-guard on their left flank, and then the retreat was changed into a flight, though the Spaniards still preserved some manner of order.

Thus fighting and pursuing, the buccaneers were gradually drawn down into the plain, and as their rear was no longer covered by the woods, the Spaniards seized the opportunity to goad upon it their two divisions, each of fifteen hundred wild bulls, at its left and right angles.

But these clumsy allies rendered the Spaniards small service.

They flew about in all directions, being astounded by the noise of the battle, and the few that did break through the buccaneer files amused themselves by tearing to pieces the colours and tossing sundry drums into the air.

When they became very troublesome they were quietly killed.

The conflict had now lasted two hours.

Nearly all the Spanish horse had been killed, the wild bulls had all disappeared, or had been slaughtered, and the foot regiments threw away their arms in despair and fled in the wildest confusion.

The buccaneers were so dreadfully fatigued that they found it impossible to go in pursuit of them.

Many of the runaways not being able to regain the city, hid themselves in bushes or among the rocks down by the seaside.

These were found, but received no quarter, as the fury and exasperation of the battle had not yet subsided in the breasts of the buccaneers.

By this time Morgan had reorganised his forces, appointed scouts, and was deliberating, on the field of battle that he had so gallantly won, upon his next proceedings, when eleven priests and one Spanish captain were brought in prisoners before him.

All Morgan's hot blood was in a ferment, and as yet quarter had neither been given nor begged on either side.

The monks fell on their knees before him in their sacerdotal vestments, and with heartrending cries and lamentations, for the love of Jesus begged their lives.

But Morgan ordered these prostrate and holy men to be pistolled slowly, the one after the other.

They were remorselessly sacrificed, and he stood calmly by and beheld the deed.

The officer Morgan spared, and from him he learned that the city was placed in a good state of defence, that it was well entrenched, the principal streets barricaded, and that in several places strong batteries had been planted.

Morgan also discovered that at the principal entrance to the city there was a battery mounted with eight heavy brass guns, manned by fifty men, and that there were altogether two hundred fresh troops in the place, and thirty-two pieces of heavy ordnance.

After taking some time to weigh his determination, Morgan ordered that in future the prisoners should be spared, and then he proceeded to review his troops.

To his chagrin he found that his loss had been much more considerable than he had at first supposed, whilst that on the part of the Spaniards was tremendous.

Six hundred and forty-seven of the latter were found dead upon the field, besides hundreds seriously wounded, and prisoners were being brought in very rapidly.

Having rested his forces for the space of an hour and a-half, Morgan, taking great care to avoid the principal gates, marched towards the city, carrying with him all his prisoners.

With all his precautions, however, his ranks were compelled to face many ramparts, from which the guns discharged upon him showers of cannon-balls, thinning his ranks at every step.

At length, however, the buccaneers penetrated to the very streets, and at last reached the market-place, but there the conflict was renewed for some time.

After three hours' hard fighting Morgan obtained complete possession of the place, and every

Spaniard who dared show himself was immediately shot down.

Morgan had conquered a realm—to-morrow he might be a king.

CHAPTER XXXVI.

MORGAN ASPIRES TO A CROWN AND MAKES A CONFIDANT OF EVANDALE.

MORGAN was by no means a merciful ruler, and his troops were not slow to follow his example.

Being undisputed owners of Panama by right of conquest, everyone took the quarters that best suited him, making the great cathedral of San Salvador the *corps de garde.*

Then commenced the usual scenes of insolent riot, one hundred mounted troopers being despatched daily into the country, man and merchandise hunting, and daily were many miserable prisoners and much wealth brought in.

Torture followed, of course, and by its means much information was gained of buried treasure.

This continued for three weeks, when Morgan, finding he had amassed considerable booty, and that he was in possession of the heads of more than one hundred of the principal families, turned his attention to other subjects.

He was in possession of a splendid state and of a beautiful city. Why should he not ape the monarch? Why not proclaim himself king thereof?

Morgan I., King of Panama, would not sound worse than other regal titles.

One evening he called Walter Evandale aside and invited him to sup with him.

The invitation was readily accepted, and the meal was delicate and *recherche.*

After it had been discussed, Morgan unfolded to his faithful lieutenant the plans he had made for the future.

Evandale strongly approved of them, and urged Morgan to lose no time in declaring himself king.

"My faithful friend, my true and devoted servant, I thank thee for thy counsel," exclaimed the great buccaneer.

"Did I not tell thee that I would stand by thee to the last, Morgan?" responded Evandale, fervently.

"Aye, aye—but don't talk of 'the last' when I seem to be only coming to the first," laughed the buccaneer chief. "And that reminds me that I have yet another matter to converse with thee on—it is the all-important subject of marriage."

"Indeed! Are you then about to make the brave Zoabinda your queen?" asked Evandale.

"No — scarcely that. I fear these proud Spaniards would hardly relish a black queen—a woman who had once been a slave, especially. Besides, I might tire of Zoabinda. She was a very fitting companion for a boisterous buccaneer, but to don the purple, and to sit beside me on the throne. Pshaw! the idea sickens me."

"And yet she has bravely helped you to win that throne, Henry Morgan," said the lieutenant.

"I don't want upbraidings, Evandale—I must teach you to play the courtier better than that," said Morgan. "Listen, now. You are doubtless aware that Donna Theresa de Guzman escaped mysteriously from my power on the night that we gave the Spaniards such a drubbing, but perhaps you have not yet heard that within twenty-four hours after that she fell into the toils again, and has been journeying with me ever since a prisoner. Ha! ha! I kept that little affair very quiet, didn't I?"

"Indeed, yes," answered Evandale, while a strange light flashed in his dark eyes. "I wonder you did not tell me of this before."

"I did not tell thee, lieutenant mine, because I shrewdly imagined that thou wast hankering after the young lady thyself, and though I have found thee faithful in most things, yet a pair of bright eyes will sometimes tempt any man from his allegiance."

"They would not have kept me very long from thy side," answered Evandale, twirling his long moustache.

"Ah! well—there are few like thee," rejoined Morgan, "and yet, now that I come to think, thou wert away from my tent all that evening, absent from my side, too, in the hour of battle; nor didst thou show thyself until we were at least six leagues on our journey."

"Indisposition kept me in my own quarters all the evening. I was from thy side in the hour of battle because a strong arm and a sharp sword were more urgently needed elsewhere, and with a score of mounted troopers I pursued the flying Spaniards so far that our horses were dead beat, and it was only with the greatest difficulty that we came up with the army again at all," said Evandale.

"Well done, my boy, I am glad to hear this of thee, for I have once or twice entertained vague suspicions that you yourself had something to do with the girl's abduction. However, she was recaptured by Rupert Russel and his troopers, who cut her escort, composed of Spanish arquebusiers, to pieces, and brought her back to me safe and uninjured; and i' faith 'twas lucky for her that it happened so, for through it she will wear a crown. I mean to wed her, and make her Queen Consort of Panama."

Walter Evandale's cheek turned of the ashy hue of marble. He bit his lip and muttered fiercely to himself—

"Fool! dotard! neither she nor the crown will ever be within thy grasp. The hour of my supreme vengeance draweth near, and will come before the regal honours."

He concealed the mingled passions which warred within his breast most completely, however, and said, with a smile—

"It is for you to will, and for your subjects and your prisoners to obey. But what will you do with Zoabinda?"

"Poison her," said Morgan, clutching his arm. "She is of no further use, so she must be removed."

Evandale experienced a feeling of intense horror and disgust at Morgan's conduct in thus treating one who had been so true and faithful to him in everything, and for whom he had professed to feel so deep a love and affection

But he still veiled his inner emotions under a smiling exterior, and shortly afterwards the conference ended, Morgan getting Evandale to promise that he himself would put Zoabinda "out of the way," and also that he would break the intelligence of Morgan's aims and aspirations cautiously to the other leaders and to the troopers, and thus gather the prevailing sentiment of the army upon the subject.

Everything turned out better than the great buccaneer chief had anticipated.

His assumption of regal power was warmly advocated by his officers and men, the former looking forward to high posts and dignities, the latter to easy quarters, high pay, and a free license for all their evil passions.

Strange to say, and this did take Morgan by surprise, Donna Theresa de Guzman listened without apparent disgust to his suit, and did not seem at all averse to share the throne and other stately honours with him. He did not know that Walter Evandale had previously gained access to the suite of rooms in which she was imprisoned, and had counselled her to play a part, promising that Morgan should never live to lead her to the altar or to become King of Panama.

Zoabinda, too, disappeared suddenly, and Evandale told Morgan that he had effectually "put her out of the way," and that "she would never trouble him more," though he would not confess that he had actually slain her.

Morgan, however, understood him to signify as much, and did not trouble to ask many questions.

Preparations were at once set on foot for the coronation, which was to be a very magnificent affair indeed.

A crown was to be made out of the gold and jewels that had been stolen from the grand altar of the cathedral of San Salvador—there was to be a throne, also of pure gold—and Morgan had a portrait painted of himself in coronation robes, whose fate we shall tell of anon.

The great day at length arrived—the streets were decked with triumphal arches and hangings of rich velvet and cloth of gold hung from windows and balconies. A thousand flags flaunted their gorgeous colours to the gentle western wind, and the public fountains threw up wine instead of water. Everything wore the outer aspect of gaiety and joy.

But the Spanish residents kept within doors, and they took no part in this vain display.

In the palace of the captain-general, hereafter to be dubbed "royal," Morgan and his officers held high revel.

In an hour he was to be wedded to the beautiful Donna Theresa de Guzman—in two hours the coronation was to take place. Then he would have gained the acme of his hopes—the height of his ambition. Oh ! he was very happy.

CHAPTER XXXVII.

THE MARRIAGE CEREMONY—MORGAN'S DISCOMFITURE AND DEATH.

LET us now enter the prison chamber of the heroine of our tale, Donna Theresa de Guzman. The long hours of the morning—the most eventful one of her life—had dragged themselves wearily past

without a visit from Morgan, though she trembled at every sound in the stone corridor without—fearing lest it might portend the approach of the great buccaneer chief, who had solemnly declared on his last visit that when next he came it would be to lead her to the altar.

Pale and agitated, the beauteous girl reclined on a velvet couch near the open window—her large, eloquent brown eyes dim with tears—her little rosy lips tightly compressed—her long, golden tresses floating loosely around her well-formed head and shading her snowy neck—whilst her taper fingers were slowly telling the beads of a golden rosary which hung from her belt.

Suddenly she started, for a hand had been laid on her shoulder.

Looking up she perceived Walter Evandale.

His entrance had been so noiseless that not until he touched her had she been aware of his presence.

"I did not mean to frighten you—Donna Theresa," he said, kindly. " My mission is to bear thee comfort and hope."

" Oh ! Heaven bless thee for all thy kindness, Walter," replied the lovely girl. " Can you really release me from the power of this cruel buccaneer ? If so, never shall I be able to repay my deep debt or gratitude."

In her excitement she would have thrown herself at the handsome lieutenant's feet, but he gently prevented her, saying—

" Kneel not to me, dear lady. I can and will release you from Morgan's power ; but not until the last moment will aid and succour be extended to thee, and then it will only reach thee from the altar itself. Fear not, my child—the schemes of Morgan shall be foiled. When next he seeks thee receive him boldly. Proceed to the cathedral without dread, and though the marriage service be well nigh ended fear not, for thou wilt never be his wife, nor will he live six hours to exercise his power over you."

" Oh ! my kind, generous friend, thou hast indeed replanted within my breast the seeds of content and hope. I know that thy sympathy is sincere, thy assurance genuine, even though I fail to see how, alone and unaided, thou canst rescue me from Morgan and his myrmidons."

" I will soon make it plain to your comprehension, lady. Many of Morgan's officers and men, disgusted at his cruelty, and indignant at his conduct towards Zoabinda, whom he has so cruelly used, have broken out into open insurrection, and have chosen me their leader. It is this band who will interrupt the wedding and save thee."

.   .   .   .

Half an hour after the handsome lieutenant had taken his departure Donna Theresa was again aroused by footsteps in the corridor without.

The door of the apartment was quickly opened, and Morgan entered the room.

He was attired in a beautiful suit of silver mail, his scarf and surcoat blazed with gold and jewels, while a magnificent crimson plume drooped over his broad-brimmed cavalier hat.

With a bow he advanced towards Donna Theresa, saying—

"Madam, I come to conduct you to the altar. The priests of your church are awaiting us, and the guests are also by this time assembling within the cathedral. Wilt come?"

He offered his arm as he concluded.

Theresa for a moment hesitated to accept it, then, recollecting Evandale's promise, she laid her hand trembling within it, and in this manner they quitted the apartment.

Three tall wax candles stood on each side of the high marble crucifix, and many more glittered as votive offerings before the shrines of the Archangel Michael and the Virgin Mary, while above the torches on all sides fluttered banners and ensigns, bannerols, and gorgeous pennons, all of which had been captured in battle.

Most conspicious amongst these was the heavy black banner of the buccaneers, with the skull and crossbones emblazoned thereon, but above it waved another flag bearing the four golden castles of Spain.

Towards the second flag many an eye was wonderingly raised, for its emblazoned arms were those of their conquered foes, and many there were ready to swear that five minutes previously no such banner was visible.

It was too late, however, to pull it down or to hazard surmises as to who had placed it there, for footsteps were heard without, and the next moment Morgan, with Donna Theresa de Guzman leaning on his arm, entered the cathedral.

They were preceded by four pages, bearing scented flambeaux, and advancing before the high altar they knelt before the officiating priests.

Beautiful indeed did our heroine look, flushed with excitement and fear lest the promised rescue should not arrive in time.

Her dark brown eyes were flashing beneath her long-fringed lashes, the dark tresses forming a marked and lovely contrast to the snow white neck and shoulders over which they floated.

She trembled violently as the service commenced and the clear intonation of the priest rang through the cathedral.

The priest had not proceeded far when a loud crash was heard, and with an involuntary start Morgan glanced round and perceived that the black banner charged with the flaunting skull and crossbones of the buccaneers—its staff broken in the middle—lay on the floor at his feet. Looking upward to where it had hung, his gaze rested on the four golden castles—the standard of Spain—which, as if in triumph, slowly unfolded itself to his gaze.

"Who hung that accursed flag up yonder above the skull and crossbones?" he thundered forth, in tones that rang hollowly through the vast cathedral, as he glared angrily around on the assembled bystanders.

No reply was made.

Every man looked supiciously at his companion, who returned his glance with interest.

"I myself inspected the planting of the flags," at length exclaimed Rupert Russel, stepping forward, "and well I know the standard of Spain was not anywhere hung up in the cathedral."

Upon receiving this assurance Morgan affected a nonchalance of manner that he was far from feeling, and exclaimed, gaily, "It matters not—we will investigate the matter hereafter. Captain Rupert Russel, raise the black flag—it is not wont to lie so low. Sir Priest, proceed with the ceremony."

Again all was silence—the intonation of the priest, the clatter of the waving censers, and the sputtering of pinewood torches being the only sounds that arose to break the stillness of the scene.

Turning to Morgan the celebrant demanded—

"Henry Morgan, King of Panama, in the name of Heaven and our blessed lady I solemnly ask whether thou art prepared to take unto thee this maiden as thy wife, forsaking all others for her sake, and her only to love, honour, and protect during the whole of this life?"

In a firm voice Morgan answered—

"Holy Mary and all the saints above bear witness to my vow that I will. May the curse of Judas rest upon me if I fail to do so!" and so saying he solemnly kissed the hilt of his sword.

A similar interrogatory was then addressed to Theresa de Guzman.

The celebrant waited for a reply, but our heroine spoke not.

Again was the question put—this time slowly and distinctly.

Morgan turned towards his victim in anger and disappointment.

She returned his gaze and answered in an unquavering voice—

"Never!"

The response was spoken in a low tone, and yet so clear and bell-like was the voice that it was clearly audible.

For a moment there ensued a dead silence—then Morgan, turning to the astonished priest, said—

"Proceed with the service, sirrah! The lady is evidently subject to occasional attacks of insanity—I mean unconsciousness—that is to say, the heat and the excitement have been too much for her. We will excuse her reply to the question."

"But I fear that we cannot do so—" began the astonished celebrant.

"Do you hear what I say, sirrah?" responded Morgan, fiercely. "Proceed at once with the ceremony, or, spite of gown and cord, I will have thee and thy fellow priests scourged through the city and then thrown into the sea. You Spaniards know very well that I am not one to threaten in vain."

Terrified at Morgan's words the priest was about to proceed with the ceremony when a deep voice, apparently from behind the altar, shouted—

"Forbear!"

And while Morgan in surprise sprang to his feet, and his officers and captains shrank back awestruck at the sound of the mysterious voice, the clatter of steel was heard, and the next moment a brilliantly uniformed cavalier—wearing a black half-mask, which effectually covered his countenance—his arms folded on his chest, stood beside the priest inside the altar rails and boldly faced the assembly.

"Henry Morgan, dastard and villain that thou art, I have arrived in ample time to frustrate thy schemes and rescue this lady from thy power. Tremble—for thy last hour has come. Lady, I have kept my promise."

As he spoke the cavalier lifted our heroine in his arms and placed her in a chair beside the altar.

He then drew his sword from its scabbard, and raising an ivory whistle to his lips, blew it.

In reply there was a loud cheer—the clatter of steel, the clank of spurs—and quick as lightning at least a hundred men rushed from behind the altar into the body of the cathedral.

But Morgan at once recovered from his dismay as soon as he comprehended the sudden appearance of this hostile body of men.

With a loud, commanding voice he called upon his officers and the grim and silent arquebusiers to drive the "scurril mob" back to the vaults from which they had just issued.

He stood firmly on guard when the masked cavalier, intent upon revenge and retribution, sprang over the altar-rail, sword in hand, to attack him, and their weapons met with a clash that echoed above the roar and din of the surrounding contest, which by this time had become general.

For many minutes the fierce duel continued, without a decided advantage being gained by either side.

The masked cavalier, in whom our readers will have no difficulty in recognising Walter Evandale, found ample work cut out for him, whilst his hundred followers, fighting with heroic courage against numbers trebling their own, soon found that the chances of their overcoming their foes were very much against them.

At length the buccaneer pikemen contrived to get into line, and then their phalanx was unpenetrable.

Vainly did the mutineers rush madly on the bloody pikeheads—in vain did sword and dagger gleam in the ruddy torchlight, and seek to hew a passage through that compact living mass of disciplined and steady valour.

Every time the malcontents advanced upon the serried ranks they appeared to recoil therefrom like an ocean wave from a rock of granite, and ere long the pikemen made a terrible onward rush, while the vast cathedral resounded with their heavy tramp.

Bravely competing to the last, the followers of Evandale were driven back inch by inch to the vaults from which they had only just emerged.

Meanwhile, Walter Evandale was in a sore strait.

He had found Morgan more than his match. A resounding blow, though turned aside by the cap of steel he wore beneath his broad-brimmed sombrero, had made him feel faint and giddy, but he nevertheless fought gallantly on.

Anon Morgan signalled to his assistance two of his followers who were close at hand, and Walter Evandale, with his back to the altar-rails, in order to prevent either of them attacking him in the rear, was bravely defending himself against the three, though evidently getting feebler every instant.

Without a chance of much longer being able to protect himself from their combined attack he still kept doggedly on.

Just at this supreme moment, Harry Seaborne, who, with his ten Spaniards, had hung upon the rear of Morgan's army and harassed it whenever they had a chance, burst upon the scene from their hiding-place, which was also in the vaults below.

He had collected together quite a respectable body of Spanish soldiery, intending to make one final effort to break down Morgan's mighty power, when the clash of steel from above, mingled with cries and oaths, apprised him that the buccaneers were fighting among themselves, and that now was the time if ever to attempt the recapture of the city.

Immediately he caught sight of Morgan and Evandale lunging fiercely at each other, while Donna Theresa was being supported by the priest, he understood the situation in a moment, and ranging himself on Evandale's side, the conflict raged anew.

The unlooked for accession of strength sufficed to turn the tide of battle in Evandale's favour, and eventually Morgan was stricken down and nearly all his followers were annihilated.

.   .   .   .

"Dog! villain! infamous wretch! You slew my father on his own doorstep, you crucified my mother on the roof of our once happy hacienda, you thrust my three infant brothers and sisters into a heated oven and baked them to death with slow tortures, and then you caused a great hole to be dug, and therein every horse, servant, and slave on the estate were buried alive. Ha! ha! have you forgotten all this?"

Evandale had been hacking, hewing, and thrusting at Morgan all the time he had been speaking, and as he concluded he plunged his sword deep into his foe's chest.

Walter Evandale knelt down and placed his knee on his foeman's chest.

"I hail thee, great King of Panama and husband of the most beautiful maiden in New Spain!" he exclaimed, derisively. "This is a nice bridal bed—this is a fitting throne for a warrior. Why, a rat would choose a better!"

"Evandale," gasped Morgan, "why have you spared me so long? Why have you fought by my side, and ofttimes protected my life at the hazard of your own?"

"Because I had to wait patiently until your life was precious to you. When I first attached myself to your person you were reckless of it and appreciated it as of little value, so for years I have been helping you to fill up and raise a cup of happiness to your lips, not one drop of which I have intended you to drink. Ha, ha! by this time thou wert to have been a happy husband and a glorious king, and now, instead, thou art dying like a poisoned rat in a drain. At the portals of the earthly heaven you have sighed and sinned for I have avenged father and mother, sisters and brothers, by despatching you straight to that nethermost hell which is yawning wide to receive thee!"

Morgan uttered a deep groan of agony.

His eyes were almost starting out of their sockets with horror.

"Ha, ha, ha! this is a rare revenge," laughed Evandale, "and well worth waiting for all these years. But I have sworn that thy death shall be one of agonised torture. I will hack thee limb from limb, and suffer thee to bleed to death here, surrounded by the dead—Spaniards whose sons and daughters you have so pitilessly tortured and murdered, and your own brave buccaneers, whom you have so mercilessly ruled."

"Oh! spare me—spare me. Mercy, mercy!" cried Morgan.

"Aye! such mercy as the tiger shows to his prey —such mercy as you have thousands of times meted out to others!"

.   .   .   .

Harry Seaborne commanded that a gibbet should immediately be erected in the great city, and that the bodies of Morgan, Rupert Russel, and Captain Kydd should be hung thereon.

This was immediately done, for Panama was now again in complete possession of the Spaniards.

On the chest of Morgan was affixed a placard whereon was written "Justice to Thieves!" and underneath it was propped up the full length portrait he had only a few days previously had painted of himself in his coronation robes, those robes that he was destined never to wear.

On this picture someone chalked the word "Coward," and the populace hacked and hewed at it as it leant against the upright of the gibbet until it was nearly undistinguishable.

And there hung the three atrocious buccaneer chiefs, above heaps of rare Etruscan vases and shattered statuary, rifled jewel caskets, rich suits of armour, swords, and halberds, and robes of velvet and cloth of gold, that had been thrown out of the adjoining houses by their riotous followers only a few days previously—followers who now lay cold and stiff in death.

.   .   .   .   .   .

Not many days after Morgan's death Harry Seaborne restored his daughter to Don Pedro de Guzman and claimed his reward. Evandale assisted at the ceremony as best man, and was always a honoured and welcome guest whenever he visited our hero and his wife—Donna Theresa—at Panama, of which splendid city Harry Seaborne was appointed governor by the Spanish authorities as a recognition of the many services rendered, and as a reward for his brilliant and daring deeds.

THE END.

www.ingramcontent.com/pod-product-compliance
Lightning Source LLC
Chambersburg PA
CBHW081211170626
46811CB00010B/3247

9781535811552